BITTERSWEET
blood

A NOVEL OF *THE ORDER*

BITTERSWEET blood

A NOVEL OF *THE ORDER*

NINA CROFT

This book is a work of fiction. Names, characters, places, and incidents are the product of the author's imagination or are used fictitiously. Any resemblance to actual events, locales, or persons, living or dead, is coincidental.

Copyright © 2013 by Nina Croft. All rights reserved, including the right to reproduce, distribute, or transmit in any form or by any means. For information regarding subsidiary rights, please contact the Publisher.

Previously released on Entangled's Edge imprint — February 2013

Entangled Publishing, LLC
2614 South Timberline Road
Suite 105, PMB 159
Fort Collins, CO 80525
Visit our website at www.entangledpublishing.com.

Select Otherworld is an imprint of Entangled Publishing, LLC.

Edited by Marie Loggia-Kee and Liz Pelletier
Cover design by LJ Anderson
Cover art from Dollar Photo Club

Manufactured in the United States of America

First Edition February 2013

To my sister, Anne, who introduced me to vampires.

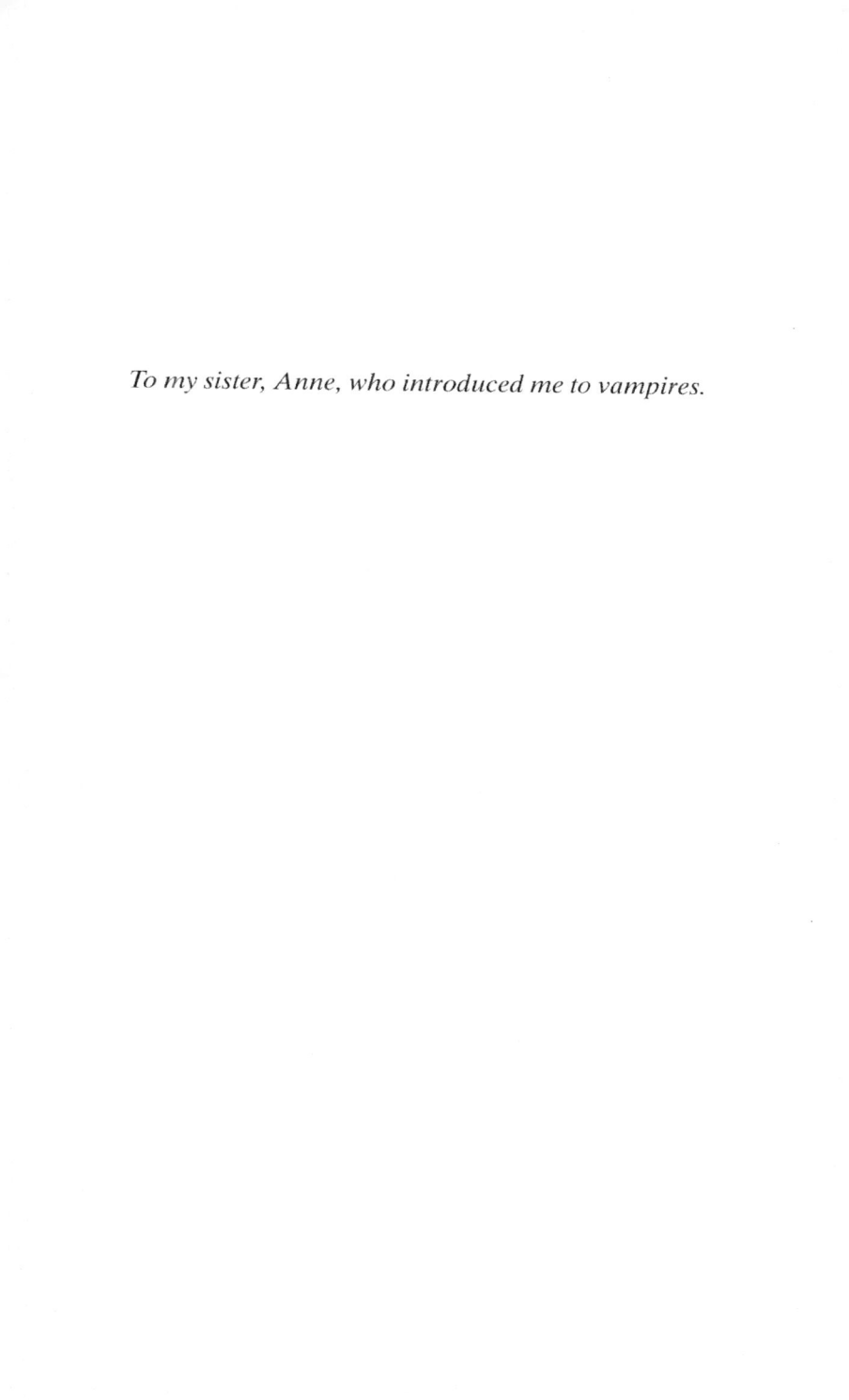

Part One

BREAKING ALL THE RULES

Chapter One

Rule Number One: Never question the past.

Tara took a single step into the alleyway and stopped.

Up ahead, something shifted in the shadows and a waft of warm air carried the stench of dirty smoke and rotten eggs to her nostrils. A prickle of unease shivered across her skin.

No way was she ending up dead in a dark alley before she had a chance to break Rule Number One. Wrinkling her nose against the smell, she held her breath and backed out into the bright lights of the main street.

And straight into something solid and unexpected.

For a second, she thought she must have hit a brick wall. A brick wall that hadn't been there thirty seconds earlier.

"Are you okay?"

A brick wall that talked.

Swallowing the lump in her throat, she turned.

Her eyes were level with his chest and at first all she registered was his immense size. Taking a slow step back, she forced her gaze upward. In the artificial light, he was leached of color, with black hair pulled into a ponytail, and skin so pale it appeared white. She went still as silver eyes captured hers. For a second, she stared mesmerized, unable to drag her gaze away from the stranger.

"Are you lost?" He spoke again, breaking the spell.

"No. Yes. Maybe." She waved the map clutched in her hand. "I was considering a short cut."

A short cut to the railway station and a fast train away from here. For the last ten minutes, she'd been dithering. Should she go ahead, break Rule Number One, and perhaps come to a messy and premature end? Or should she run away and try to forget the stupid rules had ever existed?

"A short cut down a dark alley? Has no one ever told you it's dangerous to wander down dark alleys alone?"

Was there some subtle threat beneath his words? Did he look vaguely menacing for a moment? Or was it merely her overactive imagination playing games with her? He was just a man—a tall, powerfully built man, but quite respectable in his sleek, dark business suit and red tie.

Still, a little voice in her head whispered to her to turn and walk away—though perhaps not down the dark alley.

But something held her back.

All her life she'd been afraid. Aunt Kathy had brought her up to fear just about everything, and she'd done a brilliant job. But Aunt Kathy was dead, and Tara refused to live like that anymore.

"Well?" he murmured and she realized he was waiting for an answer.

"Actually, yes. I'm quite aware of the dangers. But I have an important meeting and my mind was on other things." *Like running away.*

He considered her for a moment. "Where is this important meeting? Perhaps I can help."

"CR International. You know it?"

His lips curved into a slow smile and suddenly she

realized how devastatingly attractive he was. "You mean the CR International building behind you?" A faint trace of amusement tinged his voice.

She pursed her lips but turned slowly. He wasn't kidding. It stood directly opposite, on the other side of the street. An immense structure of steel and smoky glass with CR International in big gold letters over the door. How the hell had she missed that? "Oh…thank you."

This was it. Either she'd discover the truth, or she'd be blasted by a bolt of divine retribution. Time to find out which.

She took a few steps but couldn't resist glancing back over her shoulder. The man still stood, hands in his pockets, watching her, a strange almost hungry look in his eyes.

"Overactive imagination," she muttered and headed across the street.

A young man sat behind the reception desk; handsome, with dark red hair like a fox and blue eyes that perfectly matched his shirt.

"I'm Tara Collins," she said. "I have an appointment with Mr. Grant."

"I'll let him know you're here." He reached for the phone beside him, but it rang before he picked up, and he sent her an apologetic glance. "One moment." As he listened, a startled expression flickered across his face. "Sure, Christian. No problem."

He put the phone down. "Ms. Collins?"

Tara nodded.

"I'm afraid Mr. Grant can't see you tonight."

Tara sagged with relief and bit back a "halleluiah." She'd done her best, but now she could legitimately put off breaking Rule Number One just a little while longer. Like forever maybe.

"Absolutely no problem," she said. "Shall I make another appointment? Perhaps in a couple of weeks? A month? A year...?"

A year sounded good.

He smiled, showing perfect white teeth. "No need. That was Mr. Roth—the owner of the company—he'll see you instead. I'll take you up myself as access to the thirteenth floor is restricted."

He called one of the security guards over from beside the door and spoke with him quietly then came out from behind the reception desk.

"My name's Graham. If you'd come with me..."

She followed him, not to the bank of elevators where a few people waited, but into a smaller one around the corner. Inside, there were just two buttons, one pointing up and one down. Graham pressed the up button, and they rose smoothly. When the doors opened, he didn't exit. Instead, he pointed to a set of black double doors opposite.

Tara stared at them, unable to shake the feeling that this was the point of no return. What if Aunt Kathy had been right? What if there was a very good reason not to question the past?

"Go ahead," Graham murmured from beside her. "Mr. Roth doesn't... bite."

Tara scowled at the faint thread of amusement in his voice—it seemed as though everyone was finding her funny today. She stalked out of the elevator.

This floor appeared deserted, and hushed. Her feet made no sound on the thick carpets as she walked toward the imposing doors. Without giving herself any more time to think, she pressed her finger lightly to the smooth black metal and the door swung open. Inside, the room was in semi-darkness, the only light spilling in from the floor to ceiling windows that lined the far wall.

Perhaps no one was home.

She hovered in the doorway, unsure whether to stay or

go, when a man spoke from inside.

"Come in, Ms. Collins."

The voice was low, husky, and vaguely familiar. She hesitated a moment more and then took the few steps inside. Behind her, the door swung shut. The air was cool against her skin and she glanced around.

"Lights," she muttered. "Lights would be good here."

A faint click, and warm light filled the room. Tara blinked a couple of times then her gaze locked on the figure seated behind the huge steel desk.

The man from the alley. Why wasn't she more surprised?

"You know," she said. "You could have introduced yourself."

A small smile curved his lips. "And spoil the surprise?"

Yeah, right.

He stood slowly, then came around the desk to stand in front of her, one arm outstretched. Tara fought the urge to hide her hands behind her back; something about this man set her on edge. Of course, it could be that the whole "breaking the rules" thing was just screwing with her mind, that right now, she was predisposed to see weirdness in everything.

She grasped his hand firmly, intending the greeting to be brief, but his fingers tightened around hers. Her gaze shot to his face. He wasn't a handsome man; his features were too harsh for that, with pale skin stretched tight over hard bones. But his silver eyes held her mesmerized as he lifted her hand. For a moment, she was sure he intended to kiss it, but he merely inhaled deeply. Something flashed in his eyes, something hot and hungry, and a shiver ran through her. Then the expression vanished as if it had never been.

"I'm Christian Roth."

"So your receptionist told me." She gave a tug. "Could I have my hand back?"

He smiled and released her, then gestured to a chair in

front of his desk.

"Why don't you sit down and tell me how I can…help you." He waited until she was seated, then returned to his own chair. "So, Tara Collins, why do you need a private investigator?"

This was the moment she'd built herself up for over the last six months. She'd even practiced the words in front of the mirror. But now, at the last second, they didn't want to come out. She cleared her throat. Took a deep breath. She could do this.

"I want you to find out who I am."

There, she'd done it. Broken Rule Number One.

She sat very still, staring at her hands. Her aunt had always been a little vague about the actual consequences of breaking the rules—just that they'd be dire. Tara had always imagined some sort of fiery bolt from above. Now she waited for it to crash down and annihilate her.

Nothing happened.

"So, you're not Tara Collins?"

"Yes. No. I don't know. I've always been called Tara Collins. But I don't know who she is or who my parents were or where I came from."

"Perhaps you'd better explain a little more."

She wished she could. Really she did. But she had no explanations; nothing she'd discovered since her aunt's death made any sense. "Maybe I should start at the beginning."

"A good place to start."

Was he mocking her? But his expression was bland and she decided to give him the benefit of the doubt. "I was brought up by my Aunt Kathryn. At least I always thought she was my aunt. We lived in a house on the Yorkshire moors. Aunt Kathy was a little…eccentric." And that was the understatement of the century. "She never left the house and she would have preferred it if I never left, though sometimes

I would…"

"You would?"

Sometimes she would sneak out and hide on the moors, high above the nearby village, and watch the people go about their normal lives, and dream of being part of that. But that sounded pathetic and for some reason she didn't want Christian Roth to think her pathetic. "Sometimes I would go out, but mostly I'd stay. It was an odd life, but I didn't know any different, and I was happy, at least when I was younger. Then six months ago my aunt died."

The familiar sense of loss washed over her. Her aunt's death hadn't been sudden—she'd been ill for a long time—but it had been the end of everything Tara had known.

"And?"

Her hands gripped the edge of the desk in front of her. "And I found everything she had told me was lies."

"Everything?"

"I don't think she was even my aunt. I don't know who she was, or why she brought me up. After she died, I found papers, but there was nothing about her. It was like she never existed." She glanced at his impassive face. "My whole world was a lie. Everything I was brought up to believe in." All those stupid rules she had followed for the last twenty-two years.

"So what is it you'd like me to do?"

She frowned. Hadn't she been clear? "I told you, I want you to find out who I am. Who my aunt was and why she was looking after me." When he remained silent, she continued, "I have money to pay you. The house was in my name and I have all sorts of investments. I've got copies of the paperwork here. I thought it might help."

She took out the folder containing the meager amount of paperwork she'd been able to find about herself and her aunt and placed it on the desk in front of him. She watched as he flicked through the file, his eyes widening. Hers had almost popped out of her head when she'd seen how much money her aunt had stashed away, all in Tara's name.

Christian closed the file and sat back. "Why do you want to know?"

It was a good question, and one she'd asked herself many times. She had a life now. She had friends, was going to college, getting real qualifications. She had a chance of that normal life she'd always dreamed of. But while she'd love nothing more than to forget the past, she couldn't. All the time, in the back of her mind, the questions niggled.

Why had her aunt lied? What was she hiding? What was so bad that Aunt Kathy had concealed them away in that big old house on the moors? And what was it with all the stupid rules? The list of questions was endless and she needed answers.

"My life has been pretty odd until now and I just want to be normal. But what if I'm not?"

"So really, you want me to find proof that you're normal?"

She smiled; she'd come to the right place after all. "Yes."

There was a light tap on the door. She glanced over her shoulder as Graham peered inside.

"Christian—"

"What is it?"

"Piers Lamont is in reception."

"Okay, Graham. We've finished here for the moment."

Graham closed the door behind him and Christian rose to his feet. "Well, Ms. Collins—"

"Please, call me Tara."

"And you must call me Christian. Well, Tara, I'll read through the papers and see where we can go from there. Perhaps you can come back in a few days and answer any questions that come up."

She stood. "Do you think you'll find anything?"

"I'm sure I will, and don't worry," he added. "There will be an explanation."

Tara searched his face, trying to decide if he was telling the truth. Or was he just trying to placate her, because really he thought she was crazy, and he wanted to get her out of there fast? But his face was bland, impossible to read. Suddenly she felt drained. She'd done it, broken the rules, and now she had to live with whatever they found.

"Tara?"

"Yes?"

"One question before you go. How did you choose me?"

For a moment, she considered lying—after all, she had just said she wanted to be normal. Then she shrugged. "I didn't choose you. My cat did. He's called Smokey and I've had him all my life."

He scrutinized her as though wondering what to say next, or perhaps whether to say anything at all. "And just how did…Smokey, choose me."

"Well, he didn't pick you *personally*, just your company. He put his paw right on your advertisement." Christian regarded her with a strange expression in his eyes, and she hurried on, "I don't want you to think I'm crazy or anything, but Smokey is actually super bright and I did look you up on the internet afterward."

"Very…sensible."

Why did she get the impression that "sensible" was not the word he was thinking of right now? Perhaps it was time to leave.

He must have decided the same, because he strode past her and opened the door. Graham waited on the other side.

By the time she entered the elevator, Tara was grinning like the mad woman Christian no doubt thought her to be. She'd done it—broken Rule Number One—and hadn't been struck down by a bolt from above. Then again, maybe it was a delayed reaction. Maybe that bolt would hit her as she walked out the door. Her grin faded.

"Are you okay?'

The elevator had stopped, but Graham watched her, a slight frown on his face.

"Sorry?" she said.

"Mr. Roth can be overwhelming when you first meet him."

"He was very kind. I'm just a little worried about what he'll find out."

"I'm sure it will be fine." Graham pressed the button and the doors parted. A man stood waiting, and Tara's mouth fell open.

He looked like a rock star. An enormous rock star. Shoulder length blond hair pulled into a ponytail, blond designer stubble, lots of black leather. She had a brief impression of him smiling at her, before Graham nudged her out of the elevator.

The rock star inhaled deeply as she passed. "Mmm. Sugar and spice."

Her feet slowed, but Graham somehow maneuvered her, not very gently, across the reception area. She glanced over her shoulder. The rock star was definitely smiling.

The cold air hit her face as Graham escorted her from the building.

"Mr. Roth told me to make another appointment in a couple of days' time."

"Friday," he said. "Seven o'clock."

"I can take time off, come during the day, if it's easier."

"Mr. Roth prefers evening appointments. Seven will be fine."

He disappeared back into the building. Glancing at the dark alley opposite, Tara took a deep breath and set off down the brightly lit street.

Now for Rule Number Two.

...

Her cat?

Christian Roth stared at the closed door. He'd lived a long time, and very little surprised him these days. But her *cat*?

He inhaled, catching the lingering scent of her on the air. It was mouthwatering; a sweetness tinged with a sharp, bitter flavor he found intoxicating. He'd spent the entire interview wondering whether she tasted as good as she smelled.

She was also ravishingly pretty, with that bright blond hair and huge green eyes. But that wasn't usually enough to catch his attention. There was something more, something very different about Tara Collins. He just couldn't work out what.

Yesterday, someone had left him a very cryptic message, suggesting he should meet her. He'd been undecided. Then earlier this evening, Piers had called and told him there'd been a demon sighting close to his building. Hunting demons wasn't Christian's job anymore, but he'd gone as a favor. He'd tracked the demon to the alley opposite and then been totally distracted by a delectable blonde who'd crashed into him and sent his senses reeling.

She'd had the same effect when she walked into his office. For the first time in what seemed like an age, his hunger had risen. Even now, his gums ached with the need to feed. If it hadn't been for Piers's imminent arrival, he'd have gone hunting tonight with little Tara Collins as his prey.

But Piers *was* on his way. First the phone call, now a personal visit. Piers was head of the Order of the Shadow Accords, the organization that policed the supernatural world, and whatever he wanted, it was unlikely to be good news. Still, Christian couldn't deny the twinge of excitement that twisted his guts. He'd made the right decision to leave the Order, but he missed the exhilaration of the chase, the thrill of the kill.

Graham stuck his head around. He had a slightly frazzled look in his eyes, no doubt from the unexpected visitor; Piers tended to have that effect on humans, even ones like Graham, who had spent time around their kind and knew what they were.

"He's here," Graham said.

"Send him in."

"Another thing—Piers saw your new client in reception, and I'm guessing he liked what he saw."

"Shit." He'd have to warn Piers off, which was bound to pique his interest.

What was so alluring about Tara Collins?

Piers was dressed in his usual gear, black leather pants and a long black leather coat. Tall, around Christian's six-foot-four, he was lean and hard, and beneath the coat, he'd be armed with enough firepower to take down an army of demons. He looked exactly what he was—a killer.

He grasped Christian in a huge bear hug, and clapped him on the shoulders. Then his hands fell away, and he stepped back.

"Christian, you look like shit." A slow grin spread across his face. "In fact, it's worse than shit—you look like a businessman."

"I am a businessman."

"A *boring* businessman."

Christian didn't bother to deny it.

"You also look hungry."

"I haven't fed in a few days."

"Days?"

"Weeks then." Christian shrugged. "It's not a problem."

"Talking of eating, I ran into someone coming out of the elevator. Young, blond."

"Leave her alone."

"She smelled delicious."

"She's a client. I don't want you eating my clients. Now, what brings you here?"

Piers shoved his hands in his pockets and wandered across to the windows to stare out at the lights of the city. He appeared outwardly calm but Christian knew him too well. Something was bothering him and Christian had to curb his impatience as he waited.

Piers turned back to face him. "I want you to come back."

It wasn't anything he'd expected and he frowned. "Not going to happen. I left the Order twenty years ago—for good."

"Come on, Christian, you know it's not that simple."

"Can't you cope? You want me to come back and take over?"

"Hell, no," Piers said. "I like being the boss. We'll take you on as a consultant." His eyes drifted down over Christian. "You look like a consultant. Besides, don't you miss it?" Piers moved behind the desk, sat in the huge leather chair, and spun. "This is fun, but it hardly compares to hunting demons." He came to a halt facing Christian. "How can you live like this?"

"Easy."

Piers considered him for a moment, head to one side, weighing his next move. "Gabriel's dead."

Impossible.

Shock ripped through Christian. And following close on his disbelief came a wave of regret. The emotion was unexpected, and he turned away to give himself time to think.

Gabriel was the youngest of the Order's agents, but he'd still been strong. He should have been stronger than anything he came up against.

"We need you back, Christian."

"Tell me what happened to Gabriel."

"We don't know what happened to him. He went out on a call last Friday night—a typical minor demon sighting—and vanished. He never called in. Nothing."

"So how do you know he's dead?"

"What else could it be? We haven't heard from him in five days. Besides, Ella confirmed it. You know she's never been wrong."

A ripple of distaste ran through him at the mention of the Order's tame witch. Ella had long ago given herself over to the dark practices, but she was powerful, so the Order protected her.

"She also believes something big is coming," Piers said.

"Another war?"

"She couldn't say. But there's more. It was Ella who told us to come to you."

Christian's eyes narrowed as he processed that piece of information. Not good news. "Why?"

"Again, she couldn't say, just that you had an important part to play."

"Couldn't say, or wouldn't? Does she know more?"

"I don't think so, but you know Ella—she has her own agendas."

"You were fools to keep her on. I told you that when you took over. You should have eliminated her after the last time."

"She's useful."

"She's evil."

Piers smiled. "That's rich, coming from you."

Christian pursed his lips. It was an ongoing argument between them. "Do you really believe we're evil?"

"Good, evil, who knows? By most peoples' standards we are. So, are you coming back? Will you help?"

"I need to think about it."

But it was a lie—he didn't need to think. Excitement unfurled deep inside him, rising to the surface and mingling with the hunger that already stirred in his blood. He knew he'd go back.

Piers grinned. "You'll be back. Just don't take too long." He got up, nodded, and left the room.

Christian sank into the chair behind his desk and rested his head on the back of the seat, staring into space. So few emotions touched him now, but he recognized sadness. Gabriel had been one of his, the last of his offspring.

Christian had left The Order after the last demon war, sickened by the carnage, but also aware of the darkness rising within himself, of the part of him that reveled in the slaughter, that loved to slake his hunger with demon blood.

So he'd stepped down, pursued a different life, a life among humans.

Now Gabriel was dead, and Christian would have his revenge. He'd hunt down whatever had taken Gabe, kill them, and drain their blood. It was a long time since he'd feasted on immortal blood. Humans were fine, but nothing beat the blood of a demon.

His hunger rose. The office suddenly seemed like a cage. He needed to get out into the night.

Graham glanced up as he entered the outer office. "You have a finance meeting in half an hour," he said as Christian paused by the desk.

"Cancel it."

"Where are you going?"

Christian smiled, with a small flash of fang. "I'm going hunting."

Chapter Two

Rule Number Two: Never drink alcohol.
So what was next?
Tara touched the chain she always wore around her neck, rubbing her fingers over the familiar heart-shaped crystal. Perhaps she wasn't ready for Rule Number Three yet, but she was meeting Jamie and Chloe at a bar, and planned to have a damned good go at Number Two.

The bar was a trendy place done up like an old-fashioned pub, with wood paneling and horse brasses hanging on the walls. It was popular with the after-work crowd and the steady hum of voices met her as she pushed open the door. It took her a moment to locate her friends in the dim light. They were arguing about something but shut up as she approached. They both smiled brightly.

Tara frowned. "Everything okay?"
"Great," Chloe said. "And I love your hair."
"You really think it's all right?" Tara ran a self-conscious hand through her hair. She'd gone out that morning with it down to her waist. Now it was cut off blunt, level with her

shoulders.

"It's gorgeous. That long fringe is very sexy, makes your eyes look enormous."

Chloe and Jamie were new friends; Tara didn't have any old ones. She had literally bumped into Jamie on her first day in the city. Nothing in her life had prepared her for London, and Jamie had helped her from the start. After six months, it was as if she'd known him all her life.

Chloe lived in the apartment below Tara.

"Jamie was just telling me that I'm a bad influence," Chloe said. "That you're a nice girl, and I shouldn't try to change that."

Tara took off her coat and perched herself on the red leather stool opposite. "I don't want to be a nice girl."

"Hah!" Chloe grinned. "I told you so."

Jamie frowned at her. "She doesn't know what she wants. She's obviously still in shock from her aunt's death." He stood up. "I'll go get you a drink. You want a coke?"

"No. I'll have a..." She didn't know what to have. Chloe was drinking a pint of something dark and not particularly appetizing.

"Guinness," Chloe supplied.

"You do not want to drink Guinness," Jamie said.

"I'm determined to break Rule Number Two tonight. So accept that, or sit down, and I'll get my own drink."

"Rule Number Two?" Chloe asked.

"My aunt had all these stupid rules. Rule Number Two was never drink alcohol."

Chloe's eyes widened. "You mean you've never had a drink? Not ever?"

Tara shook her head.

Chloe regarded Tara curiously. "Your aunt sounds like she was crazy. Why did you stay so long?"

"I'd planned to go to college when I was eighteen. But

Aunt Kathy got ill, and I couldn't leave her. I was all she had and, rules or not, I loved her."

Still, it had given Tara insight on how love could be used against someone, and she never wanted anyone to have that sort of power over her again. An unexpected vision of Christian Roth flashed through her mind, and a wave of heat washed over her.

"What are you thinking?" Chloe asked. "You've got a funny look on your face."

"Nothing. You know, I think I'll have a glass of white wine."

Jamie didn't appear happy about it, but he went off to the bar without any more argument.

"It's quite sweet really," Chloe said. "Jamie and you, I mean. It's like he wants to look after you."

"I don't need looking after."

Chloe patted her arm. "Of course you don't, sweetie. How did it go with the private investigator?"

"I never got to see Mr. Grant."

"You didn't?"

"He couldn't make it. I saw Christian Roth instead. He's the owner of the company."

Chloe gaped at her. "You *saw* Christian Roth?"

Tara nodded. "Do you know him?"

"No one knows him. At least, if they do, they don't talk about it. He's like this totally mega-rich recluse. Absolutely gorgeous, or so the rumors go. There's always stuff in the papers about him but never photographs. I can't believe you got to see him. What was he like?"

"He was very nice."

"Very nice?" Chloe said, her voice rising in disbelief. "I can't believe anyone would actually get to see Christian Roth and have the nerve to say he was 'very nice.' Come on, spill the beans, tell all."

"Tell all what?" Jamie placed a very small glass of wine in front of Tara, and another pint of Guinness for Chloe.

"Tara had a meeting with Christian Roth."

"Really? That's...interesting."

"Interesting?" Chloe shook her head. "It's not *interesting*. It's amazing."

Tara inspected her drink. She thought about taking a sip but decided to put it off a little longer. After all, breaking Rule Number Two was a momentous occasion, and she was determined to treat it as such. Instead, she considered what to say to Chloe.

"Christian Roth was..." She paused, unsure how to express what she'd felt about it, yet equally unsure she wanted to put it into words. "The rumors were wrong. He isn't gorgeous, at least not in any normal way, but there was something about him. It's more than looks, there's this sort of aura."

Chloe sighed. "That, my friend, is pure power. He runs that company single-handedly, and it's huge. The Investigations side is only a tiny part. And yet, he took an appointment with you. It's unbelievable, and not a little strange." She considered Tara for a moment. "Maybe he caught a glimpse of you coming into the building and liked what he saw. Did he make a pass?"

"No, he didn't!" But Tara remembered the hot look in his eyes as he held her hand, the energy that had leapt between them at his touch.

"So is he going to take the job?" Jamie asked.

Tara nodded. "I left some papers with him. I'm going back in a couple of days. He reckons there will be some sort of logical explanation for what my aunt did."

"Oh come on, Tara," Chloe said. "Logical? What sort of person keeps their kid in total isolation? And uses moral blackmail to make them stay."

"She was ill," Tara said gently.

Chloe ignored the interruption. "I bet he finds out that she lost her own baby or something and decided to grab another one."

"I suppose it's possible." But something told Tara the solution wasn't that simple.

Chloe continued, "Why don't you do a search on old kidnapping cases and find out if any babies went missing around that time?"

"It can't do any harm," Jamie added. "You might even be able to do it on the Internet."

Tara felt her interest rise. At least it was something she could do herself instead of sitting around waiting. "I'll do it," she said. "Now, to breaking that rule."

The wine was pale golden. She raised the glass to her nose and breathed in the light, fruity fragrance. Glancing up, she found Jamie watching her intently. She held his eyes as she brought the glass to her mouth and took a sip. The wine was cool, not sweet but tart, and refreshing. She swallowed, felt the liquid slide down her throat. She smiled at Jamie. "See? Absolutely no—"

She stopped mid-sentence and frowned. There was a sharp, bitter aftertaste that burned in her throat. She was about to comment on it when something went pop inside her head. Flames flickered in her belly and a wave of wild exhilaration washed over her. Alcohol was even better than she'd expected. She wanted to get up, run, scream, rip something to pieces, preferably with her teeth. And she was hungry, ravenously hungry. She wanted meat.

Which was weird because she was a vegetarian.

Still, she needed to get up. She put her hands on the table and pushed. Nothing happened. She seemed to have no strength in her arms. She stared at Jamie and Chloe, who watched from across the table, eyes wide with shock.

"Tara, what is it?"

She licked her dry lips. "I want—" The words stuck in her throat, she could hardly force them out of her mouth. She gripped the edge of the table until her fingers hurt. The world was shrinking, a black mist encroaching around her until all she could see was a small circle of light that framed Jamie's face.

"Tara?"

His voice sounded as though it was a long way off. The circle shrank to a pinprick and everything went black.

Chapter Three

Christian woke as the sun went down over London.

He stretched, reveling in the feeling of well-being—he hadn't felt this alive in decades. He'd hunted the previous evening, and his body was replete, filled with power. But it was more than just the feeding. Piers had been right. He missed the excitement of heading the Order, and now he had the chance to go back.

There was also his newest client, Tara Collins. His mind filled with the intoxicating scent of her. The sensible thing would be to keep their interactions strictly on a business footing. Relationships with humans never worked.

Only trouble was, he was bored with being sensible.

The Order and Tara Collins. What to do?

He stood in front of the open closet and knew he'd made his decision when he pushed aside the formal business suits and pulled on his old Order gear.

He paused on his way out of the building to talk to Graham.

"Nice outfit," Graham said, his gaze running over

Christian's long black leather coat.

Christian placed the file he'd gotten from Tara on the reception desk. "I want you to look at this. Find out what you can on the aunt."

"Sure, boss."

It was still early when he walked into the bar, and most of the tables stood empty. Slow music played in the background, and the lights were dim. Ella's scent lingered in the air, sharp and acrid. Christian found her sitting on one of the stools that lined the back wall and took a moment to study her. She hadn't aged in the thirty years he'd known her, and he wondered who'd paid for that—all magic had a price, and Ella had never been too particular about who paid it.

She'd dressed to impress in a skintight dress the color of fresh blood. It showed off her perfect figure, slender yet with all the right curves, but then Ella was unlikely to leave that sort of thing up to nature. He wondered what she looked like shorn of all the spells. Some sort of raddled old hag was his guess, complete with warts on her nose.

She wore sheer black stockings and crimson stilettos. Her legs were crossed and one foot bounced in the air. Glancing up as he approached, her sullen expression was replaced by a curving smile that didn't quite reach her dark eyes.

Christian strode over and stopped in front of the table. "You came."

"The great Christian Roth calls and everyone comes running."

He raised an eyebrow, but didn't reply.

Ella shrugged. "Piers ordered me to come and give you anything you want." She stared up at him from sultry eyes, hot and sensual. "What do you want, Christian?"

Shuddering in disgust, he made no effort to conceal the reaction, and she scowled.

"You could at least make an effort to be pleasant. You

asked for this meeting, after all." She wiped the frown from her face with practiced ease and smiled again. "Come on Christian, honey, we could have fun together. You liked me once."

"Let's be clear about this." His voice was ice cold. "Be thankful I left the Order when I did. If I'd stayed, you would have died twenty years ago."

The smile slid from her face, and for a moment, fear showed in her expression. But she quickly regained control. "Don't be so sanctimonious, you've killed—countless times. Why look down on me for doing the same thing? The Order knows I can't do my work without making some sacrifices."

"And are all the sacrifices you perform for your work?" Christian grabbed her chin between his finger and thumb, forcing her to look into his eyes. He studied her pale flawless skin. She had to be in her sixties—she could have passed for twenty-five. "Been sacrificing virgins and bathing in their blood, Ella?"

"Don't be disgusting. I use anti-wrinkle cream—it can take years off a woman."

He released his hold on her chin. "We might both kill, but our reasons are worlds apart."

"But then, you hardly need to worry about wrinkles. And neither would I if you'd agree to my request."

"Females never survive the transition." She'd come to him more than thirty years ago, asking to be changed, to become a vampire. That she could even think he would consider it was crazy.

Her expression became eager. "I've been working on a spell—"

He eyed her coldly. "I would tie you to the stake and light the match myself before I would consider turning you. Or allowing you to be turned."

"Bastard!"

"Without a doubt. And now the pleasantries are over, perhaps we can get down to business." He slid on to the stool opposite her. "Are you going to tell me what's going on?"

"I thought Piers had already told you. I don't know what more I can add."

He forced down the anger that threatened to overwhelm him. "Just tell me what you saw."

"Not a lot. The night Gabriel disappeared, I saw him in a vision. I warned him not to go. He didn't listen." Her eyes glittered with malice. "You taught him too well, Christian. He's never trusted me, and that's your fault. If he'd listened to me, instead of you, he'd still be alive."

Christian ignored the taunt. "Piers said the demon was only a minor one, that Gabe should have had no problem sending it back. So what happened?"

"How should I know? At a guess, they're getting strength from something way more powerful." She took a sip of her wine. "From what I've picked up, the lesser demons are hunting for something. This isn't just normal mischief. Someone is sending them across and whoever it is, they're lending them power."

"Who would be strong enough to do that?"

"Not many. Probably one of the seven. Could be your old friend, Asmodai."

His eyes narrowed at the name, and he felt the familiar surge of hatred at the thought of the demon prince. "Have you any proof of that?"

"None, but it makes sense. He hates you, probably not as much as you hate him, but he still hates."

"Piers told me that you believed I was involved."

"I saw you, straight after the vision with Gabriel—the two are obviously connected."

Christian didn't like her, but he sensed she was telling the truth. He also knew he had all the information he was going to get tonight. But did Ella really believe Asmodai was involved, or was she just trying to wind him up? It was hard to tell. She hated Christian, but she also wanted him, wanted what she believed he could give her, and that made her dangerous.

He stood up. "If you discover anything else, you'll let me know."

"Of course, oh Lord and Master."

Christian ignored the sarcasm. His cell phone rang as he left the bar. He glanced at the caller ID. "Piers?"

"Things are just getting better and better," Piers said.

Christian sighed. "What is it?"

"I just received a tip-off. Apparently the Walker is around."

Christian's fingers tightened on the phone. "Are you sure?"

"That's what the man said. The Walker's been seen, and he's hunting."

"Hunting what?"

"My informer didn't have a clue, but he reckoned we'd want to know."

Too right, he wanted to know. Unlike demons, the fae had little desire to come to earth. They tended to hold humans in total contempt, along with anything else that wasn't pure fae, and the Walker was the worst. He was also an assassin, and had no right setting foot out of the Faelands. What the hell drew him so far from home?

Gabriel was dead, one of the seven probably involved, and now the Walker was abroad. Was it all tied in or mere coincidence? Coincidence seemed unlikely. He didn't believe in coincidence.

"You still there?" Piers asked.

"Just thinking. You need to set up a meeting with the fae."

Piers swore. "Yeah, I'd already decided that, but I hate fucking fairies."

Christian agreed. At least you knew where you were with a demon. The fae were tricky. He ended the call.

There were a few people he could talk to who might have information. Or he could return to the office, but that held no appeal. He headed off into the night.

...

Dawn was close by the time he returned to CR International. Graham, as he'd expected, was still at the reception desk.

"Good night?" Graham asked as he came through the doors.

"No," Christian growled. "A complete fucking waste of time."

Graham raised an eyebrow, and Christian shrugged.

"Fae problems. I spent most of the night trying to find out just how big, but I don't seem too popular. I couldn't find anyone who might talk. They all seem to be avoiding me."

"Is that significant?"

"Probably. Definitely. How about you?"

"I looked up that information you asked for, about Kathryn Collins."

Christian forced his mind from the night's findings or rather lack of them. "Aunt Kathy?"

"Yeah, Aunt Kathy. You're not going to believe it. And you aren't going to like it."

Christian sighed. "Give me the file."

Graham handed it over and Christian flicked through the contents. "You're sure about this?"

Graham nodded.

Christian thought about Tara Collins. What was it she'd said she wanted? A normal life? He suspected he wasn't the only one who wasn't going to be pleased about this information. That was, if she ever got to the point of even believing it.

...

The young red-haired man, Graham, was at the reception desk when Tara came through the sliding doors of CR International at seven o'clock on Friday night. He looked up as she stopped in front of the desk and regarded her curiously. A slight sense of misgiving niggled at her. She ignored it and smiled with forced brightness.

"Hello," she said, "I have an appointment with—"

"I remember. You can go right up."

"I can?"

He nodded.

"Don't you need to come?" she asked.

His lips curved in a smile, and he shook his head. "Not this time."

Within minutes, she stood outside those huge double doors, her stomach churning, her pulse thundering.

It wasn't entirely the thought of seeing Christian Roth again—though that came into it. The truth was, she was still shaky from her bout with Rule Number Two. One teensy sip of wine and she'd blacked out. She'd eventually woken four hours later, to find herself on a trolley in the local ER.

In the two days since, she'd almost managed to convince herself it had been some sort of allergic reaction to the alcohol. Almost but not quite, because she clearly remembered those few seconds before she'd blacked out. The wild exhilaration racing through her veins. It had felt so good. Even now, if she closed her eyes she could feel a residual buzz humming in her blood. That was so not normal.

She'd raised a hand to knock when the doors swung open

and Christian stood before her.

Tonight he hadn't bothered with a suit, but was wearing black cargo pants and a black button-down shirt. He looked lean and mean, and heart-stoppingly beautiful. Which was strange. Last time she'd been so sure he wasn't handsome, now she couldn't look away. She made a lingering sweep of his body before forcing her gaze to his face.

"You look different," she said.

A flicker of amusement flashed in his silver gray eyes. "I've been eating well," he murmured. "Come in."

He stood back and gestured for her to enter. Tara hesitated, then took a deep breath and stepped past. She stood just inside the door and listened as it clicked shut behind her. "Right, shall we get on with this?"

"First, can I get you a drink?" he asked.

Tara shuddered at the thought of alcohol. She wasn't ready to face that particular challenge just yet. "I don't think so."

"A coffee, something to eat?"

"This isn't a social call, Mr. Roth."

"I thought we'd decided you would call me, Christian." He circled, his eyes sliding over her. "I like your outfit, by the way, very nice. Black suits you."

"Er, thank you." He was standing too close, and she edged away and sat in one of the upright chairs in front of the desk, clutching her bag on her lap.

He took the seat opposite her and regarded her through half-closed eyes. His gaze lingered on her mouth then dropped lower to focus on her throat. Tara refused to twitch under his stare, however much she wanted to.

After a minute, he smiled. "You seem more confident this evening."

"I am. I've decided I'm being stupid worrying about all this—there's bound to be a rational explanation."

"There is?"

"Yes. My friend, Chloe, thinks maybe Aunt Kathy kidnapped me as a baby."

"Why would she do that?"

A flicker of irritation jabbed at her. "Because she lost her own baby, or maybe she couldn't have one. I did a search on the Internet and found all these cases." Reaching into her bag, she pulled out the papers. She handed them over and his eyes widened at the hefty file. "I'm convinced I'm in there somewhere. So I thought maybe you could concentrate your investigation on these."

He stared at the file. "Let me get this straight, you want me to investigate all these missing persons. Have you any idea how long that would take?"

"I told you I have the money."

He opened a drawer in his desk, dropped the file in, and slammed it shut. "In the meantime, I do have some information regarding your aunt."

Tara had been leaning toward him eagerly, now she drew back in her chair. A lump formed in her throat. She tried to swallow it, but it stuck somewhere halfway down. This was what she wanted, wasn't it? Why did she feel afraid? She bit down hard on her lower lip, tasted the sharp metallic taint of fresh blood.

She swiped her tongue over her lip, wiping away the drop of blood, and Christian stood abruptly, shoving back his chair. He crossed the room to stare out of the window, his shoulders tense, fists clenched at his side. Then the tension drained from him, and he swung around to face her. His gaze flickered to her mouth, then away, but not before she saw the heat in his eyes.

What was up with him?

It was weird, but she had the strangest feeling he was thinking about kissing her. Probably more delusions.

Tara forced herself to break the silence. "So, what did you find about my aunt?"

"Are you sure you won't have that drink?"

"Yes," she said impatiently. "Just tell me, please."

"Do you have a photograph of your aunt, a recent one?"

"Sure." After searching in her bag for her purse, she removed the small photo she always carried and handed it to him. Christian glanced at the picture briefly, then returned to his desk and opened a file. Taking out a photograph, he compared it to the one Tara had given him, before handing the second photo to Tara. "You agree that this is your aunt?"

"Of course it is."

"That's a photograph of Kathryn Collins. A photo taken nearly twenty-three years ago."

Tara studied both pictures. "But she looks exactly the same."

"I know, but then the dead don't age."

"What?" She must have misheard that last comment.

"The photograph I just gave you was taken over twenty years ago," he repeated. "Shortly before Kathryn Collins was killed when a drunk driver ran her car off the road."

The room went out of focus. Tara closed her eyes, trying to make sense of what he was telling her. A woman with the same name as her aunt, who looked identical to her aunt, had died over twenty years ago. There had to be an explanation. She opened her eyes to find Christian watching her, his face expressionless.

"Let me get you that drink," he said.

"No!" A drink was the last thing she needed. She took a gulp of air. "I'm all right. I just need to think this through." Her brain latched on to the obvious answer. "Identical twins?"

"How would that explain the fact that your aunt didn't age? Because she didn't, did she? Think back, Tara, remember your aunt when you were young. Was she really any different?"

Her aunt had just always been her aunt. Tara closed her eyes and pictured her first memories. Aunt Kathy explaining the rules when she was little, then again at regular intervals all the time Tara had been growing up. And each time she looked the same. Even her aunt's hair had never changed although Tara could never remember her going near a hairdresser.

She rubbed her temple with the tip of her finger, then pressed hard against her closed lids. She opened her eyes to find Christian still watching her. "What do you think happened?"

He crouched in front of her and ran a finger down her cheek. She shivered, his touch cool against her heated skin. Then his thumb brushed over her lower lip and she felt it as a caress low down in her belly. He was so close. If she leaned forward just a little bit…

He straightened and backed a step away. "What do you know of the supernatural?"

The question caught her off balance. "You mean, ghosties and ghoolies and…" She frowned. "I seriously hope you're not trying to tell me my aunt was a ghost."

"Actually no, I don't think your aunt was a ghost. You could touch her couldn't you? She ate and drank like a normal person?"

"Yes, she ate like a normal person. Because, you know what? She was a normal person." Albeit a rather strange one, but Tara pushed that thought to the back of her mind.

"Tara, your aunt was far from normal." He gestured to the photographs. "However much you dislike the idea, you have to acknowledge that something strange was going on."

Tara forced herself to calm down. "Okay, tell me what *you* think happened."

"The body of your aunt was never buried."

"Yes it was, I was there at the funeral."

He sighed. "I mean twenty years ago."

She felt a spark of hope. "Well obviously it wasn't buried, because she wasn't dead. They made a mistake."

"There was no mistake. I've seen the death certificate and the coroner's report—she was dead twenty years ago. The body disappeared before it could be buried. There are reports, they're all in the file."

"You're telling me I was brought up by a dead person. That Aunt Kathy was some sort of zombie?" She could hear her voice rising.

"Not a zombie, no."

"Well, thank goodness for that."

"There are other ways to reanimate a corpse."

Tara bolted from her chair. "I am not listening to this."

"You have to. The woman who brought you up has been dead for over twenty years."

She stared into his face, sure she must have heard him wrong, but no, he seemed serious. Suddenly she was furious. She took a step toward him and poked him in the chest. It was like stubbing her finger on a lump of rock and she winced. "You are so not funny."

She blamed her cat for this. Trust Smokey to pick the one nutcase private investigator in the whole of London. "And by the way," she added. "You're fired!"

She grabbed her purse and stormed away. She'd almost reached the door when he spoke again.

"Tara—"

She whirled.

Somehow, he was right behind her and she almost slammed into him. She put up her arms to ward him off and her palms flattened against his chest. He leaned forward and kissed her.

She stood there, hands splayed against his chest, while he touched her only with his lips. The kiss was slow, erotic. He tasted her with his tongue, and she let him do whatever he wished. It was over far too soon, and he stepped back.

In a daze, she opened the door and was just about to step through when he called her again. She stopped and turned.

He handed her the file, his expression sympathetic. "When you've read this, calmed down, and are willing to listen, come back."

"When hell freezes over."

She tried to calm herself as she rode down in the elevator, but bitter disappointment clogged her throat. She'd been so hopeful a private investigator would find a nice logical explanation for what had happened in her past, why her aunt had kept them isolated for so many years. Instead, she'd hired a madman, who talked about dead people as though they had the power to walk and talk and eat. A madman who'd had the nerve to kiss her. She could still feel that kiss against her lips—she'd never imagined a kiss could feel like that.

Graham regarded her as she stepped up to the reception desk, his eyes widening as he took in the red folder she clutched. Did he know what was in there? Had they laughed as they put it together?

"Would you like another appointment?" he asked.

"No," she said. "I won't be coming back, and you can return this to your madman of a boss." She slapped the file on the desk and headed for the door.

"Tara."

"What?"

"You could be in danger."

She stalked from the building. Outside, she gazed about for a moment then headed for the alley opposite—the quickest way to the train station. She hesitated at the entrance; the alley was narrow, the streetlights penetrating only a few feet, and beyond that, utter darkness.

Of course she wasn't in danger. Of course she hadn't been brought up by a dead woman. Of course there wasn't something really scary waiting for her down this alley.

And if there was, all she could say was—it had better watch out.

Chapter Four

"Well that went well," Christian murmured.

What the hell had happened to keeping his hands off her?

Though it wasn't his hands that were the problem. He hadn't been able to resist that one fleeting kiss, and she tasted as good as he'd expected. A delicious combination of bitter and sweet he'd never encountered before. If he had put his hands on her he probably would have dragged her back in here and not let her out again until sunrise.

But she didn't want that. She wanted "normal," and he was about as far from normal as it was possible to get.

Perhaps he should have kept the information about Kathy Collins to himself. He had considered that option, but was worried. Tara was obviously human—it came off her in waves—so why would she have an undead guardian? And why had the undead guardian up and died? Presumably, the spell giving her life had run out of power. But who had brought Kathryn Collins back to life in the first place and why?

There had to be a good reason, because magic like that never came cheap. Someone had paid a high price to protect

Tara. And if she didn't find out why she needed safeguarding, her chances of a normal life were remote.

Part of him liked the idea of protecting her, but he knew nothing good could come of bringing her into his world however much he might crave it. A wave of bitterness washed over him. It had been more than five hundred years since his wife and two daughters had been slaughtered in a demon attack. Christian had nearly died himself. The Order had offered him a chance to get his revenge. Since that night, he'd embraced the darkness wholeheartedly. For centuries, he'd fought demons, slaughtered demons, feasted on their immortal blood.

Until one sunset, he'd risen from his sleep to realize he no longer wanted that life. Or rather death.

He'd turned his back on the Order and tried to make a place for himself in the world of humans. But now he was bored, and he wanted more. He wanted Tara Collins. Maybe just one small taste and afterward, he would sort out whatever mess she was in, and send her on her way unaware how close she had come to the darkness.

His cell phone rang. It was Piers. "What?" Christian growled.

Piers chuckled. "Bad moment? Is your balance sheet not adding up?"

"What do you want?"

"Are you aware that there's a lot of demon activity going on tonight?"

"So, send someone after them."

"Aren't you interested where?"

Christian sighed. "Get to the point, Piers."

"They're right outside your building. Again."

"What?"

"I thought that might wake you up. I can send out agents, but I thought you might want to take a look."

Demons shouldn't even be able to pick up the fact that he was here. He'd paid a very expensive warlock a whole load of money to have the place warded, to make himself invisible.

"I'm on to it," he said.

"Let me know what you find."

Christian slipped the phone into his pants pocket, a flame of excitement burning in his belly. If he couldn't have sex with the delectable Tara Collins, fighting demons had to be the next best thing.

He went to the cupboard at the back of his office and pulled on a shoulder holster. After selecting a semi-automatic pistol, he made sure it was loaded and shoved it into the holster. He strapped a knife sheath at his waist, tied it down to his thigh, and slotted in the eight inch serrated blade. He covered the whole lot with a long, black leather coat.

Avoiding reception, he slipped out the back way. The door opened into an alley that ran along the rear of the building, and he stood in the dim light and scented the air.

There it was, the faint tang of sulfur. He inhaled deeply to determine which direction it was strongest. He set off down the alley, emerged onto the main street, and he glanced around. Another alley cut across the street opposite. Some instinct made him the peer into the darkness.

Far up ahead he could make out a figure hurrying in the opposite direction: Black coat, small and a bright head of blond hair. Christian recognized her immediately.

Had she no common sense? Even if she didn't believe in "ghosties and ghoulies," there were plenty of human scavengers who loitered in dark alleys, just waiting for people naive enough to venture down them.

He hustled after her, keeping to the shadows. He would make sure she reached her train station, and then he would go demon hunting. But as the darkness crowded around him, the strong odor of sulfur filled his nostrils.

Up ahead, Tara slowed until she came to a halt at least twenty feet from the end of the alley.

Keep moving, he urged, silently. She could still come out of this unharmed if she reached the main street—nothing would follow her there. It took him mere seconds to realize why she had stopped. A demon blocked her path. From a distance, it appeared almost human, only the dusky red skin identified it as something from the Abyss. That and the rank odor that intensified as Christian moved closer. The demon appeared oblivious to him, all its concentration on Tara. Christian drew his knife; he could take the thing down before it touched her.

A second demon slithered down the wall to Tara's right. Christian went still. His knife was raised and ready to throw, but he glanced between the two, unsure which presented the greater threat. While he hesitated, the second demon leapt for Tara. It landed catlike on her shoulders, and she crashed to the ground under the weight. Her head cracked as it hit the concrete, and she lay unmoving, the demon crouched on her chest.

A wild fury roared through Christian and he reacted without thinking. All his muscles tensed, and he flew the last few feet landing close beside them. His free hand gripped the demon's tangled hair; he ripped it away from Tara and flung it against the wall. It clambered to its feet, a low hiss emerging from the narrow, skinless lips. Up ahead the first demon drew closer, and from behind him came the unmistakable scent of a third.

He cast Tara a quick glance. Lying on her side, her hair covering her face, she appeared unconscious, but Christian could see no visible damage.

"Give us the woman, and you may go."

The first demon spoke. All three stood, side by side. Why weren't they running? They seemed unafraid, but had to know they were no match for a vampire.

"Let us have the woman, and you can go on your way, Christian Roth."

Christian frowned. "What do you want with her?"

"A little fun." The demon licked its lips. "A little food."

Adrenaline coursed through his system and his excitement rose. It had been years since he'd had a good fight. One of these lesser demons would have been a miserable waste of time, but three might give him a good workout. He held the knife loose in his hand and waited for them to make a move.

Two of them attacked without warning. Christian braced his legs and stood his ground. At the last moment, he raised the knife and impaled one through the throat. He pushed it away, wrenching the blade free, and the second was on him, grappling, its sharp pointed teeth snapping at his face. It latched onto his shoulder, slicing through the leather of his coat and sinking its fangs deep into his flesh.

The demon was incredibly strong, and too late he remembered Ella's comment that lesser demons were borrowing power from something stronger.

Ignoring the pain, Christian brought his free hand up, took hold of its throat, and ripped it away. His shoulder tore as the teeth remained locked into the muscle. Then he was free. He tightened his hold on the creature's neck, and the bones snapped under his fingers. Tossing the body from him, he spun to face the third demon. His shoulder was on fire and blood ran down his arm. He needed to finish this before he weakened.

The last demon circled him warily. It sniffed the air, muscles tensing, and Christian realized it was poised to run. He hurled the knife, taking the demon straight through the heart.

For a moment, he stood panting. Nothing moved, and he

crouched beside the body. The demon was dead. He dragged his knife free and used it to sever the head with one hard downward stroke. The scent of warm blood rose up and he swayed toward it, then forced himself back. They were dead—too late to feed now. He worked quickly, cutting off the other two demons' heads and watching them disintegrate into a pile of greasy gray ashes.

He rolled Tara onto her back and skimmed his hands over her. She moaned but didn't regain consciousness. Her face was pale, except for a dark bruise blossoming on her forehead. Rising to his feet, Christian swayed and rested his hand against the wall for balance. He was losing blood fast.

He needed to get Tara away, but there was no way he could carry her back. Besides, the streets were busy, and they'd hardly be inconspicuous. He pulled out his phone to call Graham, but at that moment a black SUV appeared at the head of the alley. The driver's door opened, and Piers grinned at Christian.

"Shame about the coat," he said. "Need a lift?"

...

Tara snuggled down. The pillow felt so cozy, soft as down, and silky smooth against her cheek. A dull ache throbbed at her temple, but as long as she didn't move too much it was bearable. She had no idea where she was, but she was definitely not in the alley, and that had to be a good thing. She thought about opening her eyes, but decided to put it off a little longer.

There were other people around. Muted voices, the rustle of clothing, but it all seemed far away. The last thing she remembered was that thing in front of her. It had come out of nowhere dressed in dark pants and a jacket with the hood pulled low over its face. At first, she'd thought it was a mugger or rapist, and she'd prepared to fight for her life.

It had come closer, sniffing the air, and a disgusting stench filled her nostrils—dirty smoke and rotten eggs. The hood had fallen back from its face and she'd gotten her first clear glimpse of her attacker.

It was red.

Not pink, but dark red. With yellow eyes.

She'd decided defending herself wasn't the good idea it had seemed a moment ago. No, running had seemed a much better option. Until something hit her from behind.

After that—nothing.

Oh God, perhaps she was in the lair of the red thing. She hoped not.

Opening one eye a fraction, she peered out through her lashes. The first thing she saw was Christian. A half-naked Christian. He still had his black pants on, but had stripped to the waist, and Tara had never seen anything quite so beautiful. His shoulders were broad, his hips lean, and the bits in between all ridged with muscle. His skin was pale, perfect with a light sprinkling of dark hair between his nipples and down his almost concave belly to disappear into the low-slung waistband. Midnight black hair hung loose around his shoulders, and there were dark shadows under his eyes.

"Graham?" Christian spoke softly, and the young man came into view. He seated himself on the end of the bed not far from Tara. He didn't even seem to notice her, simply sat, his hands in his lap, a small smile on his face. Tara had the feeling she was watching something private. That she should sit up. Tell them she was awake. Get out of there before it was too late.

Instead, she lay still as stone, hardly breathing, and watched.

Christian came up behind Graham and laid a hand on his dark red hair. He stroked his fingers through it, and tugged the head back, baring the long line of his throat. He moved in closer, rested one knee on the bed and pulled Graham back against his body, wrapping his arms around the other man's chest. Lowering his head, he licked at the throat, then his lips drew back exposing a huge pair of fangs he sank into Graham's neck.

Tara must have made a small noise because someone moved beside her. She dragged her gaze from the two men. A third man sat in a chair, his long legs resting on the edge of the bed. She recognized him as the blond rock star lookalike who'd been waiting for the elevator two days ago.

He smiled at her.

"Christian," he said. "Your guest is awake."

Christian didn't release his hold on Graham but he went still. His gaze caught hers, and held her trapped for long minutes. Then he closed his eyes and continued feeding.

Because that's what he was doing.

He was feeding.

Drinking blood.

Tara forced her mind to accept what she saw. Maybe he was just pretending. Or maybe he was insane, as she had told him earlier, some sort of supernatural wannabe, with a pair of stick-on fangs. But if he was pretending, he was doing an excellent job. She could see him swallowing as the blood flowed down his throat. Graham's face was blank, almost dreamy, his lips parted. He wasn't struggling; in fact, his whole body seemed to be straining upward. It was the most erotic thing she had ever seen, and a strange lightness filled her mind while her body grew hot and heavy.

She heard a low, masculine chuckle from beside her, and she forced her gaze back to the blond.

"It looks good, doesn't it?" he murmured. "So very, very good." His voice was low, husky, his eyes heavy-lidded, and he was staring at her greedily. "It's certainly making me hungry."

He grinned at her, flashing a pair of fangs that she hadn't noticed before. Her eyes widened. She scrambled into a sitting position and pulled herself as far from him as she could. He chuckled again and reached a hand toward her.

"Piers!"

The hand dropped, and Piers shrugged.

Christian had finished feeding. Graham sat with his eyes closed, breathing fast, but he appeared unharmed.

Christian came round and stared down at her from the side of the bed. "Are you okay?"

Her eyes flicked from his naked chest, to his face, to the blond man on the other side of her, and back to his face.

"I don't know," she said. "Am I?"

He reached forward, and she had to force herself not to flinch. For once, his fingers felt warm against her skin as he tilted her face so he could examine it closely. A brief flare of anger flickered across his expression, then it was gone.

"You'll live," he said.

She glanced again at the other man. He was sitting back relaxed in his chair, but hadn't lost that hungry expression. She shivered. "Will I?"

Christian smiled briefly. "You're in no danger here."

Tara believed him. She didn't know why, but she did. Sitting back against the pillows, she studied her surroundings. She was in a large spacious bedroom. The furniture simple but luxurious. The bed she sat on, the largest she had ever seen. "Where am I?"

"In my apartment. In the basement beneath the offices."

"In the basement?" *Of course he would live in the basement. Vampires didn't like the sun, after all.* Her brain stopped. She hadn't allowed the word into her head before. Now she rolled it over in her mind.

Vampire.

It was crazy. She needed to get out of there. But first, she wanted to know how she'd got there.

"How did I get here?"

"You were attacked in the alley after you left here." He frowned. "Has no one ever told you it's dangerous to go down dark alleys at night?"

"Actually, yes. You did." She sighed. "Anyway, it's your fault."

He raised an eyebrow. "And you reckon that because…"

"I was angry when I left here. I don't think too well when I'm angry."

"Only when you're angry?" he asked

"Hah, hah." She scowled. "So how did I get here?"

"I found you unconscious after you'd just been attacked. I scared them off and brought you back here."

She could see now that he had a rough bandage around one shoulder. "You fought those things?"

He nodded.

"Why did they want me?"

"You were just in the wrong place at the wrong time. Once they'd got a look at you—"

"A sniff more like," Piers interrupted. He leaned toward her and took a deep breath. "You smell delicious."

Tara ignored him. "What would have happened if you hadn't come along?"

Again, it was Piers who spoke. "They would have taken you to some dark, lonely place where they would have played with you for a while. Not long perhaps, though it would have seemed like an age to you, and then, in all probability, they would have eaten you."

Tara stared at him, trying to determine if he was telling the truth or trying to scare her. She decided a bit of both. "You're not a very nice person. Did you know that?"

Surprise flashed across his face, and he laughed.

"No, I'm not nice, but there aren't many people who would have the nerve to tell me that." He stood and said to Christian, "I'm going to check that everything's quiet outside. Then I'll be back to stitch your shoulder." He nodded in Tara's direction. "Get rid of her."

She glowered. "Get rid of me?"

A flicker of humor flashed in Christian's eyes. "Not permanently, but Piers isn't comfortable with humans around the Order's business."

"The Order?"

"Never mind."

"You'd have to kill me if you told me, right?" She peered into his face. "Actually, don't answer that."

He smiled and turned to Graham, who still sat at the end of the bed. "Graham, why don't you get us all a drink?"

Graham seemed to shake himself awake. He nodded, got up, and went over to a fridge against the far wall. "Beer okay?"

"Do you have any coke?" Tara asked.

"Sure." He took the tops off three bottles and brought them over. "Here Boss." He handed one to Christian, another to Tara. He sat in the seat next to the bed and drank. Tara watched as Christian took a gulp from the bottle.

"You can drink?"

"Yes. It's actually quite easy. You just lift the bottle to your mouth—"

Graham sniggered. Tara scowled but drank her own coke.

"Is there anyone who can come and pick you up?" Christian asked. "I can send one of the security guys with you, but you might feel happier with someone you know."

"Maybe. I'll phone Jamie."

His eyes sharpened on her. "Jamie?"

"He's a friend."

"A boyfriend?"

Suddenly, she remembered that he'd kissed her.

"No, just a friend. My bag—?"

Graham picked it up off the floor and handed it to her. She rummaged around for her cell phone, then glanced at Christian. He raised an eyebrow but turned away to give her at least the illusion of privacy.

Jamie answered straight away. "Where the hell are you?"

"I'm at CR international." She paused, wondering how to ask this without too much detail and without mentioning she had been wandering down dark alleys. She couldn't face a lecture just now.

"Tara?"

"Jamie, could you come and pick me up?"

He was silent for a moment. "Why do you need picking up? What have you done now?"

Tara scowled. No way was she mentioning the dark alley. "Er, I fainted again. I'm just feeling a little shaky. I don't want to go on the train on my own."

"You fainted. Have you been drinking again?"

She took a deep breath. "No, I haven't been drinking. I missed lunch, that's all it is."

He probably didn't believe her, but after a moment he sighed. "I'll pick you up in reception in half an hour."

She put the phone away and glanced up to find Christian watching her, amusement glinting in his eyes.

"What?" she asked scowling.

"He sounds more like your father than your boyfriend."

"I told you he's not my boyfriend, but I met him soon after I came to London. He sort of sees it as his duty to make sure the country bumpkin doesn't do anything stupid in the big city."

"No doubt a difficult job."

He turned to Graham. Something passed between the two men and Graham got up without a word and left the room. Tara stared after him then back at Christian. He was still half-naked, and he was still a vampire and he was sitting on the edge of the bed as if he had every right to be there. She inched away. He inched right after her.

"Is your head okay?" he asked.

"It's fine, just a little sore."

She fidgeted. She wasn't used to scenarios involving half-naked vampires and beds. Hell, she wasn't used to half-naked men and beds. Or even half-naked men and Christian was hard to ignore. There was so much of him.

"Right, I'd better get up and go meet Jamie."

His lips twitched. "You have half an hour."

"You could hear that? Don't tell me—some sort of vampire powers." She was quite proud of herself for saying the word without succumbing to hysterics. "Even so, I should get up."

He stroked down the line of her jaw. His fingers were cool now, but her skin burned where he touched. "Don't I get a reward for rescuing you? A kiss perhaps?"

Another kiss? She stared at his mouth. His lips were beautiful, but it wasn't his lips she was worried about, it was what was behind them.

"I'll write you a check," she mumbled.

He smiled as if he could see what was going on in her head. "You have no need to fear me," he said. "I've fed tonight."

"I know, I saw."

She shuddered at the memory, but it wasn't from horror. She remembered the expression on Graham's face as Christian fed. Heat flared again, low in her belly. She wasn't used to desire, but she could recognize the signs, and they terrified her. What she should be doing was running as fast as she could in the opposite direction. Instead, she stared, mesmerized as those lips lowered slowly toward her own.

Chapter Five

Tara didn't protest as Christian's hands slid into her hair, angling her face toward him. He kissed her, his tongue sweeping along the line of her closed lips.

"Open your mouth, Tara. Let me taste you," he whispered.

For a moment, she resisted, but she wanted his kiss so much. Maybe this was another vampiric power and he'd cast a spell on her. Then his lips were on hers again, and it didn't matter.

She opened her mouth, and the kiss hardened. His tongue thrust inside and without thought, her hands went up to tangle in his hair. His huge body came over her and pressed her onto the bed until she could feel his hardness through the layers that separated them.

Breaking from the kiss, he raised his head and held her gaze as he ground his hips into the softness of her belly. Heat flooded her, pooled at her core, and her eyes widened. Christian shifted lower, until he pushed against the junction of her thighs, and her whole body went up in flames.

"Oh."

He smiled, lowered his head, and kissed her again. She lost herself in that kiss, only coming back when he went still against her. Opening her eyes, she followed his gaze.

She closed her eyes again and pretended she was home and there was no six-foot-plus of half-naked vampire on top of her. And no six-foot-plus of fully dressed vampire lounging in the open doorway.

Piers watched them, an expression of amused curiosity on his face.

She shoved at Christian and tried to wriggle from under him.

"Don't move for a moment," he murmured into her ear.

She stilled.

Sighing, he rolled off her. He lay for a moment staring at the ceiling then sat up and pushed off the bed in one fluid move.

"Just wondered whether you were ready to have that shoulder stitched yet," Piers said.

Christian turned toward him. For the first time since she'd woken, Tara felt real fear. She shivered as she watched him stalk toward the other man. He moved slowly but every step radiated menace. He stared at Piers through narrow silver eyes. If the look had been directed at her, she would have shriveled up in fear.

Piers just grinned. "Well, at least you don't seem bored anymore."

Christian stared at him for a moment longer, and the tension drained out of his body.

Tara scrambled to her feet. She wanted out of there now—way too much testosterone pounded through the room.

Someone had removed her boots and coat, but she spotted them on a chair. Christian watched her, a slight frown on his face, but he didn't protest as she pulled them on.

"Right. I'm off," she said.

Christian crossed the room and stood before her. "I'm letting you go because you need time to think. When you have, come back to me."

Probably in about a thousand years, but she refrained from saying the words aloud. Instead, she forced her face into some semblance of a smile, and nodded.

He tilted his head toward her. This time, she swayed away from him, but his hand slid beneath the hair at the back of her neck and held her in place. The kiss was hard and fast, and afterward he whispered into her ear, "You will come back, Tara. We have unfinished business."

She glanced at the bed, not sure whether he was referring to that or to the search for her aunt, but she didn't feel up to asking. Perhaps it was better not to know. He stepped away, and she breathed again.

Tara headed for the door, but at the last moment, she turned and studied him. He was beautiful, but now she recognized it as the beauty of a predator, and underneath she could sense something cold, menacing.

"Are you evil?" she asked.

A startled expression crossed his face, then he shrugged. "That's something you must decide for yourself."

She nodded and left the room, ignoring Piers who stood aside to let her pass.

Graham waited for her outside. He didn't say anything, just led her to the elevator, but as they stood in the closed space, Tara couldn't stop herself from glancing at him surreptitiously. She recalled the expression on his face as Christian fed. He caught her looking and raised an eyebrow.

"What does it feel like?" she asked. "When a vampire feeds?"

He shrugged. "Vampires in general, I couldn't tell you. I've only ever fed Christian."

"What's it like?"

"Like the best sex you've ever had," he said, his expression dreamy. Then he grinned. "And I've had some great sex."

"I've never had sex."

His eyes widened. "Bloody hell. A virgin. Better not let Ella get a whiff of you."

"Ella?"

"Never mind."

She looked at him shyly. "Are you and Christian... Do you—"

"Have sex? Sleep together?"

She nodded.

"No. Christian is strictly into girls for sex. More's the pity."

The elevator doors opened and she followed him out into the reception area.

"Say, is that your friend?" Graham asked.

Jamie loitered on the other side of the glass doors, looking out of place and uncomfortable. His eyes latched onto her like a lifeline, and she smiled.

"Yes, that's Jamie."

"He's cute."

She ignored the comment. "Right, I'm off."

"Just a moment." Graham led her across to the reception desk and reached over the counter. He pulled out the red file she'd left earlier. In that long ago time, when she hadn't believed in reanimated corpses, vampires, or any of the other things that go bump in the night—or lurk in darkened alleys.

He handed it to her. "You might want to read that now."

She slanted him a rueful smile. "I doubt it." But she took the file and stuffed it in her bag.

"And here's my card. Just in case you feel the need to talk." He nodded toward Jamie. "It's best you don't mention any of this to your friends."

"Who would believe me? Trust me—you don't need

worry about that." But she took the card as well and slipped it inside the file in her bag. "At the moment, I don't want to think about it, never mind talk about it."

He smiled. "Come on, you can introduce me to your friend." He led the way out through the doors and came to a halt in front of Jamie.

"Hi, I'm Graham." He held out his hand. Jamie took it with obvious reluctance.

"Jamie," he muttered.

Graham appeared amused, but he dropped the hand and turned to Tara. "Remember, call me if you need to talk."

She nodded.

"What are you going to need to talk to that guy about?" Jamie asked as Graham went back inside the building and the doors shut behind him. He stayed on the other side of the doors and watched them.

"Sorry?" she said to Jamie.

"I asked, what are you going to talk to him about that you can't say to me?"

He sounded jealous, but Jamie had never come on to her like that.

"Nothing. I don't plan to go back. I've sacked Christian Roth from the case. I decided it was a waste of time. I'm going to do some research into the kidnappings and missing persons myself."

"So how come you were still at the offices?"

"God! What is this, twenty questions? If you must know, I wasn't. I'd left already. Luckily, Christian found me."

"Christian? Found you where? Where did you faint?"

"In an alley," she mumbled. "On the way back to the station."

"What the hell were you doing in an alley?"

She heaved a huge, audible sigh. "Leave it will you, Jamie. I fainted but I'm okay, honest, just a little shocked. I'll go to the doctors tomorrow," she lied. "I'm probably anemic or something."

Jamie's eyes narrowed in suspicion. Then he shrugged. "Let's go get you something to eat."

"A steak," she said. "I want a nice, big juicy steak."

"But you're a vegetarian."

"Not any longer."

...

Just how long was he supposed to give her, Christian wondered on waking the following evening.

A month, a week, one night?

One night sounded good. He was tempted to go and see her later that evening, but he'd promised to give her time. In most cases, he would have cleared her memory of the whole vampire thing before he sent her home last night. Piers had been pissed off that he hadn't, but Tara was different. She had her own issues, all tied up with why a dead woman had been caring for her for the past twenty-two years.

But those issues could wait. They weren't likely to be pressing, whereas Gabriel dead and gangs of super-strong demons roaming the city were. His first priority was to kill the demons or send them back to the Abyss where they belonged. Then he'd be free to pursue his little human.

How difficult could it be? He could sort out the demon problem tonight, and see Tara tomorrow.

...

The Order was housed in an office block, in the center of the business district of the city, a fifteen minute drive from his building. They rented out the upper floors to human businesses, but the building went below ground almost as far as it went up toward the sky, and it was here that the Order staff worked.

Security cleared him, and he rode the elevator down to the lowest level where Piers had his office. It had once been Christian's office, but now reflected Piers's more flamboyant personality.

"We lost another agent last night," Piers told him. "Stefan."

A shaft of pain ripped through him. Stefan, like Gabe, was one of his. He'd been a good man before death and a good vampire after. "It doesn't make sense. Why kill agents? They must know we'll come after them."

"Maybe they are getting ready for another full-scale attack. Maybe they're trying to weaken the Order."

"Picking off odd agents isn't going to do that. There has to be something more."

Piers shrugged. "It could be that the attacks are more personal. You know Ella believes that Asmodai is involved. That he's the source of the extra power. Maybe he's after you."

Christian frowned. "Why me? Why make it personal?"

"You were head of the Order during the last war. You were responsible for beating Asmodai and banishing him back to the Abyss. He must know that you wanted him killed. And look at the agents we've lost—Gabriel and Stefan. That sounds pretty fucking personal to me." He cast Christian a pointed glance. "And perhaps he knows you feel the same way about him."

"Don't go there," Christian growled.

"Look, I don't know what happened, and I don't care, but don't ever try and deny there's bad feeling between the two of you over and above your involvement in the wars."

Christian rubbed his forehead. Piers was right. It was too much of a coincidence.

"We need to capture one of these demons," Christian

said.

"Sounds like fun."

"It's not going to be easy. They're strong, and working in teams. Make sure none of the agents go out alone, and next time there's a sighting we go in force. Get one of them alive. We need to find out who's sending them and what they're after. And we need to find out fast."

Piers grinned. "It's good to have you back. I was seriously worried with all that businessman shit going in."

Christian frowned. "This is only temporary."

"Yeah, right. And afterward, you'll be going back to your balance sheets. Of course you will."

Christian didn't answer.

"There's also the little matter of the Walker," Piers added. "The two things couldn't be connected, could they?"

"I can't see a connection. The fae never leave their lands if they can help it."

"Yeah, they're too fucking superior to mix with the likes of us."

"And there's no way demons could have gone anywhere near the Faelands, or we'd have far more than the Walker to contend with. Did you have no luck arranging a meeting?"

"Not yet. If he's around he's keeping a low profile."

"Maybe the information was wrong."

"I don't think so."

Christian fought down the nagging sense of frustration building inside him—he wanted this over with.

A knock sounded on the door, and they both glanced up. Piers crossed the room and spoke briefly with the agent, before turning back to Christian. "There's been a confirmed sighting close to where you nailed those three demons last night. That's right next to your building again. Looks like it is you they're after. Let's go get the bastards."

They stopped at the weapons room.

"Remember we want them alive," Christian said as Piers strapped a sawed-off shotgun to his thigh.

"These things have already taken down two of my men. I'm not taking any chances." He slipped a couple of grenades into the slots on his belt. "Don't worry, they'll be alive." He grinned. "They might also be in bits, but they'll be alive."

...

As the vehicle came to a halt, Christian slipped out of the SUV and sniffed the air. Straight away, he picked up the rank sulfur smell of a lesser demon. Something shifted in the shadows up ahead.

"There they are," he said.

Piers came to stand beside him. "I see them. Just the two." He sounded disappointed as he drew the shotgun from the holster at his thigh. "I'm going to take out the one on the left, you bring down the second one, and we'll take it back for questioning."

"Okay, just remember, if you use that thing," Christian nodded at the gun, "we have about five minutes before the cops get here."

Beside him, Piers raised the shotgun. "Don't waste any time then."

The explosion filled the alley, and the first demon disintegrated in a shower of gore. Christian licked his lips as the warm blood sprayed across his face, a surge of power hitting his gut as the demon blood entered his system.

The second demon raced down the alley. It glanced back over its shoulder as Christian took aim. The shot took it through the shoulder, whirling it round full circle and hurling it to the ground. Christian kept his gun cocked in his hand as he approached. He slipped the toe of his boot beneath the body and flipped it onto its back.

Crouching beside the injured demon, Christian grabbed it by the hair and dragged its head back. Its eyes flickered open, yellow, no pupil, only a thin black slit down the center. The eyes were lashless and dazed; they blinked a few times and focused on Christian. The recognition was instant.

"Christian Roth."

A wave of fury washed over him. So this *was* personal. But why?

His grip tightened on the demon's hair. "Tell me why you are here. Tell me, and you can live."

"And go back to my master and inform him that we failed? It's better to be dead." It shrugged. "But our master told us there is no more need for secrecy. He wants you to know. He wants you to fear what is coming."

Christian's eyes narrowed. "Who is your master?"

"I serve Asmodai."

"Why does he want me dead?"

The vile creature stared up into his eyes, and its lips curled into the semblance of a smile revealing pointed white teeth. "Who says he wants you dead? That is not the plan—or at least not yet."

"So what does he want?"

The light was fading from the demon's yellow eyes. It coughed and a froth of blood erupted from its lips, staining black against the dark red skin. When the coughing fit was over, its head fell back, the yellow eyes staring blankly into the night sky.

Christian swore.

"Weren't we supposed to take it back for questioning?" Piers asked.

"It must have taken poison."

"Obviously. So Asmodai *is* coming after you."

"It seems that way, but we're no closer to knowing why."

Piers shrugged. "Maybe he just doesn't like you, and he's

not alone in that. I could name a dozen people who would like you dead."

"Thanks, Piers. Very helpful. Are you going to call in a squad to clean this mess up, or are you going to leave London littered with dead demons?"

"Already on its way."

Christian got to his feet. So, Asmodai was coming after him. Let him come. This time Christian would finish him off. Though he had an idea it was going to take longer than he'd originally envisaged.

In the lull following the chaos, a vision of Tara flashed across his mind—it looked as though he wouldn't be seeing her anytime soon.

Chapter Six

All Tara wanted was an ordinary life.

A life like everyone else. Was it too much to ask after her peculiar childhood?

Obviously it was.

Slumping in her seat, she stared at her laptop. Displayed on the screen were details of the last missing person case that could even remotely be connected to her or Aunt Kathy. According to the information, the missing baby had turned up alive and well a few weeks later. So the kidnapping theory appeared to be a dead end.

Tara dreaded what was next. She reached into her bag and drew out the red file Graham had given her a week ago. She didn't want to read the file because she didn't want to face up to what she knew was true.

Christian Roth was a vampire.

She'd searched her mind for alternate explanations, from hallucinogenic drugs to hypnosis—and rejected them all.

That brought her back to the red file, because if Christian Roth were a vampire, then what other supernatural beings existed in the world—like zombies.

Though Christian said that her aunt wasn't a zombie. That had to be a good thing, didn't it? Who wanted to find out that the woman who brought you up, who you loved, had been a flesh-eating monster?

Some other sort of reanimated corpse, then. Just how many kinds were there? Taking a deep breath, she opened the file.

But instead of reading, she sat back in her seat. She'd been doing her best not to think of Christian, but her best wasn't particularly good. When she closed her eyes, he was there, in her mind, as she'd last seen him—six-foot-four of half-naked vampire.

Her first ever kiss had been with a freaking vampire. What was it with her? She couldn't even fall for a normal guy.

She opened her eyes. It was lunchtime, the college library was busy, and they were everywhere—nice normal men, some of them even good looking, and none of them vampires. She banished Christian to the back of her mind, picked up the first sheet of paper in the file, and started to read.

When she got to the end, she wasn't any closer to the truth than before. The file just contained the evidence Christian had spoken of, including a coroner's report stating cause of death. Kathryn Collins had died of a broken neck at the site of the accident.

The next sheets were copies of newspaper articles, one about the accident, and a second relating to the disappearance of the body, which had been taken from the morgue the day after she died. Nobody knew why, and no clues were ever found.

What hit Tara hardest was that Kathryn Collins died leaving no family. Her parents were dead and she'd had no siblings. None. Where did that leave Tara as her niece?

Absolutely nowhere.

She rubbed at her forehead to ease the dull ache throbbing behind her eyes. This information brought her no closer to finding out who she was or where she came from.

Frustrated, she went to close the file and noticed Graham's business card. Without giving herself time to think, Tara pulled out her cell phone and punched in the number.

After a couple of rings, he picked up. "What?"

He sounded grumpy, and she almost put the phone down. Instead, she forced herself to speak. "Hello, it's Tara—Tara Collins."

He was silent for a moment. "Tara, sorry, I was asleep—not quite with it."

Tara glanced at her watch; it was almost one o'clock.

"Hey, I work nights," he said as if reading her mind.

Of course he would work nights—after all, he worked for a vampire. "Sorry I woke you."

"No problem. You want to talk?"

"Please."

"Where are you?"

She told him.

"There's a coffee shop just round the corner," he said. "Ginelli's. I'll meet you there in forty minutes."

...

The place was clean, but basic, made good coffee, cheap food, and catered almost exclusively to students. With his long, elegant frame dressed in a silver gray designer suit and a dark blue shirt, Graham appeared like some exotic creature who'd wandered in by mistake. Tara in jeans and a jumper felt scruffy next to him.

He smiled as he sat down. "So, you want to know all about vampires."

"Actually, I'd prefer to forget that they even exist. I guess that's not going to happen, is it?"

"No, probably not."

"Are you allowed to talk to me? You're not breaking any code of secrecy."

"I can tell you, but they'd have to kill me, sort of thing?" He shrugged. "There is a code. Humans who get involved with vampires either don't speak of it or they don't survive very long."

"So why are you talking to me now?"

"Christian told me to tell you whatever you wanted to know."

"But why?"

"Maybe because you need to believe in order to find out what happened with your aunt, but I don't think that's it. I think he likes you."

Tara stopped stirring her coffee. "You do?"

"I do, and that's not something I've come across in the five years I've known him. Oh, I'm not saying he's celibate or anything, but he doesn't do relationships."

"We're not having a relationship."

"No?"

"I just feel that if I'm going to keep him on as an investigator—and I'm not sure that's going to be the case—then I need to understand what he's like, what I can expect."

"So, ask away."

Tara took a sip of coffee, stirred it some more. She wanted to know everything, but that wouldn't sound very cool.

"What are they? Where do they come from? Are they a different species or were they once human? Do—"

Graham held up a hand, a slight smile on his face. "That's enough questions to start with. I'm not sure what they are, and I'm not sure they do either. I once asked Christian, and he said all they knew was that they were descended from an original group, but no one knows where that group came from, or if they do, they aren't telling. But I do know Christian was once human. A long time ago."

"How long? How old is he?"

"I'm not sure exactly. He was born sometime in the Middle-Ages, so over five hundred years, but he doesn't talk about it much."

Wow, five hundred years. What would it be like to live that long? Go through all those changes, and see so many people die. She wondered if that bothered him, or whether he just saw humans as food. "Are you human?"

He grinned. "What do you think? Yeah, I'm human."

"So how did you get mixed up in all this?"

"I'm Christian's human servant." He thought for a moment as if wondering how much to tell her. "A bond forms when a vampire feeds a number of times from the same human. I'm tied to him. I don't mind. He saved my life."

"How?"

"I was sixteen, living on the streets and I was a real fucked-up mess. One night I pissed off the wrong people. They took me down an alley, and beat on me. I was almost dead when Christian came along. I've been with him ever since."

"What do you get out of it?"

"I was a street punk—I wouldn't have lasted much longer out there." He grinned. "My mouth got me into trouble so many times it was lucky I lasted as long as I did. Now look at me."

She did. There was nothing of the street kid left in him, with his designer suits and his perfectly cut hair, his air of languid grace.

"I've got a great job," he continued. "Even if I do have to work nights. Christian has shown me a whole different way of life. All I have to do is donate a little blood now and then, and that's hardly a hardship." His face took on that dreamy expression he'd had when Christian had fed, and a wave of heat washed over her.

"Are you in love with him?"

He appeared startled at the question. "Who wouldn't be? He is seriously gorgeous, but I told you he doesn't go for guys, not like that."

"What about female vampires?"

"There are none. Not that I know of. Something to do with the process. They don't survive."

"So no little vampire babies?"

"God, no!"

They were silent for a few minutes.

"What's the Order?"

"You'll have to ask Christian about that, but I doubt he'll tell you anything. All I know is Christian was involved up until about twenty years ago. Piers Lamont, the other vamp you met, is the big boss now, but I'm not sure what they do or why. The only other person I've met from there is Ella. She used to drop by the office occasionally. She'd had a thing with Christian a long time ago and would like to have a thing again."

"Ella?"

He grinned. "She's a witch, and I mean that in the literal sense. Don't worry—she's no competition. Christian can't stand her, won't even see her."

Tara sniffed. "I wasn't worried."

"No, of course you weren't."

Tara decided to change the subject. "Do you know what was in that file? About my aunt?"

"I did the research. It's tough."

"I can't believe all this—vampires, dead aunts. I keep thinking I'll wake up and it will all be a bad dream."

"Christian will get to the bottom of it for you."

"Yes, but what will he find? All my childhood, I watched

from the sidelines, never belonging, never joining in, and I thought that was going to change. All I ever wanted was to be normal."

"You might be surprised how your view of what's normal changes. Besides, being normal isn't all that great. Boring even."

"Sounds lovely. I can't help wondering, if I could go back, would I just leave it well alone?"

"Maybe you wouldn't have had a choice. In the end, your past would have caught up with you."

"It doesn't matter. Now it's too late." She gave a small smile. "I'm scared."

He patted her hand. "Christian will take care of you."

Why didn't that make her feel better? Could it be the fact that Christian was a vampire? "And who'll protect me from Christian?"

"Do you want protection from Christian? If you were really scared, you wouldn't be talking to me, you'd be running away as fast as you could."

The comment brought her up short. She could go away, start over somewhere new. She rejected the idea. "I'm not running away."

"Good. I have to go. When you're ready to come in again, give me a call."

She nodded. "I will, soon."

He got up to go and Tara asked him one more question. "Are vampires evil?"

"I saw some bad things when I lived on the street. I learned to recognize true evil and Christian is not that. On the other hand, I wouldn't say he was entirely good either, but that would be boring."

...

Two days later, Tara headed down in the elevator, deep underground beneath the CR building.

She'd come to the conclusion that she had to return—Christian was her best bet at discovering her past. But it would be on a strict business basis. No kissing and absolutely no biting.

She would have preferred to take the elevator up to a business meeting on the thirteenth floor. Instead, she was sinking fast. Christian was down there in his private quarters, somewhere south of the sub-basement. Graham had hustled her into the elevator before she could argue.

Her knees wobbled and a queer little twist of something tightened her belly.

Get a grip. Business only.

Christian was there when the elevator doors slid open. He was fully dressed. No half-naked vampire for her tonight.

At least, not yet.

Then again, it was early.

She didn't know where that thought had come from, and she tried to put it from her mind.

He was all in black again, the business suit gone, but he looked good. It suited his pale skin and dark silky hair, which he'd left loose on his shoulders.

"Tara," he murmured her name and reached out a hand. She took it in hers, feeling that same tingle as their skin touched. He lowered his face and inhaled deeply, turned her hand over, and kissed her wrist where her pulse thundered close to the surface. His tongue stroked her skin and she trembled, half expecting to feel the sharp bite of his fangs. Before she could pull free, he raised his eyes. They were beautiful, mesmerizing, and she realized she didn't want to be free after all.

She was in big trouble. One minute in his presence and all her good intentions vanished. He smiled a slow curl of his beautiful lips and dropped her hand.

She breathed again.

"Come." He slipped a hand to her waist and guided her into his apartment.

They were in a sitting room this time. The furniture was sparse but luxurious with huge sofas upholstered in scarlet silk.

Was that to hide the bloodstains in case it got messy?

Though she was pretty sure Christian would never be so unsophisticated as to spill his food.

Candles flickered all around the room. An ice bucket stood on the small table, containing a bottle of champagne, and next to it two champagne flutes. She wouldn't be touching that. Whatever happened tonight she was determined to be conscious throughout it.

"Did Graham tell you I wanted to talk about my aunt?" She stared around the room again. "Do you often conduct your business meetings by candlelight?"

He smiled. "Are you worried what my intentions might be?"

The worry factor took second place to a slow burning rise of excitement that twisted her insides. Her blood thundered through her veins, and her heart pounded.

"Are you hungry?" he asked. "Can I get you anything to eat?"

"No." She peered at him sharply. "Are you?"

He chuckled and looked her up and down very slowly and very thoroughly, lingering, she thought, far too long on her throat. His eyes were half-closed and gleaming behind his thick lashes when they returned to her face. "You think I'm going to leap on you and bite that pretty neck?"

She didn't answer, and he prowled around the back of her, coming to a halt so close she had to force herself not to move away. His hands caressed her hair, sliding away the silky strands to bare the line of her throat.

"You smell so delicious."

Tara twitched, but his hands held her in place. His lips were on her skin and a wave of heat washed over her. Her eyes fluttered closed as his mouth opened against her throat and his tongue stroked, slow and cool against her heated flesh.

"Maybe just a little taste…" His teeth scraped her, and she braced herself for his bite. Instead, he turned her in his arms, allowing her to see the hunger burning in his eyes. So hot, so fierce that she gasped.

"See, you're quite safe with me." He lowered his lids for a moment. When he opened them, his expression was blank. "One day soon, I hope you will trust me enough to allow me your blood, but perhaps you are not quite ready for that yet."

He slid his finger down the line of her throat, pressed it against the vein, and lingered on her pulse. "Though I don't think it is only fear that makes your pulse beat so fast, and perhaps you are ready for this."

He lowered his head and kissed her. His lips were incredibly soft against hers, not demanding but requesting her compliance, and without thought her mouth opened beneath his. How easily her resolutions vanished.

His tongue slid inside. Instantly the kiss deepened, and she lost the ability to think rationally. His hand drifted up to cradle the back of her skull and held her steady while his mouth ravaged hers. Tara lost herself in the sensations coursing through her body—so new, so intense. He scooped her up into his arms and carried her to one of the huge scarlet sofas.

He sank down, pulling her onto his lap without breaking the kiss. His mouth slanted over hers, his tongue thrust into her mouth and stroked. At first, she allowed him to have his way, but it wasn't enough, and she started to move with him. At the soft glide of her tongue, his grip tightened. His hands slid over her, grinding her against the hardness of his body. It was like steel, and the muscles of her belly knotted and warm wet heat pooled between her thighs. Her body seemed to take over, and she wriggled her bottom into his hips, until he groaned against her mouth.

The air filled with a musky, feral scent, and Christian stilled. His hands gripped her arms, and he lifted her from him, depositing her on the cool silk of the sofa. He shifted as far from her as he could while staying seated.

Tara stared at him, fighting the urge to crawl across the space between them. She wanted him, needed him. She made a move, and he put up a hand to ward her off. It was like being doused in cold water.

"Why?" she asked.

He took a deep breath. "I think that perhaps you're not so safe after all."

Chapter Seven

Rule Number Three: Never remove the Talisman

She didn't want to be safe. She wanted to be in his arms. Christian smiled, his lips drawing back to reveal the long, razor-sharp canines.

"Oh."

Tara stared at them in awe. All signs of humanity were stripped from his face, revealing the cold ruthless predator beneath. The smile slid from his face, and the humanity crept back into his eyes. He laid his head against the cushions and stared at the ceiling.

"I haven't felt the urge to feed so strongly for a long time." He regarded her curiously. "What is it about you, Tara Collins? Why do you affect me like this? Perhaps we should get down to business after all, and see if we can't find out. First I need a drink."

He switched on a light and the room became brighter. "There," he said, "much more businesslike."

He rose and moved around the room blowing out the candles, then he picked up the bottle of champagne and poured himself a glass. He glanced at her, and she shook her head. After swallowing his drink in one gulp, he poured another and came back to sit at the far end of the sofa. "Don't look so worried. I have myself under control."

It wasn't Christian she was concerned about. She was the one who'd been out of control. Who'd nearly begged him to make love to her, to take her any way he wanted. And it frightened her. Falling for a vampire was not part of any plans she had for her future.

"So," Christian said, "tell me about your aunt."

Tara forced herself to concentrate. "What do you want to know?"

"Everything. What was she like, how did you live, anything you think might help us get to the bottom of this."

"I don't remember anyone else, ever. It was always just Aunt Kathy and me. Oh and Smokey, of course. That's my cat," she added.

"I remember," Christian said wryly.

"We lived in this big old house on the Yorkshire moors. It was very isolated—Aunt Kathy liked it that way. She didn't trust outsiders, which was everyone except me. We had our food delivered, and my aunt schooled me at home. That's why I'm at college now. She taught me a lot, but I don't have any qualifications.

"I wasn't supposed to leave the grounds, but sometimes I would creep away when she was busy. I liked to watch the people in the village. It's funny, I didn't realize how weird our lives were until I started watching other people."

"You never thought to leave?" His expression was thoughtful, but the pity she dreaded was absent.

"Of course I did. I told her I was moving out when I was eighteen, but she got ill, and I couldn't leave her alone. Despite everything, I loved her. She gave me the best life she knew how."

"Hmm." He sounded skeptical. "Did she ever mention the past or anything about your parents?"

Tara smiled. "You're joking—and break Rule Number One?"

"Rule Number One?"

"My aunt liked rules. Number One was never, ever talk about the past, and I didn't. It still makes me nervous to talk like this, as though I'm doing something wrong."

"Were there a lot of rules?"

"A few. Rule Number Two was 'don't drink alcohol.' I tried that, and it turns out it was a good rule. Maybe I have some sort of genetic disorder that can't cope."

"What happened?"

"One sip of white wine and I passed out." She glanced at the champagne bottle and shuddered. "I won't be trying that again anytime soon."

"You've broken rules one and two. Is there a Rule Number Three?"

Tara smiled. "Rule Number Three—never take off the talisman."

"What talisman?"

She reached beneath the collar of her shirt and pulled out the necklace. "It belonged to my mother. Or at least that's what Aunt Kathy told me."

Who knew whether it was true? Now, it seemed unlikely, and a wave of sadness ran through her. It was the one thing she had from her mother, or thought she'd had. "I've always believed that was true, so Rule Number Three wasn't hard to keep."

He rose to his feet. "Can I see?"

She held the necklace up. He took a step closer and cupped the pendant in his hand, turning it with his long elegant fingers. It was a heart-shaped locket made from some sort of opaque crystal.

"Does it open?" he asked.

She ran her nail along the seam, caught the minute catch, and the locket sprang open.

Christian dropped his hand and took a step back. His eyes were wide and fixed on the open locket still held between her finger and thumb. The contents were so familiar—a strand of her mother's hair, or so Tara had always believed, blond like her own.

"What is it?" she asked. "What's wrong?"

"It's some sort of spell," he answered slowly. "The hair has been charmed and it's powerful. This is warlock's work."

It just looked like a strand of hair to Tara. "What's it for?"

"I have no idea, but there's one way to find out. Take it off."

A wave of reluctance washed over her.

Christian watched her curiously. "What's the problem?"

"It's stupid, but I don't want to take it off." She dropped the locket and fought the urge to hide it inside her shirt.

"Maybe not so stupid—I'm guessing there's some sort of compulsion built into the charm. Which makes me even more curious about what it's doing." He thought for a moment. "Close your eyes. I'm going to take your mind off the locket, give you something else to think about."

"What else?"

"Me. Now be a good girl and close your eyes."

Tara closed her eyes. She sensed the movement as he came to stand behind her, so close his breath feathered through her hair. A hand stroked the soft skin of her neck. She shivered at the touch, and heat flared low in her belly as her body remembered the feel of him. He brushed aside her hair to bare the side of her throat and his lips pressed against her. He kissed her neck softly, opening his mouth against her. His sharp teeth scraped her skin, and she stiffened. "Christian—"

"Shh," he murmured against her throat. "I'm not going

to bite. Relax."

She tried, but relaxing really wasn't an option with his hands gliding up her body, skimmed her belly. They hovered over her breasts, hardly touching, but lightly grazing. Her nipples tightened, and she groaned. His hands again. It took her a moment to realize he was lifting the necklace over her head.

"It's off. Open your eyes."

He came to stand in front of her, her necklace dangling from one finger. His eyes met hers and something close to horror flashed across his face.

"What is it?"

He thrust the necklace at her. "Put it back on." His voice was harsh and strained.

"Why?"

"Don't argue, just put the necklace back on. Now."

She took it from him with trembling fingers and lifted it back over her head. Christian turned away, his back rigid, his fists clenched at his side.

"What is it?" When he didn't answer, she touched his shoulder. He flinched. "Christian, you're frightening me. Tell me what you saw."

For a moment he stayed where he was, his broad shoulders rigid with tension. He took a deep breath and relaxed. When he turned, his expression was blank.

"I didn't see anything."

"I don't believe you. If you don't tell me, I'll take it off again."

"Don't do that until we know exactly what we're dealing with."

"But what's it doing?"

"It's hiding something. Or rather masking something."

"What—"

He held up his hand. Tara bit her lip but shut up.

"I don't know," he said. "That's the truth. When you take it off, it's as if you're transmitting some sort of message, but who's picking it up or why, I don't know. And until I find out, you keep it on."

A cold lump settled in Tara's stomach. She'd seen something bordering on fear in Christian's eyes. What the hell did it take to scare a vampire? She thought about pushing it, but his expression was closed, and she knew he wouldn't tell her anything more. Instead, she forced herself to think through the options. "I'm not sick or anything, am I?"

He smiled. It was faint, but a smile nevertheless. "Nothing like that. Was that the first time you've removed it?"

"No, I took it off when I was leaving Yorkshire. I was upset—I'd found out most of what my aunt had told me was lies. I was going to leave it behind with everything else from that life. It was almost impossible, but I managed to take it off and hang it from the gatepost. I was halfway down to the village, and ran all the way back and put it on again. In the end, I couldn't leave it—it was the only thing I had from my mother." Her legs trembled, and she sank onto the sofa. "Do you think it matters that I took it off?"

"Probably not." He smiled. She knew it was supposed to be a reassuring smile, but it didn't work.

"What do we do next?" she asked.

"We need to go to Yorkshire."

"I don't want to go to Yorkshire."

"I think I should take a look around. See if I can get a sense of what went on there. What your aunt actually was and how she came to be. We'll go tomorrow night. There is one more thing we can do tonight. I'd rather go alone, but it might help if I have the locket, and as you can't take it off, you'll have to come with me."

"Where are we going?"

"The Order."

A shiver of excitement ran through her. Graham had said the Order was ultra-secret. There would be vampires and maybe other things. But why would Christian take her there now? What was so important about the talisman?

The familiar weight of the locket comforted her, but she couldn't shake the conviction that Christian knew more than he was saying. And what he knew wasn't good.

"Just one thing," Christian said. "When we get to the Order—"

"Yes?"

"Don't do anything and don't say anything."

Chapter Eight

The drive to the Order took them along the embankment beside the river Thames, where the lights of the pleasure cruisers glinted on the water. Then past the London Eye, the giant Ferris wheel that rotated languidly above the city, and into the business district. They finally turned down a ramp and pulled into an underground parking garage.

Christian glanced at his passenger as he switched off the ignition. She'd finally stopped shaking. She was rattled and who could blame her? He was rattled himself.

He took a risk bringing her here—Piers wouldn't like it—but he wanted one of the Order's witches to take a look at Tara's talisman. Maybe a witch would be able to identify the warlock who'd made the charm. They often left some sort of signature easily recognizable by others of their kind.

"Come on," he said. "Let's get this over with."

He was about to get out when she put her hand on his arm. She licked her lips, her small pink tongue flicking out, and he remembered the taste of her; hot and sweet with just an underlying hint of bitterness to balance. Addictive, and he wanted more. Much more.

As the memory washed over him, he had a sudden flashback to the good part of the evening. The earlier part before he'd made a huge error of judgment and decided that getting down to business was the sensible move. He should have just kissed her some more. They might be in his bed now, not in an underground car park about to face six-foot-four of pissed off vampire.

"Christian?"

"Sorry, I was miles away." Back in his bed with Tara sprawled naked on top of him. "What is it?"

"I wanted to thank you."

He smiled. "I'm just doing my job. It's what you hired me to do."

She searched his face. "Is it just a job?"

She appeared so young and so uncertain that he leaned across and kissed her on the mouth. It had been meant as a reassurance but instead of the quick kiss he'd intended, his lips lingered against hers, relishing the taste of her. *Definitely addictive.* Finally, he remembered where he was and drew back.

"Does that answer your question?" he asked.

She licked her lips again as if tasting him, and heat flared in his groin.

She nodded. "Let's go." Without waiting for him, she opened the car door and jumped out. Christian sat a minute longer, willing his body under control, then followed her.

He'd called Piers from the car, and someone waited at the elevator to escort them. Tara sized up the guard.

"Is everybody here a vampire?" she asked quietly.

"Not everybody, but most of the agents. We're actually here to see a witch."

"Ella?

Christian frowned.

"Graham mentioned her," she said.

He made a mental note to have a word with Graham. Though he *had* told him to tell Tara whatever she asked.

"Hopefully not Ella," he replied.

"Why? Graham told me you used to be close."

Yes, he was definitely going to have a word with Graham. "Not that close," he said. "And a long time ago." Why was he worried that Tara might believe him involved with Ella?

"Ella is not a big fan of mine anymore. But the Order employs other witches. Maybe we'll get lucky."

The elevator came to a halt, and the doors opened. Piers waited for them and, as expected, didn't look happy. Without speaking, he whirled and strode off down the corridor.

Christian put a hand to Tara's waist. He directed her after Piers, glancing down at her once or twice as they moved through the building. It was obvious she tried to be subtle as she stared—and failed totally.

Piers led them into his office and slammed the door.

"What the fuck is she doing here?" he demanded. "You know it's against Order policy to bring unmarked humans."

Tara stood straight and stared back, but Christian smelled her fear. And that meant so could Piers.

"Unless," Piers continued, "you plan to kill her afterward." He grinned as the little color in Tara's face fled. "I could take care of that little job if you like."

"Piss off, Piers." Christian turned to Tara. "Go sit over there for a moment while I talk to this moron."

Tara frowned at the command, but decided now was not the time to exert her independence. She sat on one of the leather and steel chairs in front of Piers's desk.

"I want one of the witches to have a look at her talisman," Christian explained. "Maybe they can identify who worked the charm."

"What do you think it's doing? And why's a human

wearing such a charm?"

"That's what I'm trying to find out."

"Okay, but you're going to wipe her memory of all this, aren't you?"

Across the room, Tara stared at the floor, hands clasped tight on her lap. As though she sensed his attention she glanced up and smiled, and something shifted inside him. Something he had never expected to feel. *Certainly not for a human.*

"Perhaps. When this is over."

"You need to mark her, Christian."

"I'm not sure she'll agree."

Piers stared at him in total amazement. "If I explain what will happen if she doesn't agree—she'll agree."

Christian stilled. His eyes narrowed and his gums ached as his fangs elongated. "Don't touch her," he growled.

"Perhaps you should explain then. It's the one safeguard we have against the humans turning on us. There can be no exceptions."

Piers spoke the truth, but the time was coming to an end when they could live in secret among humans. They should plan how to move forward when that time came rather than cling to the old rules. It was an argument he had had with Piers many times.

"I'll talk to her, but alone."

Piers nodded. "I'll go speak with Ella."

...

Tara wasn't going to admit it, but she was terrified. Had been since they walked out of the elevator and she realized she was deep underground, surrounded by the undead, and all that stood between her and a horrible end was another undead.

She watched as the two men, or rather two vampires,

spoke. Their voices were pitched too low to hear, but the exchange didn't seem friendly. Despite the difference in coloring, they were curiously alike. Both tall, pale skinned, and stunningly gorgeous. She wondered whether it was because they only chose tall, handsome men to change into vampires or if something happened during the change.

She knew, by the way they frequently glanced her way, that Piers and Christian were discussing her. Piers appeared angry—Christian must have broken a few rules to bring her here. Then again, he didn't strike her as the sort of person who bothered with rules. Ever.

Unlike herself, who had lived the first twenty-two years following a set of rules given to her by a dead woman. At the thought of rules, her hand went to her locket. She'd broken Rule Number Three, and it hadn't turned out any better than number two. What had Christian seen that was so bad? She wasn't sure she wanted to know.

"Tara." Christian held out a hand to her. She stood and walked toward him. As his fingers wrapped around hers, she instantly felt better.

"I'll leave you two to talk," Piers said.

Christian nodded. "Thanks, Piers."

He left the room.

Christian pulled her toward the desk then pushed her shoulder until she sank into the chair.

Alarm flickered through her. "I'm going to need to sit for this?"

He took the seat opposite and sat for a moment, watching her closely.

"What?" she asked.

"Vampires have remained secret among humans for thousands of years only by following a strict set of rules. One of the Order's jobs is to ensure that everyone upholds those rules."

"I guess you broke a few by bringing me tonight."

"A few. I thought it was worth it to get the information we need, but perhaps we should have had this conversation before I brought you here."

"What difference would it have made?"

"We have two ways of dealing with humans who discover our secret. The ones that survive the experience, that is. The first is to erase their memories."

"You can do that?"

"Short-term memories are easy. The longer the memory is in the mind the harder it becomes, and the more likely we are to cause some sort of permanent damage, so we try to do it as soon as possible. It's how we deal with those humans we feed from."

"Have you ever done it to me?"

He shook his head. "Sometimes I hunt, but I don't need to feed with much frequency any more. Most vampires have humans who they feed from regularly."

"Like you and Graham?"

He nodded. "Those we feed from more than once, we bind to us by the second method."

"And that is?"

"We mark them."

"Mark them with what?"

"It's not a physical mark. It's a" —he thought for a moment— "psychic mark."

"You mark their brains?" Tara shuddered. She didn't like the thought of anyone doing anything in her brain. Christian watched her closely, and she realized where this was going. "You want to mark my brain, don't you?"

"I don't want to, but I have no choice."

"You always have a choice."

"You're right, but perhaps I should set the choices out before you."

She swallowed. "Go ahead."

"The first is obviously that you allow me to mark you. I promise you the process will be painless." His eyes swept over her, suddenly hot, and she had a flashback to the feel of being enclosed within his arms. Heat coiled low in her belly as though it had been waiting for something to set it aflame again.

"You might even enjoy it." A shudder ran through her at the dark promise in his voice.

She stared into his face for long moments then broke the link between them. "And the alternative?"

The smile faded from his face. "That Piers marks you by force, and I can't promise that won't hurt."

Shock flashed through her. "You'd let him do that?"

"I don't think I would have any say in the matter. I'm strong, but perhaps not that strong. We're surrounded by over a hundred vampires. Of course, I would fight—you are, after all, my responsibility—but in all likelihood, I would die. So I think the question you need to ask yourself is would you let me mark you now, or would you prefer I'm killed and you're held down while Piers rapes your mind."

"You're trying to scare me."

"Perhaps. Am I succeeding?"

She took a deep breath. "So maybe you'd better explain this whole marking thing, because I'm not letting you into my mind without knowing what you're up to."

Amusement glinted in his eyes. "It will tie you to the vampire who marks you."

"Tie? In what way tie?"

"There would be some... compulsion involved."

"You mean I'd have to do what you say? I don't think so."

"Tara, we have the ability to make any human do as we say, it just takes less effort with those that are marked."

"Let me get this straight. You can make me do what you

want." He smiled again and nodded. "Have you?" she asked.

"No."

"Could you?"

"I believe so. What else is it you wish to know?"

She found it hard to move past the whole compulsion thing. "Tell me more about this tie."

"Your life would be bound to mine. If I were to be destroyed, in all likelihood you would die."

Her heart skipped a beat, then sped up as she realized it was the thought of Christian being destroyed that upset her, rather than her dying in response. When had she started to care about him?

"And are you planning on that happening anytime soon?" she asked.

"Not planning, no."

She could live with that. "So, last question. Is it permanent?"

"I've never tried to remove a mark. Perhaps it's possible. Most humans are happy with the benefits of belonging to a vampire."

She remembered Graham with his designer suits and his dreamy expression when he thought of Christian feeding. Then her mind focused on one word and her whole body tensed. "Belonging? I don't want to belong to anybody."

He sighed. "I think you must trust me on this one, Tara. I promise I'll not abuse the mark, and afterward, if possible, I'll remove it." He took her hands. A sense of calm washed over her, and she wondered if he were doing something to her mind. "And Tara, there are benefits."

She eyed him warily, not quite convinced that her idea of benefits and Christian's would coincide.

"You will be stronger," he said. "and live longer. I would take care of you—you'd be my responsibility."

"The stronger and living longer bits I'll take. The

responsibility thing you can keep. From now on, I'm nobody's responsibility but my own."

"So you'll allow me to do it."

"I don't see that I've got a choice." She sighed. "I can't believe you didn't think about this before you brought me here."

He appeared about to speak, but the door opened, Piers stepped in, and Christian dropped her hands.

Piers focused on Christian. "Has she agreed?"

Christian nodded. Piers studied her for a moment. She shuddered at the expression in his eyes. He wanted her, she could see that, but it was what he wanted her for that worried her most. All he said was, "Pity."

"So what happens now?" she asked. Christian had promised it wouldn't hurt, but her whole body clenched at the thought of the unknown.

"It will be done in a moment. Turn and face me."

Christian moved closer and put his fingertips to her temple. "Relax."

She stared into his eyes. For a moment, her mind opened to him, as though he were becoming one with her. Then everything locked, and she was back in her own head alone.

Christian frowned. "What did you do?"

"Nothing."

His fingers tightened on her forehead. He stared at her again but this time her mind remained her own.

"What's going on?" Piers asked.

Christian dropped his hands. "It's not working."

Piers moved to stand over them. "What do you mean 'not working'?"

"I'm not marked?"

Christian shook his head. He turned to Piers. "I can't get in. Her mind is shutting me out cold. I've never felt this sort of block before."

"Shall I try?"

Christian's eyes narrowed dangerously. "No," he growled.

"What's happening?" Tara asked.

"We spoke of compulsion, a vampire's ability to force a human to do something. I want to see if it works on you."

"What are you going to make me do, act like a chicken or something?"

He smiled though he didn't appear happy. "Nothing like that." He thought for a moment. "I'm going to make you stay seated in that chair. I want you to try and get up and walk across the room."

"When?"

"Now would be good," Piers said.

Tara got up and crossed the room. "Is that it?"

A look passed between the two men. Christian frowned but Piers turned toward her. After a moment, he shook his head. "Nothing."

"I told you to stay out of her mind," Christian snarled.

Piers held up his hands defensively. "Hey, I didn't get in."

"What's going on?" Tara asked.

"You seem to be able to keep us out of your mind. Which presumably also means we can't erase your memories."

"Is that going to be a problem?" she asked.

Piers looked at her, and his eyes were cold. "Is it going to be a problem, Christian?" The question was asked in a soft voice, but Christian tensed.

"Don't lay a finger on her," he said. "Not one finger."

"Actually, fingers didn't come into what I had in mind." Piers shrugged. "What do you suggest?"

"It may have something to do with the talisman. Maybe the magic keeps us out."

"Then she must take it off."

"Not here and not until we know more about it. Look Piers, I'll vouch for her. Keep her close, she won't betray us."

Piers regarded them silently for a moment, then nodded. "But *you* are responsible, and you mark her as soon as you can. Now, let's get Ella in here see if she can tell us something about this talisman."

The door opened and a woman walked in. Tara had been predisposed to disliking Ella but she needn't have bothered. A wave of revulsion washed over her as the woman stepped inside. Tara couldn't rid her mind of the idea she was in the presence of something evil. Dressed in black leather trousers and a black shirt that clung to her full breasts and flat stomach, Ella was a female version of the vampires, but she wasn't a vampire. She ignored Tara, her attention on the two men. Strolling up to Christian, she stroked her scarlet tipped fingers over his chest.

"You wanted me?" she purred.

It set Tara's teeth on edge. She took a step closer to Christian, only just resisting the urge to place a possessive hand on his arm. He glanced at her and back at Ella.

"Hardly," he drawled.

Ella's face hardened. Her eyes narrowed on Christian, then flicked to Tara and something dark shifted across her expression.

"We want you to look at something," Piers said.

"What?" She sounded sulky now.

"Tara?" Piers gestured to her to come forward, and Tara took a reluctant step away from Christian. Ella ran her eyes over her.

"A human? What's she doing here?"

"She belongs to Christian."

Tara didn't like the word, but at that moment, belonging to Christian sounded like a very good idea, so she didn't argue.

"She's not marked."

"No, she's not. Now can we get on with this?"

Ella shrugged. "What do you want?"

"Show her the talisman, Tara." Christian spoke softly beside her.

Tara pulled the locket from beneath her shirt and held it out. As Ella moved closer, Tara had to fight the urge to step back. She did not want the other woman to touch her.

Ella reached out but her hand dropped back before she touched it. "Can you open it?" she asked.

Tara flicked open the catch. Ella stared at the contents, her eyes widening in surprise.

"What can you tell us?" Piers asked, sounding impatient.

"Not a lot. It's powerful, but what it's doing is shrouded, part of the magic. Where did it come from?"

"That's what we want to find out. Can you tell us who made it?"

"No. For once there's no signature, which is strange in itself. As though the maker didn't want to be identified, but there aren't many powerful enough to make this charm."

"Could you do it?" Christian asked.

Ella shook her head.

"So how many could?"

She tilted her head. "Three or four, maybe."

"Can you make us a list, find out where they are, who's the most likely."

"I suppose I could. Are you going to tell me what this is about?"

"You don't need to know," Christian replied.

Ella's eyes narrowed. "You're not my boss anymore, Christian." She glanced at Piers, but he said nothing, and she shrugged again. "I'll let you know."

"Ella, I want this kept private."

She looked ready to argue but turned and stalked from the room. The door slammed behind her, and Tara released the breath she'd been holding.

"Nice lady," she said.

Piers chuckled. "No, she's not. She's neither nice or a lady." He turned to Christian. "I think you may be right. It's time for her to go."

"She's a dangerous woman to leave around," Christian said.

"Oh, I don't plan on leaving her anywhere," Piers replied with a grim smile.

"Well, don't do anything before she gets my information."

Were they calmly discussing killing Ella? Maybe she hadn't understood the conversation. Then she remembered the evil lurking behind the woman's face, and shivered.

Christian's arm curled around her shoulder. "Let's get out of here."

She nodded. She wanted to go home. She wanted her pajamas and a cup of hot cocoa and Smokey purring on her lap. She wanted to pretend everything was normal, but the normal world she wanted seemed farther from her than she could ever have believed possible.

Piers said, "Keep me informed. I want to know what happens."

Christian nodded and led her from the room. She tried to keep her eyes focused ahead, but something made her glance to the side. Ella stared at the two of them. She smiled as she caught Tara's gaze, but her eyes were filled with such malice that Tara's steps faltered, and she stumbled against Christian.

Her eyes were on Ella, and Christian followed her gaze.

"Ignore her," he murmured. "She can't do anything to you."

Tara wanted to believe him, but she felt the other woman's eyes bore into her as the elevator door closed behind them.

Chapter Nine

Christian opened the passenger door for her. "I'll take you back to your apartment."

"That's okay. You can drop me off at the train station."

He shook his head. "I want you to pick up some things. You'll be staying at my place tonight, and tomorrow we go to Yorkshire."

Neither proposition sounded appealing right now. "I've had my fill of vampires for the night, thank you, and I'm not ready for the whole basement thing."

"You can sleep in the penthouse."

"You have a penthouse?" She tried not to sound impressed.

"Yeah," he answered dryly. "It's at the top of the building."

However desirable she found Christian, she just wanted to go home. She wanted her pajamas, her cat, and that mug of cocoa. She craved the safety of the familiar. "I want to stay at home."

"It's not an option. I told Piers you wouldn't be a problem, which means I have to make sure you're not."

Her mouth tightened. "I'm not going to tell anybody. Your secret is safe and all that crap."

"Don't make this difficult."

"Or else what? Are you going to order me? Hey, didn't you forget something? It doesn't work. You can't actually tell me what to do. Well you can, but luckily for me, I don't have to do it."

"You think mind compulsion is the only way to control you?" He took a step toward her. Refusing to back down took an awful lot of effort, and Tara could feel her legs trembling with the struggle to hold them in place.

"I'm sure that there're all sorts of vampire scary stuff you could do, but you did promise you wouldn't hurt me."

He sighed. "I won't hurt you, and I won't let anyone else hurt you, but you are coming back with me tonight."

In the dim light of the underground car park, he appeared huge and solid, his expression implacable. If he wanted to, she was sure he could pick her up and put her in the car.

"Okay," she said, "but I will want cocoa."

"Graham makes excellent cocoa."

Neither of them spoke as he drove out of the underground garage and onto the street. The roads were quiet. It was almost midnight, and she needed to ask Chloe to feed Smokey and give him a cuddle each evening. Hopefully, she'd still be up.

Christian seemed to know the way to her apartment, and half an hour later, they pulled up in front of the building.

"Do you want to wait out here?" she asked and tried not to sound too hopeful.

"No."

Tara rolled her eyes. "You know I'm not going to escape out the back window and run away." Ignoring the comment, he got out of the car, walked around, and opened her door. She sighed and climbed out. "Just get one thing straight. I do not belong to you, okay?"

"I agree, you do not belong to me," he replied. She started to walk away and almost didn't hear the softly spoken, "yet."

A ripple of some unknown emotion ran through her. Anticipation or trepidation, she really wasn't sure, so she decided to ignore it. She was getting good at that.

She let them both in through the front door. A light was on in Chloe's flat, and Tara decided to go there first. Christian stopped her with a hand on her arm.

"Where are we going?" he asked. "Your flat's on the second floor."

"Do you know everything?" she snapped. "We're going to see my friend Chloe. I'm hoping she can look after Smokey for me while I'm away, because otherwise I'm not going anywhere."

"Graham can come in and feed your cat," Christian said.

She raised a hand to ring the bell, but paused. "Does Graham do everything you tell him?" She was curious as to the answer. Of all she'd learned tonight, the compulsion thing worried her the most. She had no intention of letting Christian have that sort of power over her.

"Yes," he replied.

At least he wasn't hiding it. Sighing, she pressed her finger to the bell. Nothing happened, and she leaned closer. Inside, she could hear music and someone moving about. A minute later, the door opened a crack, and Chloe peered through the gap.

"Hey, what's going on?" She unlatched the chain on the door and opened it wider, only then noticing the man standing behind Tara. Her eyes widened, and she grabbed Tara's jacket and pulled her inside, slamming the door behind them. Releasing her hold, she stared at the door as though expecting it to crash open.

"Tell me that is not Christian Roth," she whispered.

"Well I could," Tara said. "But unfortunately, I'd be lying."

Chloe's eyes narrowed. "Okay, then tell me you haven't brought Christian Roth to my doorstep while I'm wearing plaid pajamas."

Despite everything, Tara grinned. The usual Goth gear had disappeared, and Chloe wore a pair of red and black plaid flannel pajamas, and big, pink fluffy slippers. "Sorry," Tara said. "I'd be lying again."

"Oh my God, what am I supposed to do?"

"I just came to ask a favor."

Chloe shook her head. "Right, I'm with you. My brain may have left for a moment, but it's back now, honest. What do you need?"

Tara opened her mouth to speak but Chloe scurried around Tara and peered through the spy hole. "Yup, just checking, he's still there. And Tara..." She put her eye to the hole. "...he's huge." She straightened. "Sorry, but honestly, it's not often you have a hunky billionaire standing outside your door." She glanced down at herself. "And I am just so not dressed for this."

"It doesn't matter," Tara said. "Look, I have to go away for a few days—"

"You're going away with him?" Chloe nodded in the direction of the door.

"Yes. I hired him again and we're going up to Yorkshire, to my old house, to see if we can find something out up there. I wondered if you would care for Smokey while I'm away."

"No problem, but are you sure you're all right with this? You've only just met this guy, and now you're going away with him. All alone." She scrutinized Tara. "Are you okay, you look a little strained?"

"It's just been a long night, but I'm fine, and Christian's been a real gentleman. He just wants to help me find out about my past."

"Hmm, I look at him and I've got to be honest, the word gentleman is not the one that springs to mind."

Tara wanted to ask what word did spring to mind, but maybe she was better off not knowing. "Perhaps not, but appearances can be deceiving."

"Does Jamie know about this?"

"No, we just decided tonight. But it doesn't have anything to do with Jamie."

"No, I suppose not. You know we've sort of been seeing each other. Jamie and me, I mean."

"Really? That's fantastic. I—"

A tap on the door interrupted her. Obviously Christian. Tara considered ignoring him, but the tap came again. Harder this time. "We're coming," she shouted. "Have a little bloody patience."

Chloe raised an eyebrow. "I think that's the first time I've ever heard you swear."

"Probably the company I'm keeping," Tara said darkly.

"I thought he was a gentleman?"

"He is. Now, are you going to come up so I can show you where everything is?"

"Hell, yes." Chloe said. "I want to meet Christian Roth." She gave her outfit one more disgusted glance and shrugged. "Let's go."

Tara opened the door. Christian was hovering just outside. "Back off," she said.

He took a step back but smiled.

"Christian, this is Chloe, a friend. Chloe this is—"

"Christian Roth." Chloe held out a hand. "I've read all about you, Mr. Roth."

"I doubt that," Tara said.

Christian took Chloe's hand. "Please call me Christian. Any friend of Tara's is a friend of mine."

Tara rolled her eyes. How corny could you get? But Chloe seemed to lap it up. Leaving them holding hands, she headed up the stairs, let herself into the apartment, and called Smokey. He appeared out of the living room, purring and weaving between her legs. As she reached down to stroke him, he hissed and streaked away, disappearing back from where he'd come from. She turned to see Christian and Chloe standing in the open doorway.

"Are you going to invite us in?" he asked.

"Come in."

He stepped over the threshold.

"Just a minute." Tara peered around the sitting room door as Smokey's tail disappeared behind the sofa. She frowned. Smokey was normally a very friendly cat, at least with people. Could he sense Christian's true nature? That made her wonder if vampires could drink animal blood. Ugh! She made a mental note to ask him.

When she turned back, he was watching her.

"You wait here," she said. "I'll show Chloe where the cat food and so on is. Then pack a bag. I'll be back in a minute, okay?"

"No problem."

She dragged Chloe into the kitchen and shut the door behind them.

"I distinctly remember you telling me he wasn't gorgeous," Chloe whispered. "Are you mad?"

"Probably." She didn't want to talk about Christian. "Right, he has two meals a day—"

"Who? Christian?"

"No Smokey, of course. It's all in here." She opened the freezer door. "He has chicken in the morning and beef in the evening. I cook it for him, and they're all labeled. If you get the next meal out when you feed him, it should defrost, but don't leave it anywhere he can get it. In the oven is best."

"You're not going to talk about the two of you, are you?"

"There is no two of us. Now, he can let himself in and out from the roof terrace, there's a cat flap, but sometimes he gets stuck out the front and you have to let him in." She glanced up to find Chloe frowning at her. "Are you paying attention?"

"Yes, Miss."

"Good. That's all really, but if you have the time, I'm sure he'd appreciate a cuddle in the evenings."

"And who will you be cuddling in the evenings?"

"No one, I told you, it's just business."

"He doesn't look at you as if it's just business."

"How does he look at me?"

Chloe smiled. "Like he wants to eat you up."

Was it just an unfortunate choice of words? She hoped so. "I'm really grateful, you know, and I'm sorry I bothered you so late."

"I would have been seriously pissed if you hadn't. I wouldn't have missed meeting him for anything. Come on, I'll help you pack your bag."

Tara led her out of the kitchen. Christian was where they had left him by the door, but he lounged against the wall relaxed, arms folded across his broad chest. His eyes followed them as they crossed the hallway to Tara's room but he didn't speak.

"Don't you just love the strong silent type?" Chloe asked with a giggle.

Tara ignored the comment. She dragged a small bag out of the wardrobe and put in some underwear, jeans, and jumpers. She placed her own flannel pajamas on the top.

Chloe picked them up and shot them a look of disgust. "Haven't you got anything more appropriate?"

Tara snatched them from her and put them back in the case. "I'm going to Yorkshire in the middle of December and most likely the heating will be off. So, believe me, these are appropriate."

"But hardly romantic."

"I told you it's—"

"Just business, I know, but I bet it doesn't stay that way." She sighed. "It's so 'Cathy and Heathcliffe,' just the two of you alone on the moors. I bet it will snow, and you'll be stuck there for months, having to share body heat."

"We will not be sharing anything, especially not body heat."

Chloe ignored her. "Don't worry about me and Smokey—we'll look after each other. You stay as long as you like." She hunted through Tara's wardrobe as she spoke. After pulling a black silk shirt off the hanger, she folded it carefully before placing it in the bag. "Don't you have any dresses?" she asked, continuing her search.

Tara looked at her in amazement. "You hate dresses. I've never seen you in a dress."

"Yes, but I've never been on a romantic break with Christian Roth."

Tara opened her mouth. Closed it again. *What was the point?*

Chloe moved to burrowing in the drawers. "Ah," she said, "here they are." She held up the lacy black bra and matching panties they'd bought on a shopping trip, and added them to the bag. Tara shook her head but zipped up the case and put it on the floor.

"Thank you." She reached out and hugged Chloe. "I always wanted a friend. I'm glad I found you."

"Aw, that's sweet," Chloe said, and tightened her arms around her.

After a moment, Tara took a step back. "Right, that's it then?"

"Toothbrush." Chloe said.

"Toothbrush?"

"Believe me, you're going to want to brush your teeth. Probably like every five minutes. I'm always like that when I get a new man."

Tara shook her head again but went into the bathroom and filled a bag with toiletries and make-up. She added it to the case.

Christian straightened as they came out of the bedroom and took the case from her. Tara peered into the living room. It didn't look like Smokey would to make an appearance. "Smokey is behind the sofa, and the keys are on the side, over there."

"Don't worry about a thing," Chloe said. "And you" — she turned to Christian— "you look after her."

Amusement flickered across his features, but he nodded.

Tara gave Chloe one last hug and followed Christian down to the car.

Part Two

DISCOVERY AND DENIAL

Chapter Ten

"What time is it?" Tara mumbled.

"Just gone one." Graham carried a steaming cup of coffee that he put down on the table next to her.

She was on the scarlet sofa in Christian's apartment. She'd come down from the penthouse just after sunset as instructed and found Christian already up and gone. According to Graham, he'd had a call from Piers soon after he'd awakened and disappeared shortly afterward.

She yawned. "One in the morning?"

"Yes, and Christian's back."

A jolt of excitement hit her in the stomach, and she sat up, running a hand through her hair and searching the room. "Where is he?"

"You're to meet him in the underground garage. He wants to leave straight away."

They were driving to Yorkshire that night. It was a good four-hour journey even without delays, and obviously, Christian would want to reach their destination well before sunrise.

Because he was a vampire.

"I'll take your case." Graham broke into her thoughts. "And meet you down there. Drink your coffee, and there's a bathroom through there if you want to freshen up." He picked up her small case and disappeared out the door.

In the bathroom, she stared at herself in the mirror. She appeared pale, her eyes huge and shadowed, and she knew it was as much worry as sleeplessness.

There, she had admitted it to herself. She was scared of going back to Yorkshire. Scared of what she might find there. All day, she'd tried not to think about it, but was heading back to the one place she had sworn never to return to, and was doing it in the company of a vampire.

Underneath the worry was a glimmer of excitement at the thought of spending time alone with Christian. Totally inappropriate excitement. No way did falling for the undead have any part in her future. Still, she couldn't deny that deep beneath the surface was a cauldron of anticipation that threatened to overflow and set her on fire.

Unless she kept it firmly under control.

She found Christian waiting for her. He was dressed in a long black leather trench coat and leaned, arms crossed, against a black SUV. He appeared wired, like he'd taken something.

"You're not hungry, are you?" She stared at him suspiciously.

He straightened and a small smile played around his lips. The smile didn't quite reach his eyes, which gleamed with an almost palpable excitement.

"I'm fine," he said. His voice was low and dark, sending shivers down her spine. "I've fed." His tongue came out and stroked over his lower lip as if remembering something amazingly good.

Why didn't that make her feel better? She couldn't

help but wonder whom he had fed on. "Good," she said. "I wouldn't want you to get peckish on the journey."

"Sorry about the delay, something came up. Are you ready?"

"As I'll ever be."

His eyes slid over her and a slow burning heat glowed in the pit of her belly. She stared at him for long moments before closing the space between them.

"Let me take your coat," he said. "It's a long journey, and you may as well be comfortable."

Tara slipped out of the coat and handed it to him, trying to ignore the way his gaze wandered over her body. She'd dressed sensibly in jeans and a sweater for the Yorkshire December weather, but his eyes seemed to probe beneath the bulky clothes, to strip her bare.

He opened the car door and tossed her coat onto the back seat. She moved to get in, but his hand on her arm stopped her. She almost jumped.

"Relax," he murmured.

Her eyes flicked to his face in disbelief. "I can't. I thought I was leaving all the weirdness behind and starting a new life. Yet here I am."

"You'll have your new life."

"Yes, but I want a new normal life. With normal people," she reiterated. She thought about adding "not with a vampire" but that was rude. Besides, he'd never actually said he wanted her in his life. Maybe she was just a client, but even as the thought flickered through her mind, he bent and kissed her lightly on the lips.

"Normal can be highly overrated," he said.

She pulled back. "Not when you've never had it."

"There are other things you've never had," he said in that same low voice. He stepped closer, crowding her against the vehicle. His hands came up, sliding into her hair, tilting her head so she had no choice but to look up into his face. He was all dark shadows and glowing eyes in the dim light of the underground garage. He kissed her again. His lips slanted hard over hers. She opened her mouth to protest, and his tongue slipped inside. It took all of ten seconds for Tara to become mindless. All her good resolutions forgotten. She closed her eyes, her hands reached up to grasp his shoulders, and she sank into the kiss. Long minutes later, he raised his head.

Tara let out a small whimper, and her grip tightened on his shoulders. He was so close she could smell the faint musky scent of his skin. She opened her eyes as a slight smile flickered across his features.

"I told you—normal is highly overrated."

He gripped her hair and tugged her head back almost roughly. His lips were at her throat, his teeth grazing over the sensitive flesh, and her whole body tensed in anticipation as she waited for the sharp pain of his penetration. He nipped the skin between his teeth but the pain never came. Instead, he released her and she felt the slow almost languid stroke of his tongue against her taut flesh. The sensation was exquisite and without thinking, her head fell back to allow him access.

He ran a finger down her throat, and then took a small step back. "Did you know you have other veins, other places I can feed from?"

She stared at him wide eyed and he picked up her limp hand. He stroked the pad of his thumb across the thin skin of her inner arm. "One here at your wrist. And one..." He dropped her hand and reached down between them. "And one just here, between your thighs." He stroked his finger down the seam of her jeans. "Would you like that, Tara? My mouth between your thighs?"

Tara couldn't answer; she'd lost the ability to speak. Her insides were melting and threatening to slide out of her body.

He laughed softly, his hands gliding over her back, sure and firm. They splayed over her bottom and pulled her into him so she could feel every hard inch of him against her. He shifted, and the rigid line of his erection pressed against the softness of her belly. Her body clenched, and she curled her fingers into the hard muscle of his upper arms. He held her against him for a long moment. Then released her and took a step back.

He smiled ruefully. "I told myself I was going to give you time, let you sort out your personal issues before I gave you anything else to deal with. I guess I'm not very good at not taking what I want."

He stroked the pad of his thumb across her lower lip. She trembled, dropped her hands from his arms then backed against the car and breathed in slowly.

"Er, right. Hadn't we better get going?" She was proud of how steady her voice sounded. "After all, you don't want to be on the road when the sun comes up."

They drove through the almost deserted streets of London. Tara stared at his hands on the wheel, the long, elegant fingers. His sleeves were pushed up, revealing strong forearms, the skin pale with a slight sprinkling of dark hairs. He had a circle of scars, like bracelets, around each wrist, as though he'd been tied up at some time. Was it before he became a vampire?

She had so many questions she wanted to ask. How old he was, where he came from, had he a family? She made a mental note to ask him sometime but just now, she didn't feel inclined to break the silence. Despite what had happened between them, the atmosphere in the car was comfortable. So she sat back and watched the passing lights.

After a while they left the city behind and sped northwards on the dark motorway. The car was warm and she drifted off into a light sleep.

...

Christian knew the moment she fell asleep. He glanced away from the road. Her eyes were closed, her lush pink mouth slightly open. He remembered the taste of her. He'd almost lost it. All his good resolutions had vanished with the first taste of those lips. She was intoxicating.

He could blame some of it on the demon blood he'd drunk that night. He could still feel it race through his body, intensifying his senses.

Piers had called him with news that another agent had died, and they had gone hunting together. They had caught up with the demons and taken them down, sated themselves on the blood—just like old times.

Still, it hadn't lessened his hunger for Tara; he was beginning to crave her like an addiction. He'd almost bitten her back there. That was the unfortunate aspect of demon blood—it lowered his inhibitions.

What would they find in Yorkshire? What secrets would the house hold and would it reveal them? An undead guardian and a magical charm. Why? What could she be hiding?

Whatever it was, he was sure Tara was unaware of it. He thought of her desire for a normal life, and knew he had to let her go.

Three hours out of London, snow began to fall.

...

"Tara, we're almost there."

A hand touched her shoulder, and she opened her eyes. The car had stopped moving, and the interior light was on. They were cocooned in darkness, a swirling mass of snow outside, and beyond that nothing. She turned to find Christian watching her.

"Are you ready for this?" he asked.

Was she? She nodded. "Of course. It's only a house."

He switched off the light and turned the ignition. They drove slowly. A layer of snow crunched under the car's wheels, and the dark trees on either side were shadowed in the headlights' beam. Tara stared straight ahead.

"I guess you know this road well?" Christian spoke into the silence.

"Not well. We didn't leave very often. In fact, I don't remember Aunt Kathy ever leaving."

"Probably the magic that kept her alive was tied to this place."

"What? So she would have—" She'd been going to say died, but that didn't seem the right term for someone who was already dead. "I used to cut across the moors to get to the village, so this track wasn't used much. Just deliveries and things."

Up ahead she saw the wrought iron gates at the entrance to the house. "There it is," she said. "I have the keys, just a moment."

She found the big old-fashioned keys in her bag and opened the car door. Swirls of snow entered the warm interior and she shivered. "I need my coat, it's freezing out there."

Christian took the keys from her and exited the car. A minute later, the gates swung open, and he climbed back in and drove through. He halted the car at the midpoint through the gates.

"The gates are warded."

Tara could see nothing unusual. "Warded? What does that mean?"

"More magic. My guess is it's a cloaking device. Hiding what's inside."

"But there's nothing there to hide."

"No, but there was…you."

She rubbed at the point between her eyes to erase the tension. "Why would anyone want to hide me? I can't do anything different. I'm *ordinary*."

"You're not ordinary. I don't know what you are, or why someone should feel the need to hide you away, but there is something about you, something I sensed straight away. Your scent is exotic, deliciously intoxicating." He breathed in deeply, his eyes half shut. "I've never come across a human or a supernatural being who smells quite like you. No, whatever you are, you're different."

"I don't want to be different."

Christian shrugged. "We rarely get what we want. We just have to learn to accept what we are. Come on, let's get you inside before you freeze."

Chapter Eleven

The building appeared out of the darkness. Half hidden by the swirling snow, it loomed gray and huge.

"You need to drive round the back," Tara said.

Christian pulled up in the shelter of the house, and Tara got out of the car and hurried to unlock the door. It opened straight into the farmhouse kitchen. After stepping inside, Tara was amazed at the feeling of welcome that washed over her. She pressed the light switch just inside the door, hoping the power was still on, and relaxed as light flooded the room.

This had always been her favorite part of the house. For a moment, she stood and let the feeling run through her. She'd built the place up into some sort of nightmare, when in fact she had been happy in the only home she had known for twenty-two years. While from the outside the house had appeared grim and austere, the inside was warm and welcoming. It was only as she grew older that she felt hemmed-in, trapped.

A noise made her turn back to the open door. Christian stood on the threshold, snowflakes settling like stars in his dark hair. He was so big he filled the doorway.

"You need to invite me in," he said.

She remembered he'd asked the same thing at her apartment. One more vampire lore confirmed. "Come in," she said, and he stepped over the threshold.

"How does it feel to be back?" he asked.

"Actually, it feels good. I never hated the house. I just wanted to see something of the world."

"I'll go get the stuff from the car."

He returned a few minutes later with her small case and a box. He put the case next to her and the box on the table. "Graham said you might need some food, coffee and so on. This should keep you going for a couple of days at least."

"I think I may be in love with Graham." She opened the box. "You want some coffee? Do you even drink coffee?"

He nodded.

Tara put the coffeemaker on; everything was exactly where she expected. She puttered around the room, putting things away, stroking her hands over the comfortable, familiar furniture. She found Christian watching her. "What?"

"You seem at home here. I thought you hated this place."

"So did I. After Aunt Kathy died, I wanted to get as far from here as possible. A lot of it was guilt. I sort of promised her that I would stay here."

"When?"

"When she was dying, or whatever she was doing. She made me promise to stay here and to keep the rules. And I did—promise I mean—then as soon as she was gone, I packed up and left."

She poured the coffee and sank into one of the chairs, cradling the hot mug in her hands. Christian drank his coffee fast. "I'm going to take a quick look around outside, then I need to find somewhere to spend the day."

"There's a cellar."

"Sounds good."

She watched as he went out the door, closing it behind him and leaving her alone.

...

Outside, the snow had stopped falling. A couple of inches lay on the ground but Christian didn't notice the cold as he walked around the house. The clouds had also cleared, the black sky was studded with stars, and a sickle moon shone overhead, reflecting off the snow.

The house had a strange, timeless feel, and he knew there was magic at work. Powerful magic, as though they were in a bubble cut off from the outside world. He searched the area, trying to get a sense of the source.

A wall ran around the entire property. He walked toward the nearest section and put his hand to the cold stone. The hum of magic ran through it, sending a frisson of shock up his arm and down through his body. It was the same magic warding the gates. He strolled the perimeter, touching the wall with his fingertips. The circle was unbroken.

It was probably safe for Tara to remove the talisman inside the wards. He might get the chance to discover what she hid under there. Someone had paid a high price to give this level of protection, and he was betting the cost wasn't only money. Dark magic was stronger but always demanded a blood price. Whose blood had paid for this, and why?

About time they found out.

He turned back to the house. In the kitchen, Tara was slumped over the table, another cup of coffee in front of her, and a pile of blankets and pillows at her feet. She wasn't moving, and a flash of alarm shot through him. He touched her arm lightly and she shifted under his hand, moaning softly. She was fast asleep.

He sat down opposite her. Her head rested on her folded

arms, one side of her face turned toward him, and his eyes ran over the pure line of her cheek, the arching curve of her brow. There was a slight shadowing beneath her eye, and one hand clenched the talisman as it lay, still around her neck, on the table.

Someone had done all this to protect Tara. Would she still be here if the aunt had not "died"? What had gone wrong? Had the magic binding Kathryn Collin's soul to the earth failed? Or had the spell been deliberately broken? Was someone, even now, hunting for Tara?

An overwhelming need to protect her rose up inside him, hitting him hard in the gut. Tara was his to care for, and whoever came after her would have to go through him first.

Mine, the word screamed in his head.

He couldn't ever remember feeling this way—he wanted to keep her close and safe. The thought pulled him up short. It wasn't in his nature to care, certainly not for a human because a relationship could only be fleeting. He should find out whatever was after her, destroy them, and afterward, he would find the strength to walk away and leave her to her normal life.

He stroked the hair from her face. Her eyes fluttered open, and she sat up.

"Sorry," she mumbled, "I didn't sleep much last night." She took a sip of coffee and grimaced. "Cold," she muttered putting the cup down. "So did you find anything out there?"

"The whole place is warded. In effect, we're inside a spell that I believe stops anything on the outside from sensing the presence of anyone within its boundaries."

"But why?"

"I don't know, but it's probably safe to take off the talisman here."

"Then why did Aunt Kathy always insist I wear it here."

"Probably just being extra cautious. So are you willing

to try?"

"It's what we're here for, but do you think we can leave it until tomorrow night? I'm tired and... Maybe I just want to forget about it for a little while."

He nodded. "It's not long until dawn."

"Do you have to sleep during the day?"

"I no longer have to sleep, but it is preferable."

She hesitated for a moment then asked, "Do you sleep alone?"

She watched him out of those enormous expressive eyes. And he knew she would spend the day with him. All he had to do was ask, and he could have anything he wanted from her.

Her body and her blood.

A wave of heat washed over him, and for a moment his resolve weakened and a slow fire started in his belly. He shook his head—this would only make the inevitable parting harder. Only minutes ago, he'd decided they could have no future. Most of his existence, he had taken what he wanted and not thought about the price. Now he found he didn't want Tara to pay.

Did he sleep alone? He rose to his feet. "Always."

Chapter Twelve

Tara woke up in her old bed. Snow was falling again, swirling against the glass, obscuring the outside world. Chloe hadn't been far wrong—perhaps the snow would strand them together, cut off from everything. It should have sounded romantic, until she remembered the speed he'd shut the door in her face the previous evening.

Talk about mixed signals—first the kisses, then the brush off.

She should have left it when he'd told her he always slept alone, but no, she'd pushed. She hated it, *really hated it*, when people said they were doing something for "your own good." Her aunt had used the phrase all the time. Tara was quite capable of making up her own mind. If he didn't want her after all, she'd rather he came right out and said it.

Yesterday, she'd decided to keep the relationship with Christian on a strict business footing. Now, after a few kisses, she was miffed because he'd insisted on sleeping in the cellar alone. Not that she wanted to sleep in the cellar. The place was nothing but a dark hole under the ground—it should fit

Christian to perfection.

After showering and dressing in warm clothes, she went outside to decide what she was going to do. She left the gardens by a small gate that opened onto the moors, but stayed close to the house. Having grown up around here, she knew how little it took for the weather to turn hazardous. Instead, she headed toward a former haven—a huge rocky outcrop that overlooked the village below.

Standing on the edge, she surveyed the picture-pretty village. There was a pub, and a café, a post office, none of which she'd ever entered. How many days had she lain on this rock gazing down and dreaming of a normal life?

It was strange coming back here. She'd built it up to be terrible, but she'd had a happy childhood. For a dead woman, Aunt Kathy had been amazingly kind.

What else was she going to find out about herself? Had her mother, whoever she was, gotten mixed up in the supernatural world and tried to protect her daughter? And who was her father?

She remembered Christian's expression when she took the talisman off last time: Shock and fear. Would it be any better the next? It made no difference. She would remove the talisman and break Rule Number Three. But she'd persuade Christian to take her to the pub. They could have a drink together—a drink with normal people.

Well—normal people and a vampire.

...

"You want to go to the pub?" Christian stared at her as if she was a crazy woman, as if she'd asked for something weird.

"It's what normal people do."

"It may have escaped your notice, but I am *not* a normal person."

Once again, he was dressed in black, all six-foot-four of him. She doubted that the villagers of Shelby had ever come across anyone quite like him before, but she didn't want to go alone. "You can pretend, can't you?"

"You want to have a drink?"

"No, I don't want to have a drink, but that's not the point. I've never been to the pub in Shelby, or the café, or even the post office. I don't know what's going to happen when I take off the talisman, but I have a feeling it isn't going to be any kind of normal. So first, I'd like you to take me to the pub, and we can both pretend for a couple of hours."

"Are you asking me on a date?" His eyes settled on her mouth. He was going to kiss her, she was sure of it, and small flames flickered to life in her belly. "Will I get a goodnight kiss at the end of it?"

Tara swayed toward him until he was so close she could see the black circle around his silver eyes.

He stepped back and shrugged. "I don't see why not."

Disappointment tore through her, and it took her a moment to realize he'd agreed. "Right, I'll go get changed."

Christian raised an eyebrow. "Will I need to change?"

"No," she said, looking him up and down. "You're perfect as you are."

...

They drove down into the village and parked outside The Coachman's Arms. As they stepped into the pub, all faces turned to stare at them. Perhaps it would have been a good idea for Christian to change his clothes after all, though Tara doubted he possessed anything that would blend in with this particular setting. With his tall, broad figure and the black leather trench coat, he appeared exotic and a little dangerous. In fact, he stood out like a panther at a garden party. He couldn't even take the coat off as she had seen what was underneath.

"I don't go anywhere unarmed," he'd replied when she suggested that he might want to leave the gun behind. At that point, it had occurred to her that she might have been better off leaving *him* behind, never mind the gun.

The pub was small and snug with a long wood bar at one end and a small spattering of tables. The walls were dark red with horse brasses hanging from hooks and pictures of the moors. Christian had to duck as they crossed the room to avoid the low wooden beams. She found an empty table and pushed him toward it. "Sit down. I'll get us a drink."

She bought Christian a beer and herself a Coke and could feel the barman's eyes—along with everyone else's—on her as she made her way back across the room.

Christian took his drink and eyed her glass as she sat.

"What?" she said. "I like Coke."

"Some supernatural beings react to alcohol."

"In what way?" She wasn't sure she wanted to hear this. Why couldn't they chat about the weather or something?

"Demons go crazy. It brings out their darker side."

"It's a good job I'm not a demon, then. I just passed out, and that was bad enough."

He looked around the bar. "Do you know any of these people?"

"I recognize some of them. Most people have lived here all their lives."

"So they would have been around back when you were born?"

"I suppose so. Do you think they might remember anything?"

"Newcomers are always noticed in these sorts of places. Do you want to try?"

She did. A pang of excitement jolted through her at the

thought that someone might remember them coming all those years ago. There were only about fifteen people in the pub. Some, like the barman, were too young but most were quite elderly. She wasn't very good at approaching people, a hang-up from Rule Number Four—never talk to strangers—but there was one man seated at the bar who caught her eye and raised his glass. He appeared to be in his fifties, so he should remember her moving here with her aunt. Without giving herself time to think, she got to her feet and walked across to him.

"Hello," she said.

He nodded. "Evening."

"I wondered if you'd mind talking with me for a moment. My name's Tara, I used to live at the house on the tor."

"I know the house."

God, this was hard. "Can I buy you a drink?"

Glancing at the barman, he raised his glass. The barman poured him a pint and put it down in front of them.

"Would you mind talking to my friend as well?"

He looked across at Christian, who, to give him credit, wasn't doing anything obvious to draw attention to himself. "No problem."

Christian stood as they approached and nodded. They all sat down.

"I'm Ted Carter," he said.

"Christian Roth."

"Well then, what can I tell you?"

"My aunt died recently—"

"Aye, I know, and we were all sorry for your loss."

"Thank you. My aunt was a very private person and didn't tell me much about my family. I was wondering if you remember when she came here."

"Of course I do. It was the talk of the village for a while. Not that she ever gave us much to talk about, she kept to herself." He paused and took a sip of his drink. "Well, they both did."

"Both?"

"Your aunt and your mother. At least, I presume it was your mother. She was pregnant at the time, heavily pregnant, and she had a look of you about her."

Tara went still. For some reason, it had never occurred to her that someone would remember her mother. "Can you tell me about her?"

"Not much to tell, I'm afraid. I only saw her once, but she did stick in my mind. She was beautiful, the most beautiful thing I've ever seen." He seemed lost in thought for a moment, a small smile playing across his features. "I think we all fell in love with her just from that one sighting. She was like something from another world, too good for this one." He shook his head. "It's not like me to be fanciful, but she had that effect." He gave a rueful smile, pulled himself back from the past, and focused on Tara. "She was a lot like you, you know. A tiny little thing. With hair so blond it was almost silver and long, right down her back. Like yours used to be when you lived here, and her eyes were the exact color of yours, like new spring grass."

Tara blinked back tears and took a gulp of coke. "Sorry," she said. "But no one's ever spoken to me of my mother before. Can you remember anything else?"

"She carried a big gray cat, cuddled it the whole time, and she seemed sad."

Had she known then that she would never see her child grow up? "Do you know what happened to her?"

He shook his head. "I told you, they kept to themselves. Bill Tyler used to do the deliveries up there. He told us once that he heard a baby crying in the house. That wasn't long after they moved here, but no one ever saw your mother again. Never saw much of your aunt either. Though we did see you."

"You did?"

"Aye, on and off we'd see you running wild on the moors. Or sitting on that big rock watching us all. Some of us wanted to do something about you—it didn't seem right you spending all that time alone, not going to school, but we were told it was all in order, your aunt was teaching you."

"Yes, she did."

"It still didn't seem right, but what could we do, and you seemed healthy and happy enough."

"I was. Happy I mean, at least most of the time."

"Good."

Tara tried to make sense of what she had learned. What had happened to her mother? Could she have given birth and simply abandoned her daughter? What could make any woman do that? Perhaps she had hated Tara's father, whoever he was, and staying with Tara would have reminded her of him every day. So she left, and maybe, even now, she was alive somewhere.

But Tara knew in her heart that her mother hadn't abandoned her. At least, not voluntarily. She knew it with a certainty, and a deep well of grief rose within her. She swallowed back the tears. How could you grieve for a mother you'd never known?

Christian had told her that someone had gone to a lot of bother to hide her, keep her safe. Her mother must have cared for her enough to try to protect her, but from what?

She ran her hands through her hair, pressing her scalp to relieve the tension.

"Are you all right?" Christian watched her closely.

"I'm fine." She shrugged. "I'll go get another round in, shall I? Mr. Carter?"

He nodded and Tara jumped to her feet and headed to the bar. When she returned, she put the drinks onto the table and slipped into her seat.

"So, I reckon you would notice any newcomers around here?" Christian asked.

"Too right. We're not exactly on the tourist track."

Christian took a sip of his beer. "Have you noticed any other strangers recently?"

Ted Carter gave him a sharp look. "Not recently, no."

Christian smiled. "How about a few months ago, around about the time Tara left."

The other man nodded slowly. "Aye, we had a few strange types asking questions around about then."

Tara frowned. "Questions about what?"

"I never spoke to them." He looked thoughtful for a minute. "Do you mind if I invite someone over to join us?"

"Of course not," Tara answered.

He crossed the room, returning a few minutes later with a middle-aged man and woman. "This is Bill Tyler and his wife, Jean." He smiled. "Jean, you might be interested to know, is the teacher at the village school, and one of the main voices calling for something to be done about you."

"You should have gone to school," the woman said.

Both men rolled their eyes as if to say, *here we go again*.

"Right then," Ted said. "Bill here was the one who spoke to the strangers."

"What did they want?" Christian asked.

Bill glanced across at Tara. "It was strange. They turned up the day after you left, but they didn't ask about you specifically, in fact, they didn't seem to know much about what they wanted. Asked if we'd noticed anything strange in the area recently." He grinned. "I said they were the strangest things we'd seen in a while. Weren't too pleased about that."

"What did you tell them?" Christian asked, and an undercurrent of darkness threaded through his voice.

Bill raised one eyebrow. "Nothing. We don't speak

to outsiders, but it was more than that. I didn't like them. Straight off there was something not quite right, like they were looking down their noses at us. Anyway, that was the first lot."

He sat back and took a swallow of his drink.

"There were more I presume?" Tara sensed Christian's impatience. She was surprised the others couldn't.

"Aye, a day later, but these seemed to know a whole lot more. Asked about anyone who had come to the area in the last twenty-two years." He took another sip of his drink. "Then they asked about your mother."

Tara sat up. "What?"

"Gave a spot-on description. They obviously knew her, but they didn't mention your aunt. Or you, for that matter." He turned back to Christian. "And before you ask, no we didn't tell them anything either."

Christian smiled.

"So," Bill said, "do you know these people?"

Christian stared into the man's eyes. Bill shook his head in some confusion. Christian turned to the others and held their gazes for a moment.

"Right," Bill said, "Where were we? Oh yes, you asked about the weather, and no it's not typical, very unusual to have this much snow, this early."

Tara looked from him to Christian. The latter smiled at her, and she realized with a jolt that she had just seen vampire powers in action. He had wiped their brains of the conversation. Without any effort.

"Okay," Bill said. "My round."

Chapter Thirteen

"That was amazing," Tara said as she let them into the house.

She'd been silent on the way home, deliberately not thinking about all she had learned earlier in the evening. Instead, she'd concentrated on the pleasure of just talking with ordinary people. They'd all been so nice, and in the end, a group of them gathered around the table, chatting and laughing. She'd learned more about the village and its inhabitants tonight than in the twenty-two years she'd lived there. She'd also come away with two invitations to dinner.

Christian had been perfectly behaved, silent for the most part. No doubt he'd wrapped himself in some sort of vampire invisibility thing. Still, dinner with Jean and Bill might stretch his normal abilities beyond the breaking point.

Tara unwrapped her scarf, took off her coat, and turned to find Christian studying her. His half-closed eyes gleamed in the dim light and for a brief second, he allowed her to see his hunger for her.

Heat washed through her, and she swallowed, hard.

Okay, maybe she'd already stretched him too far because

he appeared way beyond normal now. His smile revealed a brief flash of fangs, and the blood thickened in her veins until she could feel it thundering through her body.

His gaze still on her, Christian shrugged out of his coat, unbuckled the shoulder holster, and hung it over the back of one of the chairs. His movements were graceful but gave the impression of leashed power, barely controlled, seething just below the surface. What would he be like if he released all that power? Instead of frightening her, the thought made her temperature climb even higher.

"Are you ready to do this?" Christian murmured.

She knew he meant the talisman. Or at least she thought he did.

He stared at her throat as though he could already taste her blood. Then he moved to stand beside her, leaning his long body against the solid wooden table, arms crossed over his broad chest, his hooded eyes locked on hers.

"I suppose so, but first—"

"Yes?"

"Will you kiss me?"

Shock flashed across his features then he smiled. "You mean like the end of a date?"

"Maybe, I've never actually had a date, but I'm sort of scared of what you're going to find when I take off the talisman, and maybe you won't want to kiss me afterward."

"Come here," he ordered, his voice low, mesmerizing. She entwined her fingers with his and he tugged her closer until she almost touched him. "I can smell your blood."

"Nice."

He smiled and tucked her hair behind her ear then stroked one long finger down the soft skin of her neck. At his touch, her blood caught fire; she lifted her chin and bared her throat. He bent down and his cool breath shivered across her heated flesh. For a moment, she thought he was going to take what she offered. Instead, he kissed her where the blood pounded so close to the surface, and whispered against her ear. "Soon."

Sliding his hands around her shoulders, he held her still. His mouth hovered over hers, and she trembled in anticipation. He kissed her, just the fleeting meeting of their mouths, before drawing back, teasing her, tempting her so she leaned closer to him. She needed to feel him against her, all of him, but he held her away and kissed her again, his mouth tasting hers, lingering for a moment then retreating. It was intense, beautiful, and in no way was it enough. He raised his head and stared into her eyes.

"There is nothing we could discover that would stop me wanting to taste you," he said. "But if I do so now, we'll still be making love at dawn."

"Sounds like a plan."

He laughed and the sound rippled over her skin. "I'd be flattered," he said. "Except I'm not sure which you want more, me, or *not* taking off the talisman."

She sighed. He was right.

"You're thinking too hard." Christian interrupted her thoughts. "Come, we'll do this together." He pushed her gently into the chair and pulled another close so they faced each other, knees almost touching. "Take off the talisman, Tara."

She took a deep breath and nodded. For a minute, she held the locket between her fingers, rubbing her thumb over the rough surface, remembering all the times she had held it and thought about her mother. She lifted it over her head. As she went to hand the locket to Christian, he shook his head, and she placed it on the table.

He looked at her for a long while as he squeezed her hands in his. She tried to feel reassured, but she didn't like his blank expression. What was he hiding from her?

...

A sense of foreboding washed over Christian. Something lurked behind her eyes. She still appeared human, but it was like a thin veneer concealing some other form. He breathed deeply and the faint rank, bitter scent of rotting eggs assaulted his nostrils. Demon.

His eyes flickered around the room, searching for an explanation, but they were alone, and his gaze returned to Tara. He inhaled again. The taint of sulfur was still there, but overlaid with something exotic and sweet. It rolled around his senses, intoxicating and sensual. His cock stirred in his pants and heat coiled low in his belly. The prickle in his gums reminded him that he longed to taste her. He closed his eyes and savored the feelings. Whatever she was, it made no difference.

And whatever happened in the future, he knew he would have her this night, in every way possible. She would be his.

"Christian, what is it?"

An edge of panic floated beneath the surface of her voice. Opening his eyes, he made no attempt to hide the hunger in his gaze. He'd kept so much of his real self hidden from her, concealing his exact nature, afraid she wouldn't be able to accept him. Now he let her see beneath the mask, and her eyes widened with shock. She swayed toward him, but then shook herself and sat up straight.

"Tell me what you see," she said.

"I see nothing, but you smell..." He leaned closer and inhaled. "Delectable." He stroked his tongue along the line of her throat. "Edible...irresistible."

...

At the first stroke of his tongue, Tara's body melted and her mind ceased to function. She wanted desperately to know what he had seen when she removed the necklace. If anything, he seemed to want her more. It was an almost tangible thing between them, and a flicker of unease rippled through her.

He nuzzled at her neck, nibbling at her flesh, and tremors of pleasure shot through her. She squirmed in her seat, but forced herself to make one more try. She slipped her hand between them and pushed. It made no difference. He was immoveable.

"Please, Christian, tell me."

He sighed against her throat. Then sat back, and Tara watched, fascinated as he pulled himself under control, wrapped it around himself like a cloak. She waited, holding her breath as the hunger faded from his eyes.

"I don't know," he said. "There's something there, you're different." He searched her face. "It isn't in how you look. It's in your very essence." He shook his head. "I can't tell what it is. May I try something?"

"What?"

"Do you trust me, Tara?"

Strangely she did. She nodded.

"I want to try and get inside your head. We need to do it at some point anyway."

"We do?"

"You heard me with Piers. I promised. And you're less likely to come to harm once you bear my mark. Too many people in my world have met you now, and for some reason you're not easily forgotten."

"You won't make me do anything I don't want?"

He murmured, "I assure you that you will crave every last thing we do together with every cell of your body."

"Promises, promises..." But she had no doubt that he spoke the truth. "Okay, what do I have to do?"

"Nothing. Just don't fight me."

He took her chin between his finger and thumb, raised her head, and stared into her eyes. Tara waited for something to happen. After a minute, he released his hold and sat back.

"Well, that was a bit of an anticlimax," Tara said. "What happened?"

"Nothing. Absolutely nothing. I was sure with the talisman gone you'd be mine to take, but I can't get in. Your mind is locked up tight."

"What does it mean?"

"It could be a number of things. I don't want to speculate without knowing more."

"Why?" she asked. "Are all these 'things' unpleasant?"

"Not at all," he said, and she had the distinct impression that if not lying outright then he was being stingy with the truth. "But it's been a long evening for you and there is one more thing we can do tonight."

"And that is?"

His eyes roamed over her before setting on her throat. "I can taste you."

"Taste me?"

"Drink your blood." His voice dropped, low and dark. Sharp prickles of sensation shot through her body, stiffening her nipples to hard little nubs, clenching the muscles of her belly into tight knots of desire. She shifted in her chair and he smiled.

"We can tell a lot from a person's blood. It may reveal exactly what you are, what has been done to you. Are you willing to let me drink from you, Tara?"

She stared at him, mesmerized as the tight hold on his control slowly unraveled, letting the monster peer out from within. He smiled with a flash of fangs, and her breath caught in her throat. She opened her mouth but no sound came out, and she closed it again. Taking a deep breath, she nodded. A fierce flare of excitement gleamed in his silver eyes and an echoing surge shot through her.

This was the point of no return. She didn't care.

He stood up and lifted her effortlessly in his arms. Her body rested against the coolness of his chest as he carried her through the dark house and up the stairs. He kicked open her bedroom door and laid her on the bed. The curtains were open and moonlight streamed in through the window.

Staring down at her in the dim light, he truly appeared part monster, his pale face filled with a fierce predatory beauty. Her eyes ran down his body, snagged on the bulge in his pants, and her whole body tightened in anticipation.

He started to unbutton his shirt, and her eyes followed his movements. He paused halfway. "Are you sure? You say you don't want to belong to me, but once this is done, I'll not easily let you go."

Tara hardly heard his words. He couldn't stop now. Desire flowed through her like a living thing, but she didn't have the experience to show him how much she wanted him.

"Please, Christian," she said.

It was enough. He ripped open the remaining buttons, shrugged out his shirt, and tossed it onto the floor. He was beautiful, pale like marble, each hard line perfectly sculpted. His ribs were visible and his flat belly ridged with muscle. A line of dark silky hair bisected his stomach, disappearing beneath the waistband of his pants. She followed it down, swallowed and caught his eyes. They were hooded, gleaming beneath his lashes. He held her gaze as his hands went to the fastener of his pants and flicked it open. He paused before sliding down the zip.

Tara's heart raced, the blood thundering in her veins. His soft laughter echoed in her ears.

"Scared?" he said.

He dropped his pants to the floor and stepped out of them. He was naked now, while she was still fully clothed and burning up. She couldn't take her eyes from him. The silky hair thickened, forming a dark nest from which his cock rose proud, erect, almost vertical against his flat stomach. Pale glossy skin stretched tight, the head swollen, darkened with a faint blush of blood, and he was huge, though she had nothing to compare him to. She couldn't take her eyes off his shaft, which jerked with a life of his own.

"You look as though you have never seen a naked man before," he said. The heat rose in her cheeks, and his eyes narrowed. "Tara, have you seen a naked man before? Have you ever actually done this?"

Tara decided to misunderstand him. "What?" she asked. "Provide dinner for a vampire? Nope. Never. This is definitely a first."

He smiled at her answer, and knelt on the bed beside her. She breathed in the musky, almost feral scent of him, and a wave of dizziness washed over her. He stroked her cheek.

"A virgin? I suppose it's unsurprising considering your upbringing. But intriguing all the same."

"Hey, it's no big deal. I never got the opportunity. But it makes no difference, so don't worry that I'm going to go all weird on you. This is just sex, right?"

"Just sex?" A flicker of something flashed in his eyes. "If you say so, but I think you'll find that there is no 'just' about what we'll do together, and no, it makes no difference, but perhaps I would have been a little more discreet," he gestured down the length of his naked body, "had I known."

She looked again at his cock. It twitched under her gaze and her insides threatened to melt. She could almost feel him inside her the desire was so strong. She pressed her thighs together to relieve some of the tension, licked her lips, and heard him groan. He straddled her hips, and reaching between them, he picked up her hand, brought it to his body, and wrapped her fingers round him. He was cool and hard, the skin like satin stretched over steel. She squeezed, and his head went back. She released him and fluttered her fingers up over the swollen head. It pulsed, and he groaned again. He put his hand back over hers, stopping her movement.

"You're wearing too many clothes." He gripped the sides of her jumper, slid it over her head, then traced the black lace on her bra. "Pretty."

He trailed one long finger over the soft swell of her breasts. His nail dragged across the swollen nipples, and lightning flashed to her groin. He repeated the action, and her hips rose of their own accord. Slipping a hand beneath her, he flicked open the catch of her bra, peeled the straps down her arms, and tossed it to the floor. He sat back on his heels and covered her breasts with his large hands. His palms were cool against the fiery heat of her skin. For a moment, they squeezed then drew down to frame her breasts as he took one pouting nipple between his teeth. She went wild beneath him as pleasure shot through her body. His hands held her still with ease as he kissed and licked her breasts, sucking on the sensitive nipples.

She thought she'd explode as the sensations rushed through her and settled in the hot, swollen place between her thighs. She needed something, anything, and her hips bucked against the restraining cage of his body.

"Shh," he said against her breasts, while his hands glided down over her belly and stoked the fires inside her. They moved lower and he cupped her denim-covered sex in his palm, his fingers pressing upwards to her core.

She strained against him.

It wasn't enough.

She needed him inside her.

He slipped open the fastener of her jeans, slid down the zip, and tugged her jeans and panties down over her legs. He paused to pull off her boots and socks, and she was free.

The cool air brushed her skin. Raising her head, she stared down the line of her naked body. He stood at the foot of the bed, clasped a hand around her ankles, and dragged her legs apart. A slow smile spread across his features as he drew the scent of her arousal into his nostrils. "You smell divine."

He knelt between her open legs and trailed one hand up the inside of her thigh, his fingers stroking over the thin skin. "I can feel the blood in your veins," he whispered.

Chapter Fourteen

Tara went still as Christian lowered his head and kissed the exact spot where his fingers had been. His lips parted over her skin and flames shot upwards to the junction of her open thighs. She wanted to cry out with the need that thundered through her. Instead, she bit down on her lower lip and tasted the sharp metallic blood on her tongue.

Christian raised his head slowly, sniffed the air, his eyes focusing on the drop of blood that clung to her lips. He moved, faster than she could have believed possible, and he was crouched over her, his hair falling about his shoulders, his lips drawn back to reveal the razor sharp fangs. She should have been afraid, but instead she licked the blood from her lip with the tip of her tongue.

Hunger flared in his eyes, the silver now streaked with crimson, and a low growl trickled from his throat. He closed his eyes. When he opened them, he had regained some level of control.

"You're playing with fire," he said.

He lowered his body onto hers so the hard length of his

erection pressed into her belly. His hands moved up to cradle her face, the pad of his thumb running over her lower lip. Tara flicked out her tongue, teased him, and his body jerked. Leaning close, he kissed her. Tara opened her mouth beneath his and his tongue thrust into her.

She rubbed her hips against his straining erection.

"Slow down," he said against her lips. "Or I'll lose control."

"I don't care."

He laughed softly and the sound moved across her body like a caress. "I can see that, but you're small and I'm—"

Tara glanced down the line of their bodies and a flicker of fear shot through her, cramping the muscles of her belly. "Not," she finished for him.

"I'll make sure it's good for you."

She breathed slowly and forced herself to relax.

"Good girl."

He slipped a hand between their bodies, stroking over her breast and belly, down through the soft curls at the base. He parted the lips of her sex with skillful fingers, fondling the already saturated folds. One long finger slid inside her, and her muscles clenched tightly around it. He withdrew and slid the finger now slick with her juices higher. He teased and tormented her, his finger gliding lazy circles around the hard little point of her desire. Tara's thighs fell open, and she heard his low masculine chuckle. She didn't care—she had to have this. She pushed up against his hand. At last, he touched her there, and she cried out. He rubbed his finger over the tight little nub, pinched it between his finger and thumb, and she screamed as her world exploded.

He played her mercilessly, waiting for the tremors to subside, touching her again, sometimes softly, then increasing the pressure until she was mindless with pleasure. She hardly noticed him shift up her body, positioning himself between her wide-open thighs. Only when she felt the huge swollen head of his cock nudge the opening to her body did she come back to herself. She shifted to accommodate the sheer size of him as he stared into her eyes.

"Give me your throat, Tara," he said.

She raised her head and bared the long line of her throat. Her whole body tightened, anticipating his penetration. With one fluid move, he plunged deep inside, and a fierce stab of pain shot through her. Tara threw back her head to scream as Christian sank his fangs into the soft flesh of her neck.

The scream caught in her throat. He pinned her effortlessly, and after a few minutes, the pain subsided, and she calmed. He filled her completely, but he hadn't yet moved. As she relaxed, he shifted his hips, grinding his pelvis against her, giving her a flash of the pleasure she'd felt moments ago. The last of the pain vanished. She moaned, and he loosened his hold. His fangs were still buried deep in her vein and now she felt the slow drugging pull as he drank her blood. It tugged at places deep inside her as he started to move. The drag of his cock as he withdrew created exquisite sensations, and the push as he filled her completely stoked the fire at her core.

The mouth locked at her throat held her immobile, and she gave herself up to the sensations building inside her. Moving more easily within her as her tight muscles accustomed themselves to his invasion, his speed increased, still controlled but powerful. She wanted his lovemaking to go on forever and at the same time, she needed it to end.

He released her throat, and suddenly she could move again. He rose up above her, fierce and wild, her blood staining his fangs crimson. Withdrawing from her almost completely, he held himself poised until his muscles strained with the effort.

"Are you ready?" he asked.

She nodded, and he smiled, his eyes not leaving hers as he shoved into her hard. She gasped, but her body rose up to meet him and her legs wrapped around his waist as he drove them both over the edge. She clung to him as she exploded the second time, and still he kept moving as the orgasms rolled over her. Finally, when she could take no more he went rigid above her as his own release thundered through him.

...

Christian gazed down at the woman beneath him. Her eyes were closed, and she appeared unconscious. Had he pushed her too far? She'd seemed to be with him all the way. He stroked his tongue over the small wounds to quicken the healing, and felt for her pulse. It was strong and steady. He rolled onto his side, propped himself on one elbow, and watched her sleep. Her blond hair lay tousled, her pink lips open, her cheeks still flushed with desire.

She shifted uneasily, and he reached out a soothing hand, caressed her cheek, wrapped his arm around her, and pulled her to him. She didn't wake, but her body snuggled into his as though it belonged there. He held her back curved into his chest, curled his arm around her, and took one sweet breast into his palm. Lowering his head, he found the soft place where her shoulder met her neck and breathed in deeply. He caught again that same whiff of sulfur overlaid by a deep rich sweetness. He'd tasted the same delicious mix in her blood and now her life source buzzed through his system like a drug.

Demon blood.

Intoxicating.

He hadn't wanted to accept it, but the truth was impossible to deny. He could smell it on her. Taste it in her blood. It appeared that his little human was not a human after all. Or at least not completely human. Maybe there was human in there, but there was also demon, and something else that gave her a sweetness he had never before encountered.

He tightened his grip on her. He'd hated demons for so long. Devoted his life to keeping the earth free of their taint.

Now he might very well be in love with one.

The irony struck him hard. He'd never believed in love, but this must be it. He wanted to keep her close, keep her safe, lose himself in her body. He wanted to protect her from pain, and this little piece of news would cause her a whole shit load of pain. How was he supposed to tell her that her normal life would never happen?

His hand tightened on her breast, and she shifted in her sleep. He massaged her gently, grazing his palm over the nipple. It tightened to a hard nub against his hand and he took it between his finger and thumb tugging until she moaned and wriggled her warm little bottom against him. His cock hardened and his balls ached viciously. He wanted her. He couldn't feed again yet, but he was desperate for the taste of her on his tongue.

He slipped a hand down between them, pushed between her thighs, and found her still wet, warm and slippery.

"Christian?" she whispered his name as he pushed one finger up inside her. He stroked the soft skin of her bottom then wrapped a hand around one slender thigh, lifting it to give him access. He opened her gently, and his cock slipped inside her as though it belonged there. He nuzzled her neck, grazed the skin with one razor sharp fang, and lapped at the beads of blood that welled from the wound as he moved inside her.

...

Tara came awake fully as his fang grazed her skin. Christian was behind her, curved around her spine, wrapping her in a warm, sensual glow. He was also buried deep inside her, his arms enfolding her. One hand tugged at her engorged nipple while the other gently stroked her swollen clit. She was on fire as he thrust slowly. She wanted it to go on forever but she craved the release he could give her. She let herself go, giving herself up to the sensations building inside her until she was free and flying.

She slept again afterward. When she woke, he was still beside her and she was wrapped in his arms. She felt different and realized something fundamental had changed deep within her mind. Whether from his lovemaking or feeding, Christian had forged a connection between the two of them, like a low hum, whispering through her brain. Tara found it strangely comforting.

She knew that soon she was going to have to ask him what he had discovered but for a little while, she wanted to forget.

"Where did these come from?" She stroked her fingers around the scars that circled his wrists.

His eyes followed the movement. After a minute, he gripped her hands, settling them palm down on his naked chest and pressing them down with his own. His skin felt warmer now, smooth as satin under her fingers, but he wouldn't distract her so easily. Tara wanted to know everything about him. Where he came from, what his life had been like before he died. Graham had told her Christian didn't talk about his past but she refused to be put off.

"I thought you healed all scars?"

He sighed. "Not those that happened before we were changed."

"So you got them before you were turned into a vampire?"

Christian rolled onto his side, trapping their hands between their bodies. It brought his face close and his breath feathered across her cheeks. "You don't want to talk about this," he said against her skin.

A shiver ran through her but she shook it off. "Actually, I do. I want to know, and it will take my mind off my own problems for a little while."

He drew in a deep breath. She thought he was going to refuse her, but he pulled himself up, dragging her with him so he rested back against the headboard. He tucked her under his arm, and she relaxed against him.

"I was born in 1502."

Her eyes widened in shock. "1502? That makes you—"

"A lot older than you. If you want to hear this, I suggest you stop interrupting. It's not a story I've told before."

"Sorry," she mumbled. "Go ahead."

"My parents were rich by the standards of the day. I grew up in a manor house. I was betrothed at thirteen and we married when I was eighteen and Elizabeth fourteen."

Tara opened her mouth to say something. Christian shot her a look, and she closed it again.

"We were happy. Over the next few years, we had two daughters. A son would have followed, but it was not to be. My family was murdered. I didn't know it at the time, but the Earth was in the middle of one of the demon wars. A particularly long, drawn-out war. They happen every so often, and we normally manage to put them down without too many problems, but there are always human casualties. My family was targeted because of me."

He rested his head against the wall behind him, and stared into space. It was such a long time ago but he obviously still felt the guilt.

"If the demons killed them, how could you be responsible?"

His smile didn't reach his eyes. "Not so much now, but during the wars in the Middle Ages, demons and the fae recruited humans to work with them. They can sense when a person is susceptible to their ways and approach them with promises of rewards. I wasn't, but it was common knowledge I'd had problems with the church. I was against many of their practices and spoke out, believing my position would protect me. So perhaps I drew the demons to me. When they realized I would never work for them, they killed my family out of spite."

He shook his head. "I'll probably never know the details, but I found out later they were killed on the orders of a demon called Asmodai. He's one of the seven princes in the Abyss, and I suppose I should be flattered that he came for me himself. After the murder, the church leaped at the chance to have me arrested. I blamed myself after my family died, and didn't care what happened to me.

"I was imprisoned, although my position kept me alive for three years. Three years in a dungeon chained to a wall in the darkness, thinking about what had happened." He held out his hands to show the scars on his wrist. "That is when I got these." He lifted himself away from her and twisted to show her his back. A fine tracing of silvery scars ran over the whole length of it, marring the perfection of his skin.

Tara stroked her finger over the scars with a trembling hand. "What happened?"

"My family connections stopped them from permanently maiming me, but they felt they had a duty to beat the devil out of me. At the time I believed I deserved it."

Tara blinked away a tear. It slipped out and rolled down her cheek.

Christian picked it up on his fingertip. "Don't cry for me," he said. "It was a long time ago, and in a way, the imprisonment is what kept me alive. Had I been free, I would have gone searching for death and no doubt found it."

Tara couldn't bear the thought of him alone in the darkness with only his guilt to keep him company. "How did you get out?"

"I didn't. Well, the man I was never left that cell. After three years, the church sentenced me to death. I was to be burned at the stake as an emissary of Satan. I remember thinking I liked the irony of it. The night before I was to die, I had a visitor. He said he could free me, give me a new life, immortality if I wanted it. I answered that I didn't want a new life and immortality at that point seemed a burden rather than a prize, but he told me I would be fighting demons. He belonged to a group that protected the Earth, and I could be part of that. I could hunt down the killers of my family, and all I needed to relinquish was my mortal life and my soul. At that point, I wasn't even sure I had a soul worth saving. So I agreed, and received the vampire's kiss."

"So the one who approached you was from the Order?"

He nodded. "He was the head of the Order of the Shadow Accords."

"Did you manage to get the demon that killed your family?"

"We've had a couple of run-ins. I've beaten him once or twice, but you can't destroy one of the seven forever, at least not here on earth. You can kill the body but they just re-manifest in the Abyss."

"You must really hate demons."

He cast her a look she didn't quite understand. "I did. For a long time, I hunted them and destroyed them when I could, but I found that all hatred runs out in the end. So after the last wars, I left the Order."

"But you're back there now."

"I wouldn't be, but it seems that Asmodai is back, and he's after me."

She frowned. "You personally?"

"He's picking off agents close to me."

"Why should he do that?"

Christian shrugged. "I was in charge of the Order during the last wars when he was banished back to the Abyss. It's unusual for a demon to bear a grudge—unlike the fae—but for some reason, it's gotten personal for him. It's always been personal to me."

"What were they like, your wife and daughters?"

"It's so long ago that I can hardly recall their faces. Things were different back then. I liked and respected Elizabeth but love was not a part of our marriage. It was arranged, as was the way at the time. My daughters were different, I loved them, but they were young, I barely saw them."

. . .

Her eyes filled with compassion for a five-hundred-year-old wound that had healed long ago. But as Christian watched, her expression changed. A grim determination settled on her face, and he knew what was coming.

"So," Tara said, "are you going to tell me what you saw? What you tasted?"

He could see the anxiety in her eyes, and he didn't know how to tell her. She wanted so much to have a normal life, and he was about to put an end to her hopes forever. He opened his mouth to speak, and his cell phone rang.

Christian put her gently from him and swung around to sit on the edge of the bed. He pulled the phone from his pants pocket and flicked it open. It was Piers.

"We have a meeting with the fae."

"When?" Christian asked.

"Tomorrow, midnight."

"How melodramatic. You found them?"

"I didn't need to in the end. They came to us. Apparently they have something they want us to do."

"Any idea what?"

"No, but it's connected to you somehow. They're insisting you're present at the meeting."

"Insisting? Since when have the fae had the right to demand anything of the Order?"

"Actually, I didn't argue very hard. I thought it might be a good idea if you're present."

"Why?"

"Me and the fae don't exactly hit it off. It might be a good idea to have you there as a buffer."

Christian sighed, but he realized Piers was right. Diplomacy had never been Piers's strong point and with the demons up to something, it was probably best not to rile the fae any more than necessary. "Okay, I'll be there."

He broke the connection. "We have to leave," he said to Tara.

"We're going back to London?"

"Yes, I have a meeting tomorrow night." He pulled on his clothes as he spoke but was aware that Tara watched him through narrowed eyes.

"So, are we going to talk about what's going on here?"

"I think it might be better if we wait until we're back in town. Give me a little time to think it over. I don't want to tell you something now, get you all riled up, and just have to take it all back later."

He knew from her fixed expression that it wasn't going to be that easy.

Chapter Fifteen

Christian reached out and ran a hand through her hair.

Tara knew he meant it to be soothing. Instead, the caress made her scalp prickle. She gritted her teeth. He was lying. He knew something, and he wasn't telling her.

All her life her aunt had told her, "listen to me," "I know best," and Tara had listened, believing she'd had her best interests at heart. Look how well that had turned out.

Crap! That was how it had turned out.

Her aunt had died—or did whatever it was that reanimated corpses did—leaving Tara alone, without a clue. Why couldn't she have told her before it was too late instead of leaving her to blunder on in total ignorance.

Now, here was someone else expecting that just because she cared about him, she would quite happily do whatever he said and not ask any awkward questions.

Not going to happen.

He waited for her answer, but obviously so confident that she would go along with anything he asked.

She had run the gamut of emotions tonight. She'd been

worried, wildly excited, scared. Now the first flicker of a deep-rooted anger rippled through her. It felt good. It had been part of her life for so long, simmering under the surface. She'd tried to suppress it, but it had grown, feeding on all the things that stood in her way. Her breathing slowed until she took long deep breaths, and with each intake of air, her anger intensified. She opened her eyes and smiled. Yeah, she was pissed—well and truly pissed. He didn't want to get her riled? Well, it was too damn late!

"I'm not going anywhere." Surprise flickered across his face, and a wave of savage satisfaction ran through her. "I'm not going anywhere until you tell me what you know."

"We're going back to London. Now."

"*You* might be going back to London, but until you tell me what's going on, I'm staying here. And unless you want to force me, you're going to have to live with that."

For a moment, he studied her as though he seriously considered the force thing. He eyed the distance between them, but Tara stood her ground. Finally, he relaxed and nodded.

"Okay, get dressed. I'll make you a coffee, and see you in the kitchen." He left the room and closed the door behind him.

As soon as he agreed with her demand, Tara wished she could retract it. She stared at the closed door, wanting to call him back.

She dressed slowly, repacked her bag, and carried it down to the kitchen. She put it by the back door, and took a seat opposite Christian. He pushed a mug across to her. Picking it up, she held it close to her nose and breathed in the aromatic scent of the coffee. She took a sip, it was scalding hot, and she put the mug back down.

"Is it so bad you can't tell me?" she asked.

"No," he said, shaking his head. "What is it you want to

know?"

"The spells around the house and the talisman, what are they hiding?"

"They're hiding you."

It wasn't the answer she had been expecting, though maybe she should have been. The spells around the house might have had some other purpose, but the talisman could have only ever have been for her.

"Why, what's so special about me? I'm just ordinary. Aren't I?"

His eyes wandered down over her. "No, there's nothing ordinary about you."

A shiver ran through her. "I'd really like to believe you meant that in a good way. But you don't, do you?"

Shoving his chair back from the table, he rose to his feet. He thrust his hands in his pockets, cocked his head to one side, and considered her.

"Neither good, nor bad. We are what we are. I've had a long time to accept this, and still sometimes, I wonder if I should exist at all. But perhaps that's something you still have to learn."

"Of course that might be easier if I knew what it is I'm supposed to be accepting. What am I?"

"When I said I wasn't entirely sure, I was telling the truth."

She gritted her teeth. "Then tell me what you think."

"You have demon blood."

For a brief moment, she presumed she'd misheard him. Her gaze shot to his face. He appeared deadly serious, and she took a deep breath. She could cope with this. Couldn't she?

"Explain exactly what you mean by 'have demon blood.'"

"You're part demon."

"Which part? Forget that question." She picked up her

coffee and drank it slowly. Her mind flashed back to those things that had attacked her in the alley that night. The red skin and yellow inhuman eyes. "You mean I'm part one of those things that attacked me."

"Perhaps, but there are lots of different demons."

She scrutinized her hand still holding the mug of coffee. Her flesh was pale, creamy, not red. "I can't be part of one of those. I don't look anything like them."

"Not all demons are the same. Those were lesser demons. Some—the more powerful ones—can almost pass for human."

"You hate demons. They killed your family." Her eyes stung and her throat clogged. She'd told herself she could cope with anything and now it seemed like she'd been lying to herself. She blinked away a tear, but another spilled over her lashes.

Christian sank into the chair beside her. He swiped the pad of his thumb over her cheek, wiping away the moisture. He uncurled her fingers from the empty cup and put it on the table, but kept hold of her hand, stroking across her palm. "I don't hate you."

How could he not? Demons had murdered his family, were even now murdering his friends. More tears spilled over and this time she didn't try to stop them.

"Sorry, I made you tell me this and now I'm being all pathetic." She rubbed her hand across her eyes. "I'm all right now, honest. I don't know what I was expecting, but not that. I don't want to be a demon."

He tugged her toward him, picked her up, and sat her on his lap. She turned her head into his chest, her hand clinging to the soft, slippery silk of his shirt. Leaning back in the chair, he let her cry. She wasn't used to crying—she hadn't cried after Aunt Kathy's death. Now she let herself go.

He stroked her hair. "You're not a demon. You just have

some demon blood. I'm not even sure how much. Maybe it's just a tiny little drop."

She sat up and wiped her face. "You're just saying that to make me feel better, aren't you?" He nodded and she almost smiled. "So how much of a demon am I?"

"I'd say half."

"So was my mother a demon?"

"I don't think so. From what we were told at the bar, it sounds unlikely. There are female demons, but I've never heard one described as beautiful before."

A little ray of hope glimmered in her brain. "So I'm at least half human?"

He remained silent, and she twisted round so she could see into his face. "Just how human am I? If I'm half-demon and not half-human what else can I be?"

"I'm not sure, but at a guess, I'd say you have fae blood."

"Fae as in fairy?"

He nodded and put his face close to the curve of her neck. "You smell sweet and you taste even sweeter. I've never drunk fae blood, but I've smelled them before, and you smell of fae."

She stared at him in disbelief. "Forget the fae bit for a moment, but I'm part demon. I bet I taste disgusting."

"Actually, vampires love demon blood."

"They do?"

"We find it intoxicating." He licked her neck. "We can't get enough—it's like a drug to us. Yours is even better, bitter mixed with sweet. You're unique."

She sighed. "I don't want to be unique. I want to be normal." She slid off his lap and sank back onto her own chair. She needed a clear head. "I don't understand how I can be what you say yet feel like a human. What makes a demon a demon, or a fae a fae?" She frowned. "I'm too small to be a demon."

Her talisman was still on the table where she had placed it earlier. Now she reached across and picked it up, dangling it from her finger. She lifted the chain over her head and settled the heart against her chest. A sense of containment washed over her and for a moment, she had to fight the urge to remove it again.

"I don't look like a demon. I don't feel like a demon. What's to stop me forgetting all this and just getting on with my life?"

"You don't think it's going to be that simple, do you?"

"I don't see why not. If I hadn't decided to investigate in the first place, I wouldn't know any of this. What if I'd never come to you? For that matter, even if I'd gone to another private investigator, I'd probably never have found all this out."

"So, if you'd never met me, you would still have the chance at that nice, normal life you want so much." For the first time, she heard a thread of anger in his voice. "Come on, Tara, accept it, that was never going to happen."

"If I keep the talisman on, I can stay hidden, get on with my life."

He cast her an exasperated glare. "There's more going on here."

"There is?"

"Do you really believe it was coincidence that you turned up at my office? You needed a private investigator, and you end up picking the one agency in the country with ties to the supernatural community. I don't think so."

"Coincidences happen."

"Why do you think your mother went to so much trouble to hide you? Magic like this doesn't come cheap and chances are she paid for it with her life."

Tara's mind whirled in circles, searching for a way out. "If my mother did go to that trouble, and if she did die for it, perhaps I need to honor that and stay hidden."

"It's too late for that. There were already people hunting for you here."

"We don't know they were looking for me."

"You took off the talisman and a day later strangers appear here asking questions. Do you think the two things are unrelated? And do you think they've stopped searching?"

"Yes, but I did take it off. They came, they couldn't find me, and it's been months. If I keep it on, maybe they'll never find me."

"What happened to breaking all the rules?"

She ignored the comment. "Or I could stay here. You said yourself the house is safe."

"So, now you plan to shut yourself up in the one place you've spent your life trying to escape from."

Her anger flared again. "I don't want to be a monster."

His eyes went blank, his mouth twisted into a snarl, giving the brief flash of fang. "You mean, a monster like me? So you don't like monsters? You seemed to like me well enough when I was inside you. Are you regretting that?"

Heat flushed her skin at the reminder of what they had done together. Her chest tightened. "I don't regret it." She reached out a hand to him. "I don't know what to do. All I understand is that this changes everything."

"Actually," Christian said, "it changes nothing. You have always been what you are. The only difference is now you know." He picked up her case. "We need to leave."

...

Half an hour into the journey, Christian finally managed to unclench his fingers from their grip on the steering wheel. He rolled his shoulders to ease the tension, opened his mouth, then closed it again as he realized he had no clue what to say. His original anger had faded to something less easy to identify.

He'd thought he knew how she would react to the news that she wasn't entirely human. He'd thought she would be upset, but he hadn't thought she would try to pretend the whole thing didn't exist, including him.

He realized something else—since he'd found out she wasn't human, he'd started to believe there could be a future for them together.

He could never have a long-term relationship with a human. They became puppets, slaves as he took away their free will. Some, like Graham, accepted this and believed the advantages outweighed what they lost, but he would never want that with Tara. He would have left her before it came to that.

Tonight, she proved that he could not control her mind. If she stayed with him, it would be because she wanted to, not because she couldn't leave him.

Unfortunately, it looked as though she didn't want to stay with him. He was a "monster," and a constant reminder that she was a monster as well. She'd no doubt prefer to pretend he didn't exist along with the rest of the truths that didn't fit with her neat little ideas of a normal life.

His hands tightened on the wheel again. He decided he was angry after all. Angry and hurt. And underneath that, he wanted her again, desired her blood and her body. As they got nearer their destination, he realized he didn't want to let her go, didn't want to leave her.

But he wasn't being fair. The revelation must have been an incredible shock and Tara needed time to think it through.

He would give her that time, but she also needed to be aware that this was far from over. He would leave her tonight with the same ache in her body he felt. He would make her remember how good it had been and trust she would come to him of her own free will.

She wasn't immune to him. She stared out of the window, but he could feel her sidelong glances every few miles.

He'd wait. But if she didn't come to him, he'd go and get her. He wasn't letting her go. She'd been warned, and now she was his.

...

They were silent on the way back to London. She was aware of Christian beside her, angry with her, radiating a freezing iciness that sliced at her heart.

She'd hurt him, and hadn't considered that possible. She hadn't thought about what would happen between them after they made love. A relationship with a vampire hardly fit into her idea for the future. Had she imagined she could sleep with Christian and just walk away, get on with her life?

She could still feel the slight ache in her body where he had filled her so completely, the slight ache in her throat where he'd drank from her. Without thinking, she touched the scar at her neck. Then jumped as Christian spoke.

"It should heal within twenty-four hours. You won't even know I was there."

She glanced across at him, but he'd already turned his attention back to the road. His expression was closed, his hands grasped tight on the wheel. She stared out of the side window. They had left the motorway and were entering the city. She would be home soon. Then what?

She'd told him she needed time alone to think this through. Now, at the thought of him leaving, a flash of pain ripped through her. But he couldn't stay; in less than an hour the sun would rise, and Christian needed to be back in his basement away from the light of day.

For a moment she had the urge to tell him she'd changed

her mind. Beg him to take her with him. She bit down on her lower lip to stop the words coming out. She needed time alone—this close to Christian she couldn't think.

The car pulled up in front of her apartment building. Christian got out without a word, and fetched her case from the trunk. Tara followed him out. Standing by the car, she breathed in the night air, crisp and dry after the dampness of Yorkshire.

"I'll see you to the door," Christian said. "There's something I need to say before I leave you."

She nodded and followed as he led the way. Suddenly cold, she huddled into her jacket and dug her hands into her pockets. Christian appeared unaffected by the temperature.

She let them into the building, up the stairs, and they both came to a halt in front of her door. He put down the case and turned to her.

"I'm leaving you here because you're right. You need to come to terms with what we discovered tonight."

In the back of her mind she'd harboured the secret hope that he would insist on taking her with him. That he wouldn't be able to leave her behind. She berated herself for being so stupid.

"And you need to come to terms with what we did together tonight."

A wave of heat washed over her. She fumbled for the right key. She couldn't find it and rested her forehead against the cool wood of the door. A hand touched her shoulder, and Christian turned her toward him.

"Don't think this is the end," he said. "I'm expecting you to come to the right decision. You need to accept what you are."

She opened her mouth to say something, but he put a finger to her lips. "I want you to be clear why I'm letting you go when everything screams that I should keep you close.

You need time alone, and I believe you'll be safe as long as you wear the talisman. Don't take it off."

Tara's hand went to the chain at her throat. "That's not all, is it?"

"I don't want you anywhere near Piers. You're still unmarked. He'll see you as a threat."

She shivered. "And do what?"

"He'll do nothing. I won't allow it, but it will be easier if I keep the two of you apart. However, I don't like you here alone. I'm going to send some of my people over to watch over this place."

"Vampires?"

"No not vampires. They'll need to watch in the daytime as well. Demons prefer to hunt at night, but they can move around in the light of day."

"Anything else?"

"Just one thing." His voice was no longer expressionless, but dark and low; it caressed her sensitive ears, sending tremors down her spine.

"What?" she whispered.

"Something to help you come to the right decision." He clasped her hands, slipped them inside his coat, and pressed them against his chest.

Beneath her palms, she felt the hardness of muscle and bone, and she curled her fingers into him.

He whispered in her ear, "Did you like what we did tonight? Did you like having me deep inside you?" One hand released hers and trailed over the small wound at her throat. At the touch of his fingers, that rhythmic tugging tightened the muscles of her belly.

"Here," he whispered, rubbing the pad of his thumb over the small mark. His hand slipped between them, pushing between her thighs to cup her sex. "And here."

Unable to prevent the instinctive movement, Tara

pressed herself against his palm. She clutched the soft silk of his shirt and whimpered as his clever fingers moved against her, tormented her.

He stepped back. For a moment, she clung to him, and then her hands fell to her sides. He studied her, his gaze heavy with desire. "Let me know when you'd ready to finish this."

Turning away, he walked back down the stairs and out of the front door. Tara ran to the window and stood, fists clenched, as he got in the car and drove away. She watched until the car disappeared into the night and she knew for certain that he wasn't coming back.

She shook as she let herself into the apartment. The place was silent. There was no sign of Smokey although she opened all the doors calling to him. In the kitchen she found food set out, but no cat.

Smokey was probably out hunting on the heath, but she wished he was there. She could have done with his comforting warmth. Instead she curled up alone on her bed, hugging a pillow to her chest and trying not to think of Christian.

But when she finally slept, his image still filled her mind.

Chapter Sixteen

"Have I mentioned the fact that I hate the fucking fae?" Piers asked as they exited the elevator onto the open rooftop.

Christian ignored the comment. All his senses were alert, but the roof appeared deserted, and nothing moved in the shadows. He glanced at Piers. He'd been preoccupied with his own thoughts, but now, for the first time he noticed that Piers looked pissed.

"I mean," Piers continued, "with a demon you know where you are, what to expect—"

"Them trying to kill you?"

"Yeah, but at least they're up front about it and you get a good fight. Hell, demons are fun. The fae on the other hand don't know what fun is, and they certainly don't know how to have a good fight. They're more likely to wait until they can stab you in the back or bore you to death with all that purity of the blood shit. And that magic stuff, what's with that?" He shook his head in disgust. "Man, I hate the magic."

Christian had to agree. The fae were tricky. The one point in their favor was that they kept to themselves. That was the thing about thinking you were better than everyone else—you didn't want to mix. In his years running the Order, he'd never had much contact with them.

"Have you ever met the Walker before?" he asked.

Piers nodded. "Oh yeah, I've had the pleasure, more than a few times, and boy was that fun. What about you?"

"Once. At the end of the last wars. They'd been trying to recover something the demons had stolen from them. They wanted our help."

Piers grinned. "I bet it hurt them to ask for that. Did we give it to them?"

"We never found whatever it was." Christian shrugged. "They weren't happy, but there wasn't a lot they could do about it."

"What did you think of the Walker?"

"Very focused. Ruthless. I was glad when they went back where they belong."

"So you don't like them any more than I do. Though I have to admit they are good for one thing." Piers's eyes gleamed in the darkness. "Have you ever tasted fae blood?"

"It's against the Accords," Christian said.

"This was before the Accords were signed."

"You're that old?"

Piers nodded. "And it was wild times back then. Pretty much a free for all."

"And the fae blood?"

"The sweetest thing you have ever tasted." He licked his lips and grinned. "You can understand why a demon will break the Accords to get some of that."

Christian stepped out of the shadows and searched the open area in front of them. The night was clear, and up here, high above the city streets, it was quiet. Far below, the constant hum of the city continued as normal.

"Perhaps I should tell you," Piers said, "the Walker and

me, we have some history."

Christian swung around to face him "You do?"

"Hmm.

"Is it going to be a problem?"

"Probably."

"And you only thought to mention this now?"

"Hey," Piers said, "the fae approached the Order for this meeting not the other way round. So they can take what they're given or fuck off back to fairyland where they belong."

Christian rubbed a hand across his temple. He wanted to get this meeting over with and get back to Tara; he was worried about her. No, it was more than worried. He needed to see her. It was less than twenty-four hours since they'd parted and it was already too long. He shouldn't have left her at the apartment; he should have kept her close where he could protect her.

He stopped short at the thought. Turned it over in his mind. It felt right, and a wave of excitement rippled through him. He'd never had a woman of his own. Not since his mortal life before he was turned. For a moment, he felt a flicker of doubt. He'd been unable to save Emily or their daughters. Could he do any better now? He had to—Tara was his.

"Christian. We've got company." Piers gestured across the rooftop to where a faint figure was taking form. It glowed with a pale luminescent that faded, leaving the Walker standing before them. He could almost pass for human: a tall human, wand-slim, with silver-gilt hair down to his shoulders and a long slender face with high cheekbones and a sharp blade of a nose. His expression screamed arrogance, which changed to disgust as he took in the two figures. His eyes blazed hatred at Piers.

The air filled with a sweet subtle scent that caressed Christian's nostrils and made his fangs ache to feed. The fae stopped a few feet from where they stood. Ignoring Piers, he bowed formally to Christian. Christian returned the gesture and heard Piers snort in obvious amusement.

"I am approaching the Order to report a breach of the Accords," the Walker said.

"Unfortunately, I am no longer with the Order. You need to speak to my colleague here. I believe you already know each other." He gestured to Piers and a slow hiss came from the fae.

"Hi, Walker," Piers said, waggling his fingers. "Long time, no see."

"Blood taker," The Walker replied. "I would do much not to deal with you."

Piers shrugged. "Don't then. Come on," he said to Christian. "Looks like this meeting is over."

The Walker turned back to Christian. "Do you know what this man was? A hunter of our people. He stole our blood."

"And what were you, Walker?" Piers asked. "Back in the good old days?"

"I was a protector of my people."

"You were an assassin."

"Assassins are paid. I was never paid for killing your kind. I did it for pleasure."

"Ditto," Piers said.

Christian's muscles tightened as he watched the two circle each other. Piers opened his coat and placed his hand on the pistol at his thigh. The Walker flung back his cloak and his hand rested on the hilt of his sword.

"Nice outfit," Piers said, "It's good to see you're making a real effort to blend in here."

Christian sighed. "Piers, could we get to the point here?"

"Hey, I'm not the one who called this meeting."

"No, but as head of the Order you have a duty to listen to emissaries from either side. Hear what he has to say."

"Yeah, a duty, right." Piers frowned. "You know it was a lot more fun in the old days. We could have just drained him dry."

"I doubt that very much," the Walker replied. "I could take you both."

Piers stepped forward, showing fully elongated fangs. "You want to try?"

"Fuck this," Christian muttered. "Both of you, get a grip."

The tension stretched out, straining, humming in the air, until Christian was sure it would snap. Easing his hand beneath his coat, his fingers gripped the knife hilt at his waist. He was unsure if they could take the Walker, but it looked like they were going to find out, and a slow roil of excitement tightened in his gut.

Piers stepped back. "One day, Walker. One day, I would very much like to try, but perhaps not today. Now, tell me what you want."

For a moment, the Walker's tall figure remained rigid, then the tension drained from him and Christian released his grip on the knife.

"I seek the Order's help," The Walker said.

Piers laughed. "So you thought you'd try a little charm, did you? Well my friend, you suck at charm. So tell me how can we help the mighty fae?"

"During the last war the demons stole something from us."

Piers raised an eyebrow. "And you want us to get it back?"

The Walker shook his head. "You promised your help in recovering what the demons stole. We made a deal, we would depart to our lands in peace in exchange for you returning the item to us. You banished the demons, but what they stole was never recovered. You failed."

Piers raked a hand through his hair. "Are you going to

get to the point?"

The Walker pursed his lips. "We are giving you a chance to redeem yourselves, to make good on your promise."

Piers rolled his eyes. "Did I mention, I hate the fucking fae?"

Christian decided it was time to take control and get this over with. He would trust Piers to watch his back in a fight any time, but he should have remembered that diplomacy had never been his strong point. "Walker, tell us what the fae require."

The Walker nodded. "There is one we seek. One who has the ability to enter both the Abyss and the Faelands."

"Is this a demon or a fae? I've never heard of someone who can cross both the boundaries."

"It shouldn't be possible. This being is an abomination and needs to be destroyed. We are asking for your help in this matter."

"Do you know where they are?"

"Not yet, but we are hunting them and they will be found. Must be found before the demons discover them, and use them to infiltrate our lands."

"They wouldn't do that," Christian said. "It would break the Accords and cause another war."

"Your faith in the demons is quite amusing," the Walker replied. "Are you aware that they are targeting you personally?"

Christian's eyes narrowed. "You know this? How?"

"We have our contacts. Have you not lost agents? You must have noticed even with an imbecile in charge."

Piers lunged toward him and Christian stopped him with an arm across his chest. "Stop it. Can't you see he's trying to wind you up?"

Piers took a deep breath and relaxed. "You can let me go now, I'm cool."

Christian dropped his arm and turned to the Walker. "Let the Order know when you have any information, we'll see that it's done."

"You pledge the word of the Order on this."

"We do."

The Walker nodded. "Thank you. You will hear from us soon."

He walked away, his figure fading until only a faint drift of mist remained, and soon that, too, was gone.

Christian stared at the empty rooftop. "Well, that went well. I'm so glad you decided to shelve your personal prejudices and behave in a professional manner."

"Fucking asshole. I told you, I can't stand the fae. Except to eat of course, then I like them a lot."

Christian wasn't interested in the fae right now. Or at least not pure fae. He had a flashback to the taste of Tara's blood, the unique blend. Bitter and sweet. Demon and Fae. He glanced across to where the Walker had vanished. What did the fae hunt? A being who could travel to both the Abyss and the Faelands. He wasn't sure there was a connection, but the unease twisted in his gut.

"You staying here all night?" Piers asked.

Christian shook his head. He needed to increase Tara's protection and get someone looking into this abomination of the fae's. "I'm out of here."

Chapter Seventeen

Smokey strolled in through the open door and leapt onto the sofa. Tara was worried about him—he'd been back for brief visits since she'd returned from Yorkshire, but he appeared unsettled. He'd stay for an hour or so, as if reassuring himself that she was fine, and then he'd disappear again.

He'd never taken to London. In fact, he would probably jump at the chance to return to Yorkshire, if that was what she decided to do.

She tried to imagine going back to her old life and incarcerating herself in that big gray house on the moors. She knew, in her heart, that it wasn't an option. Not now that she had sampled life, mixed with people, and had grown to be part of something.

Besides, it would be a life without Christian, and she was beginning to fear that wasn't an option either. It had been four days, and she wanted him with a desperation she hadn't known existed. She could still feel him in her mind, fainter now, at times almost absent, but he was always there, forcing her to remember.

He'd told her she needed to accept what she was, and she was trying, she really was.

"I am a demon," she said to herself.

Smokey leapt up onto her lap and rasped his rough pink tongue over her hand in sympathy. She couldn't believe it. Each morning she woke and rushed to the mirror, checking for signs of change, some indication she was something other than human. She'd searched her face and could see nothing even bordering on demonic.

She tried again. "I am a demon, and I'm in love with a vampire."

Smokey hissed and jumped from her lap.

"You're right. It's not good, but this isn't about being good. It's about being honest."

Smokey cast her a disgusted look and stalked out of the room. She watched him go and frowned. He hadn't been right since she got back from Yorkshire. She wanted to ask Chloe how he had been while she was away, but Chloe hadn't been home.

She must know Tara was back, because she hadn't been around to feed Smokey, but Tara hadn't seen a sign of her. She'd gone to her apartment, phoned her cell phone—nothing. Maybe someone had called her away on a family emergency, but Tara was sure she would have left a note. She flicked open her cell phone and tried the number again. It rang but no one picked up.

She was getting a bad feeling about this, and convincing herself it was simply the demon thing turning her paranoid didn't make her discomfort go away.

There had to be a reasonable explanation for Chloe's absence. She punched Jamie's number, but he didn't answer either, and she tossed the phone down in disgust. Chloe had never spoken of her family, so there was no one else Tara could contact.

Five minutes later, her cell phone rang. It was Jamie.

"I'm coming right over," he said and disconnected before she could answer. Tara stared at her phone for a minute then put it down.

"I am a demon," she said.

Jamie arrived within minutes. Tara let him in, feeling a wave of relief she now had someone to share her concerns with—though Jamie was obviously already worried enough on his own. There were deep shadows under his eyes, and his mouth was held in a tight line.

"What is it?" she asked.

"Chloe's missing."

Shock reverberated through her to hear it spoken aloud.

"Are you sure?"

He nodded, and Tara swallowed down the fear that rose in her throat.

"Come through to the kitchen," she said. "I'll make us some coffee. You look like you need it." She put on the coffee maker and turned to face him. He'd slumped on the chair by the table, his head in his hands.

"Jamie, what is it? What's happened?"

His eyes were bleak, and panic clawed at her insides.

"I think someone's taken her," Jamie said.

"Why should anyone take her?"

He ran a trembling hand through his already ruffled hair. "We were supposed to see each other the night you came back and she never showed up. I went to her apartment, and there was nobody there. I came around here and nothing. I haven't been able to reach her on her cell."

"Me neither, but I thought maybe she'd gone to visit her family or something."

"She wouldn't, at least not without telling me. We'd become quite close."

"I know, she told me." Tara made the coffee and put a

mug down in front of him.

"I've searched for her everywhere. I checked her college—she hasn't been there. I even managed to track down her mother. She hasn't heard from Chloe in over a month. I don't think they're close, but Chloe definitely wasn't there."

"I'm sure there's an explanation. We've just got to think it through."

Jamie shook his head, his expression desolate. "I don't think so. I think someone has taken her, and it's all my fault."

"How can it be your fault?"

"I—" He stopped, bit his lip. "Nothing, it doesn't matter, but I still think she's in some sort of trouble."

"Should we go to the police?"

"What will they do?" Jamie asked scornfully. "They'll just tell us she's over twenty-one and probably off partying somewhere."

"And you don't think she could be?"

"No!"

She laid her hand on his arm. The muscles were locked tight under her fingers. "I know she's not out partying. I was starting to worry myself. So if we can't go to the police, what can we do?"

"I think you should go and see Christian Roth."

"What?"

"He's an investigator, isn't he?"

She'd forgotten that, but of course he was, and he had a whole company to call on. They could look for Chloe.

A wave of excitement washed over at the thought of contacting Christian, and she realized that she'd been subconsciously searching for an excuse to see him again.

Guilt followed closely on the excitement—that she should get what she wanted because Chloe was missing.

"Well?" Jamie asked, and she could hear the thread of impatience in his voice.

She nodded. "I'll do it."

He relaxed, and a slight smile flashed across his face. "Thank you." He picked up his coffee and drank it quickly. After putting the mug down, he stood, crossed to the window, and stared down at the street. "It's almost sunset."

Tara glanced at him sharply. Why should he have mentioned that? But he didn't add anything further, just came back and sat down again.

She picked up her phone but paused before pressing the number. "Do you want to come with me?" she asked.

"No. I'm going to look a few more places, talk to more people."

She spoke to someone on reception at CR International. It wasn't Graham, but they appeared to recognize her name, and told her to come in that evening. Christian would see her. She put the phone down. "I'll see him tonight."

"Good. I'll take you over there safely before I go off."

"I don't need an escort."

"Yes, you do. Chloe's missing, and I'm not letting you loose on the streets of London."

Tara could have told him she didn't need an escort because she already had one. Christian had done as he'd promised, and there was at least one person watching her at all times, more than one for the last day. They made no attempt to hide from her, and in fact acknowledged her presence if she left the apartment, then trailed her at a discreet distance.

The thought of the guards made her think of something else. Could Chloe's disappearance be tied to what was going on in Tara's life? It made no sense. At least she desperately hoped it made no sense. She couldn't bear it if she was the cause of harm to her friend.

The sun was setting as they came out of the tube station, turning the sky red and tangerine. As they hurried along the embankment, Tara was aware of Christian's man trailing them, but Jamie seemed oblivious, his mind obviously focused on Chloe. He was clearly rattled and that worried Tara more than anything. He'd always seemed so laid back and relaxed.

At the glass doors, he kissed her cheek. He appeared so forlorn that she hugged him. "It will be all right. Christian will help us, and together we'll find her."

For a moment, his hands tightened around her then he stepped away and nodded.

Tara hesitated before the door, a ripple of apprehension running through her. She'd spent so much time thinking about her feelings for Christian but hadn't considered what Christian's feelings about her might be. He'd said he wanted her to come to him, but he'd also been angry with her. How did he feel about her now? How would he react to her asking for his help?

The sky darkened to purple as the sun set behind the tall buildings. Deep in her mind, she sensed another presence. Christian was awake.

Chapter Eighteen

Graham grinned as she approached the reception desk.

"It's good to see you," he said. "Perhaps we'll get some peace now. Christian's been a nightmare for the last few days."

"He has?"

"Yeah, on the phone every five minutes to the guys watching you. Must have driven them crazy."

She suddenly felt amazingly happy. "He was?"

He nodded. "I'll call up and let him know you're here. He's in the office."

Christian didn't seem particularly pleased to see her. Seated behind his desk, fingers steepled, face expressionless, his eyes never left her as she walked across the huge expanse of floor. Her nerves tightened with every step, and the excitement building inside her since she'd spoken to Graham oozed away.

He was beautiful. She had tried not to think too much about him, because she wouldn't be able to stay away if she did. Now she couldn't stop staring.

He seemed to have lost the business suits and with them, any sign of the businessman she'd thought him to be. He looked lean and mean—a hunter, dark and dangerous, and every cell in her body yearned toward him.

It took a physical effort to come to a halt in front of the desk when all she wanted to do was crawl straight over it and into his lap. For a moment, she seriously considered it, then she glanced into his face; it was cold, stern, and remote.

Maybe Graham had it wrong and Christian just saw her as some sort of responsibility. Or he'd thought the whole thing through and decided he did hate her after all. Because she was a demon. Horror flashed through her as she searched his expression.

"Graham said you needed help." Christian spoke into the silence between them, and she jumped.

"Sorry?"

"You have a problem you believe I can help you with."

"I do?" She shook her head to get her brain working but couldn't shift it from the idea of Christian hating her. "Do you hate me?" The question popped out before she could stop it.

He frowned. "What?"

"You've thought about it haven't you? About me, I mean, and you've decided that I'm some sort of evil demon monster, and you hate me."

"Tara," he said, "what are you talking about?"

"You and me. You told me to come to you, but now I have, and you're so cold, and it must be because you've realized I'm a monster, like the monsters that killed your family." She blinked, her eyes stinging. "I'm sorry, I'll go."

He knocked back his chair and rose to his feet. "Stay where you are."

Tara had been about to turn tail and run but, at his words, she stopped. Her eyes ate him up, her fingers itched with the need to reach out and touch him.

He walked around the desk. As always, the grace of his movements filled her with awe. He stopped in front of her and her eyes searched his face. His expression was no longer blank, but wary.

He reached for her, his hands gliding across her shoulders, and pulled her to him.

Tara stood on tiptoes and raised her face for his kiss, and his lips came down on hers with a savage desperation.

She lost herself in his kiss. Gave up her mind to him, but she needed more. Her hands slid to his hips, up over his lean belly and rib cage. They came to rest against his chest, and the muscles contracted under her touch. She dug her nails into the softness of his shirt, and he went still above her. For a moment, he held her against him, then his hands dropped from her shoulders, and he took a step back.

"Did that feel like I hate you?" His voice held a ragged edge. She licked her lips to get the last taste of him and shook her head.

"No, it's just Graham said—then you seemed so cold and you have every reason to hate me."

"I have no reason to hate you."

"Maybe."

"I was perhaps a little disappointed that you'd only come to me because you have a problem. You do have a problem, don't you, Tara?"

"Oh, God! It's Chloe. Christian, you have to help us. She's—"

"Tara, slow down and sit down." Instead of leading her to the chair by the desk, he took her hand and led her to the black leather sofa. He pushed her gently down. "There," he said, taking the seat next to her. "Tell me."

Tara took a deep breath, tried to sort out the facts. "You remember my friend Chloe? You met her that night at my apartment."

"Of course."

"Well, she's disappeared. She hasn't been home, and she's not answering her cell phone. Nothing."

"When did you last see her?"

"That night when we left for Yorkshire."

He frowned. "Does anyone else know about this?"

"Yes, Jamie. He was supposed to see her the night we came back, but she didn't turn up. He's been everywhere he can think of, spoken to anybody who might know or have seen her, and it's as if she's vanished."

Christian leaned back on the sofa, his head resting on the cushions, and stared into space.

"What are you thinking?"

"I'm thinking that it's unlikely your friend's disappearance is anything to do with the other things going on in your life right now. But I don't like coincidences and the timing is…suspicious." He pulled out his phone and punched in a number. "Piers?"

Tara listened while he explained what had happened and finished with, "Can you find out if there was anything going on around there four nights ago?"

He put the phone down and turned to her. "He'll get right back to me. We'll wait, see if he comes up with anything, then decide our next move."

"Thank you."

His long legs stretched out in front of him. Without thought, Tara laid her palm on his thigh. The muscle tensed beneath her fingers, and his hand came down and rested on hers.

"I'd hoped you would come to me because you couldn't stay away." He picked up her hand and rubbed his fingers along the sensitive skin of her palm. "Each night I've awoken and fought the urge to come to you. Claim you. Force you to accept what you are and what we could have." He brought her hand to his mouth and kissed her fingers, stroked his velvet tongue along each one until tremors ran through her body. "Each night I stayed away by telling myself you needed time." He sucked one finger deep into his mouth, and Tara moaned with desire. He bit down with his teeth and heat flashed through her. She sat immobile, melting as he placed her hand back on his thigh, pressing it down with his palm.

"I wanted to come to you," she said. "In fact, I never wanted you to go in the first place."

"I believe you want me, but I also think that you're far from happy about that. You'd still prefer me to be a nice, normal person." There was a definite sneer in his voice when he spoke the word "normal." "You still can't accept what I am."

"Yes. No." She frowned. "Maybe. I have accepted what you are. It's me I have the problem with. But I'm trying." Flickers of anger stirred within her. "Is it so difficult to understand? Having demon blood has taken away everything I thought I wanted. I have to come to terms with that, but I'm working on it, okay?"

"How are you working on it?" he asked, sounding genuinely curious.

"Every day, I stand in front of the mirror and chant, 'I am a demon,' fifty times. I am a demon," she added for good measure. "There you see, I've been practicing, and now I can say it without hysterics."

"Very impressive.

"Well," she said. "If you liked that one, how about this—'my lover is a vampire.'"

She watched him as she spoke the words. Flames leapt in his eyes and he reached for her, pulling her onto his lap and burrowing his head in her neck. His mouth was at her throat, fangs scraping across her flesh. He didn't bite.

"Am I your lover?" he murmured against her skin.

Her body tightened in anticipation, and she realized she wanted him to bite her, wanted to feel him inside her. Deep inside.

"I hope so," she replied. She wriggled around until her knees rested on either side of his hips and her breasts brushed against his broad chest. Raising her head, she offered her throat to his hungry gaze.

He pressed his finger over her pulse point, and the blood throbbed in her veins.

"Are you sure?" he asked. "I taste you one more time, and I'll not let you go."

For a moment, she hesitated—was this what she really wanted? Staring into that lean predatory face so close to hers she saw the hunger clear in his silver eyes, and knew she was past the point of having a choice. "That sounds good to me," she murmured and kissed him.

He kissed her back, his lips moving down the line of her jaw. One large hand slipped around the back of her neck, tipping her head to give him access to her throat. He pulled her closer and she went willingly, trusting him implicitly. Her breasts tightened in anticipation, and a pulse throbbed between her thighs. "Please, Christian."

He kissed her skin softly. His mouth opened, he swiped his tongue over her, steadied her with his hand on her head, and his fangs sank into her throat.

This time she had no urge to fight him. Eyes closed, she gave herself over to the rhythmic tugging that pulled at places deep within her body.

As she relaxed against him, his hands settled on the curve of her bottom. His fingers stroked through the denim of her jeans, then moved to her hips and pulled her down harder into his lap. The hard length of his erection pressed against her core, and she rocked on him, reveling in the sensations that washed through her.

After long minutes, Christian stopped drinking. He licked at her throat, and then sat back, pulling her with him. She snuggled into his body and felt him relax beneath her.

They lay entwined, until the purr of the phone jolted her upright.

"Piers."

Christian listened. After a minute, he replaced the phone. "Piers has heard nothing."

"That's good news isn't it?"

"Probably." He sighed. "I'd love to carry you downstairs, take you to bed, and make love to you all night long, but I think we should go make a visit to your place to see if we can find out anything about your friend."

Tara sat up. "You think something bad has happened?"

"I don't know, but it seems odd that she should disappear at that particular time."

A wave of foreboding welled up inside her, and she forced herself to ask, "You think it's something to do with me, don't you? This is my fault."

"I don't believe in coincidences. We know someone is hunting you, but if they know where you live, why not take you? Why turn up when you're not around and take your friend?" He stroked her hair. "Maybe she left for a while, forgot to mention it."

Tara bit her lip. She was starting to feel very bad about this. "You don't believe that, do you?"

"No, not really."

"So, what do we do?"

"I'll see if I can't pick up any trace of anything unusual at your place. If we do, maybe we can borrow a couple of Piers's hellhounds. Try and track her."

"Hellhounds?"

"They're the best creature for tracking. The Order keeps

a pack, but hopefully we won't need them."

As Tara scrambled off his lap, he made no attempt to hold her. She sank in the corner of the sofa, hugging her knees to her chest and worrying her lower lip. She tried to give herself the courage to ask the question that had been haunting her since her return from Yorkshire.

"Why did my mother go to so much trouble to hide me? Who wants to find me? And why? What do they want me for?"

"I don't know. I think our best lead will be finding the warlock who made your talisman. He may be able to identify your mother."

"Your old girlfriend was looking into it wasn't she? Have you heard anything?"

He shook his head. "I'll get Piers to sort it out. Chase up Ella. Now, let's go see if we can find your friend."

"Okay, but maybe I'll give Jamie a call first. Make sure he hasn't found anything new."

Jamie didn't answer so she put the phone back in her bag.

"You can try again later. Come on."

Five minutes later, she sat beside Christian in the black four-wheel drive in the underground garage. He reached forward to turn on the ignition when his cell phone rang.

He flipped it open. "Piers?"

He listened for a moment, a frown forming on his face.

"I'm just leaving," he said. "I'll wait ten minutes—give your guys time to get here. Tell them to make sure nothing follows us, and let me know how it goes." He disconnected and spoke to Tara. "They're picking up demon activity again, lots of it."

"Where?"

"Right here."

A shudder ran through her as she remembered the last time. "Are they coming after you?" He was silent for a moment, and Tara started to feel distinctly nervous. "What is it? What are you thinking?"

He appeared to come to a decision. "Actually, I think they may be coming after you."

"What?"

"We know there have been demons watching this place, but they've been discreet, never staying long enough to get picked up and only one at a time, like they didn't want to be noticed. The only times they've appeared in numbers is when you're here."

A ripple of unease ran through her. She'd tried to tell herself that as long as she wore the talisman she would be safe, hidden. That the people hunting for her wouldn't find her. Unfortunately, it seemed like they already had.

"How would they have found me?" she whispered.

"I don't know." He ran a hand through his hair. "Maybe you were picked up by one of the demons watching this place."

"How would they recognize me?"

"Perhaps the people in Yorkshire weren't quite as silent on the subject as they made out. If they were offered enough money, one of them might have talked."

"I just wish I knew *why* they wanted me."

Christian put his hand on her arm. "Whatever the reason, I won't let them get you."

She believed he would do his best to protect her, but he couldn't be there all the time. What kind of existence could she have always looking over her shoulder wondering when they might catch up? And then what?

She tried to keep the fear from spilling into her eyes, but Christian must have seen, because he pulled her to him and held her tight against the hard strength of his body. "We'll find out and we'll stop it. Whatever it takes."

Chapter Nineteen

"Do we have to worry about these demons?" Tara asked as they drove out of the building.

"Piers will have people out there by now. He's kept agents close since we found out that they're targeting me. They'll stop any demons from coming after us." He put a hand on her thigh, squeezed. "I told you I'll take care of you."

"I don't want you to have to take care of me. I'm never going to be normal—I've accepted that, but it doesn't mean I've resigned myself to hiding for the rest of my life." Something occurred to her. "Just how long will my life be? Presuming, that is, that I don't come to a messy end in the next five minutes."

"Have a little faith," he murmured.

"You said demons don't die. Will I?"

"I think it's unlikely."

"So, I'm what, like some sort of immortal being?"

"Probably."

She frowned. "How will I know?"

"You won't die."

"Right," she snapped. "So I'll just wait around and see, shall I?"

She looked out of the side window. The tinted glass made her feel a little better, knowing nothing could see her, but there appeared nothing strange going on. No gunfire, no screams, and soon they were away from the building and driving through the evening traffic toward Hampstead.

She pulled her mobile out of her bag and tried Jamie again. There was still no answer.

Tara couldn't seem to rid herself of the feeling of dread as they pulled up in front of her apartment building. She didn't know what would be better—for Christian to find something, or for there to be no trace of anything bad. Where would they go next if they found no trace of Chloe here?

"Can we go look at your friend's apartment first?" Christian asked as she let them into the building.

"I don't have keys," she said.

"It's not a problem."

Tara led the way to Chloe's apartment. She rang the bell in case Chloe had returned but wasn't surprised when there was no answer. Christian examined the lock for a moment. He put his hand against it and pressed. It took no apparent effort, and the lock broke with a sharp crack. He pushed and the door swung open.

Chloe's bag lay on a small table in the hall. Tara picked it up with trembling fingers. Chloe would never go anywhere without it. She peered inside. Everything was there, Chloe's purse, her cell phone. Tara put the bag back while Christian opened all the doors that led from the hallway, peered in the rooms.

After a few minutes, he returned. "There's no sign of anything here. Let's try your place."

As he pulled the door closed behind them, Tara pointed to the shattered lock.

"Should we leave it like this?" she asked.

Christian shot her a surprised glance, and considering all that was going on, a broken lock did seem a little low down on the priority list. "I'll send someone over to fix it," he said.

Tara led them upstairs and unlocked the door to her apartment.

"Why don't you go pack a bag," Christian said, "while I take a look around."

"Why do I need to pack a bag?"

He turned to her, and she saw the grim resolution in his face. "You are not staying here."

"Where am I supposed to stay?"

"With me. Now go pack a bag. This is not negotiable."

"I can't go. I have to look after Smokey."

"Take the damn cat with you, whatever, but you are not staying here."

Tara thought about arguing for all of about ten seconds. Then the fight oozed out of her, and she realized how afraid she'd been at the thought of coming back here, staying alone. The certainty had been growing in her since she'd seen Chloe's bag in her apartment. Something had taken Chloe while she'd been here feeding Smokey.

Her mind flashed back to those things that had attacked her in the alley. Had something similar taken Chloe? Piers's words echoed in her head, *They'll play with you and then eat you.*

Chloe had been gone for four days. If the demons had taken her, maybe Tara should be hoping her friend was already dead.

A wave of nausea washed over her. Running for the bathroom, she slammed the door, fell to her knees, and threw up in the toilet. Her stomach was almost empty, but she wretched and wretched until nothing remained.

After flushing, she stood shakily and caught sight of

herself in the mirror. Nothing had changed; she looked the same as always. She poured a glass of water and drank it, then brushed her teeth.

Anything to put off going outside and facing Christian.

She was terrified of what he'd discover about her friend. Her skin was clammy, her knees weak and she sank down onto the edge of the bath. Her head ached and she pressed her fingers to her eyes to relieve the pressure.

Maybe there was still a chance. Maybe the demons would use Chloe as a hostage and wouldn't actually hurt her. Taking a deep breath, she got to her feet.

Christian lounged against the doorway into the kitchen. He straightened as he saw her emerge and gestured into the kitchen. She went through and found he had made her coffee. Sinking into a chair, she cupped the hot mug in her hands.

"Tell me," she said.

"You haven't taken off the talisman here?"

She shook her head.

"Then I'm pretty sure demons have her. I can sense their presence, faint, but it's here."

A shaft of pain stabbed her. She bit her lip, not trusting herself to speak until she was under control.

"Why would they take her?"

"Maybe they came for you and found her instead. She may still be alive, Tara. If they've taken her to get to you, they might not harm her too much."

"So they might be willing to do a swap. Me for her?"

Christian's face closed up. "That is not an option."

"I think that's for me to decide."

"We'll find her, and if she's still alive we'll get her back. I'll call Piers and see if we can get the trackers on to this right away."

Tara needed to do something; she couldn't face sitting around thinking about what Chloe might be going through—

she wouldn't allow Christian to shut her somewhere safe while he hunted.

Christian was speaking softly on the phone. He glanced at her, then turned away and lowered his voice. Tara tried to tell herself that it wasn't more bad news, but couldn't rid herself of the dread lodged in her middle.

She sipped her drink to get rid of the bad taste in her mouth, but the coffee made her sick, and she put it down. Her bag needed to be packed and she had to find Smokey. There'd been no sign of him since they'd arrived, and she couldn't bear to leave him here alone.

Christian made no move to stop her as she left the kitchen. Smokey was nowhere to be found, and in the end, Tara gave up and went into the bedroom. She remembered the last time she'd packed this same bag. Chloe had been next to her, joking and full of life, and finally the tears spilled over. Tara sank onto the bed and sobbed. When she stopped, she found Christian regarding her from the open doorway. He had his blank face on, and the fear inside her spiraled out of control.

"We have to go to the Order."

"I haven't finished packing."

"Leave it. We'll sort it out later."

"And Smokey's not here. I have to find him."

"I promise we'll come back for the cat, but we need to get over there now. They've found Chloe."

"I don't understand. Who's found her?"

"The Order. I don't have all the details. We'll find out once we get there, but the description fits Chloe. And we need to get over there fast."

Chapter Twenty

This would be bad, and Christian didn't know to make it any easier.

He would have preferred to drop Tara at his place, where she would be safe, but he wasn't convinced she would stay put. And Piers had been blunt; if they wanted to talk to the girl, they had better get there fast.

He cast a sideways glance at his passenger. Tara appeared so small huddled in the seat, her arms wrapped tightly around herself, her face pale. He wanted to hold her, tell her it would all be all right, but he knew that wasn't the case.

He sighed. "Come on, let's get this over with." He came around and opened the door for her, and she climbed out. At least she'd stopped shivering.

He led her toward the elevators and frowned as he noticed Piers in the shadows by the doors, one shoulder resting against the wall, his arms crossed. He appeared relaxed, but Christian could sense his tension. His eyes were fixed on Tara, and he did not look happy.

"What the fuck's she doing here?" he asked.

"Just leave it, Piers," Christian growled. "Where's the girl?"

"You're too late," he said. "She died ten minutes ago."

Christian put his arm around Tara as she sagged against him. "Thanks Piers," he muttered.

Piers raised an eyebrow. "You brought her here. I did warn you. If she can't take it, you should have left her at home. Where she belongs."

Tara tugged at his arm. "Is he talking about Chloe?" Christian could hear the edge of panic in her voice. She was close to losing it. "Tell me. Is it Chloe?"

"I don't know."

"Well let's go and find out, shall we?" Piers said.

Christian held her in the crook of his arm as the elevator descended deep below the building. She seemed to have gone somewhere within herself.

"Why did you bring the girl here?" he asked Piers softly. "You don't usually bother with humans."

"This one was a little different."

Christian frowned. He hated it when Piers went all cryptic. "In what way?"

"Well, for one thing, she's got Christian Roth written all over her. Literally. I thought you'd want to see. Besides, she was still alive. I thought she might be able to tell us something." He pursed his lips, studied Christian for a moment. "You know this is shaping up into some sort of vendetta, and you're the target. Just what was this girl to you?"

"If she's who I think she is, then nothing. She's Tara's neighbor, I only ever set eyes on her once. It doesn't make sense."

"Like just about everything going on around here."

The elevator stopped and the doors opened. Piers led them out and down the corridor to the medical center. He stopped in front of a door.

Christian turned to Tara. "Wait here. Let me check if it is Chloe first. If it isn't, there's no reason for you to see this."

Tara shook her head. It was what he'd expected and he resigned himself to coping with the inevitable fallout. He'd seen demon kills before, and this wouldn't be pretty. And if they'd killed the girl to get at him for some reason, they would have made sure it would make an impression.

Piers glanced between the two of them. "Christian, this is not a good idea."

"I'm going in," Tara said. She sounded determined and her small hand slipped into Christian's and gripped it tight.

Piers shrugged. "Okay, but if you throw up, you clean it up."

He pushed open the door. Christian followed him through and the scent of fresh blood hit him straight away. Fresh blood and charred flesh. He squeezed Tara's hand.

They were in a small room, bare but for two beds and some medical equipment that had been pushed out of the way.

On one of the beds lay the naked and mutilated body of a young woman. He heard a sound beside him and reached out just in time to prevent Tara from collapsing to the floor in a dead faint. He picked her up in his arms, held her tight. Thankfully, she was unconscious. Crossing the room, he laid her on the empty bed, and she curled in on herself, moaning softly. He stroked her face, but she was still out, and he turned back to the body.

He stood over the bed and stared down at the corpse. Chloe was clearly recognizable; her face had hardly been touched, just her lips bitten through.

She'd been tortured, probably raped, though it was hard to tell because the damage was so bad. "Christian Roth" was branded into her flesh, not once but on every available piece of skin. She'd also been partially devoured, chunks of flesh bitten out, leaving open wounds. Her wrists and ankles were scarred by red raw bracelets.

"She was alive when you found her?"

"Hard to believe, isn't it?"

"Did she say anything?"

"Couldn't really." Piers gripped Chloe's jaw and opened her mouth. Her tongue was missing. "Bitten off, by the looks of it." He let her go and stepped back. "So, who hates you enough to send you this little present?"

"Probably any number of people, but why her? She's nothing to me. Why go to all this bother for someone I hardly know? All the others were close to me; this one makes no sense."

"Unless she wasn't the one they were after."

Christian hadn't wanted to think about that. Now he forced himself. They had taken Chloe from Tara's apartment. He was becoming more and more certain it had been Tara they'd come for.

He'd thought this was somehow linked to what they had discovered in Yorkshire. But what if it had nothing to do with who Tara was, except that she was close to Christian.

He had a vision of Tara lying across that bed, her body mutilated and burned, and a wave of fury surged through him so strong that Piers took a step back.

If someone had wanted to hurt him, they would have succeeded beyond measure. He cast another glance at Chloe and gave silent thanks that she had died in Tara's place.

"What are you thinking?" Piers asked.

"That they got the wrong woman." He nodded at the body on the bed. "She was at Tara's place while we were away. They came for Tara and took Chloe by mistake. I doubt they even realized it. But it still doesn't make a lot of sense. I've only known Tara for a short while. Why would anyone connect her to me or even think I cared enough for it to matter?"

"And does she matter?" Piers gestured to the unconscious girl on the other bed.

"Oh, yes," Christian said softly. "But the question is who would know that? I will find out, and they will be very, very sorry."

A small moan came from Tara. Christian dragged a folded sheet at the end of the bed to cover Chloe's body. He crossed the room, sank down to the bed beside Tara, and stroked a finger down her face.

"I'll leave you to deal with her," Piers said. "I hate hysterical women. Oh, and Ella has the information you need, if you want to see her before you leave."

He opened the door, but paused in the doorway. "By the way, did you mark her?"

Christian shook his head.

"Are you going to tell me why?"

"No."

Piers opened his mouth to argue.

"Just leave it, Piers. I'll vouch for her."

Piers nodded once and closed the door behind him.

...

Tara didn't want to wake up. Something terrible waited for her on the other side of consciousness, and she clung to the darkness.

But whether she liked it or not she became aware of someone seated beside her. It was Christian, and his fingers stroked her hair. It felt good and she pushed against his hand. Anything to delay the moment.

The air in the room hung heavy with the scent of blood and something else, like cooked meat. Icy cold washed over her and she huddled into the bed. Suddenly, she knew what that foul stench was—Chloe, or what was left of her. Beautiful

Chloe, reduced to charred meat.

A roaring filled her head, and threatened to erupt in a scream of denial. Chloe was dead and before she died, she had suffered days of unthinkable torment. And it should have been her. It should have been Tara lying there.

She wanted to cry, but she was way past tears. She wanted to crawl into Christian's lap, hide herself in his hard embrace, but nothing could ever comfort her for this. She would have to live with it forever. The pain would eventually fade, and she would be able to live again, but Chloe's death would always be part of her, and would change her forever.

She would find out who did this and make them pay.

She opened her eyes and stared straight into Christian's. Usually he was so careful to hide what he felt, but now he allowed his outrage to show, and beneath the outrage, she recognized fear. He was afraid for her. That's what caring for people did.

"Are you okay?" he asked.

Tara shook her head. She wasn't sure she would ever be okay again. Easing his hand away, she sat up and forced herself to look at Chloe. Someone had covered the body with a white sheet.

She pushed herself off the bed. Her legs trembled, but she steadied herself and stumbled across to Chloe.

She stood over her for a minute then drew back the sheet. Chloe's face was almost unmarked; her eyes closed as if she were sleeping. Tara forced herself to lower the sheet further. Christian moved up behind her but she ignored him. She needed to do this.

She touched one of the wounds on Chloe's breasts, tracing a finger over the charred writing—Christian Roth. She turned and buried her face in his chest, wrapped her arms around him, and held on tight as if he could keep her safe in this terrible new world she found herself in. "This was my fault," she said. "She would be alive if she hadn't been my friend. It's because of what I am, isn't it? It's somehow tied to what you told me in Yorkshire."

"Actually, I don't think it's anything to do with what you are, and it's not your fault. It's mine. Someone is coming after me, killing the people I care about. I think they came for you because I care about you, and Chloe was taken by mistake."

"Who would even know about me? Why would they think my death would cause you pain?"

"Perhaps because it's true."

The words filtered through the fog of pain clouding her mind, warming her frozen emotions.

Christian frowned. "The question is, who would have passed on that information to my enemies?" He stared down into her eyes, his own cold and predatory. "I will find out and they will pay for this. Come on, let's get out of this place."

Tara cast one last look at the body on the bed. "What will happen to her?"

Christian shrugged. "It doesn't matter. This," he gestured at the body, "isn't your friend. She's gone."

"Gone where? I never used to believe in heaven and hell. Aunt Kathy called all religions fairy stories, but I believe in hell now. So is there also a heaven? Do people have souls? What happens after they die?"

"People have souls."

"Yes," she said, "I remember now, you told me you gave yours up when you became a vampire."

"And there's a heaven, though I've never been. It's rumored that the higher demons came from there. Fallen angels banished from God's sight."

"I can't believe that. Nothing that was once good could have done this."

"It's not that simple. This was an act of true evil, but not all demons would do this, and many would speak against it.

All races have their share of psychopaths and killers. Humans are no different. You want a job done and they're there for the hiring. My guess is the people that took Chloe were no more than hired hands."

"Hired by whom?"

"We'll find out, but until we do you stay by my side."

She could do nothing more for Chloe here and she let Christian lead her out of the room.

Piers waited for them outside the door, his face expressionless.

"Where's Ella?" Christian asked.

"There's a problem."

"She doesn't have the information?"

"That's not the problem."

"Then what is? Stop being cryptic, Piers, I'm not in the mood."

"I told her you were here to see her. She seemed surprised. Especially when I mentioned Tara was with you. And not nice surprised either. I didn't think too much about it, but she was stopped a few minutes ago trying to leave the building."

Christian appeared calm but beneath she sensed a raw, savage fury.

"How come they stopped her?" he asked.

"They wouldn't have normally, but I've upped to emergency status. From now on, no one leaves or enters the building without my authorization."

Tara put her hand on Christian's arm and he glanced down at her. "What's happening?" she asked softly.

"I think we may have found our traitor."

"Ella?"

He nodded. Tara thought back to her meeting with the witch, that last glimpse of her as they left the building and the malicious hatred on the other woman's face. That someone she hardly knew would hate her so much sent a ripple of shock through her. The shock was followed by a wave of rage so strong she almost staggered under the force.

"Where is she?" she snarled, and Piers glanced at her, amazement on his face. He raised an eyebrow at Christian, who shrugged.

"I've got her in the holding cells. She's ranting that she hasn't done anything, and that she didn't know about the lockdown."

"Maybe she needs to believe that's the only reason she's being held. I need the information she has first. Let me talk to her."

"I'm going with you," Tara said. "This is about me, and Chloe was *my* friend. I promise I'll be good, stay quiet."

She held her breath, waiting for his reply. After a moment, he nodded. "Okay."

Piers led them into a lower area where the walls were bare concrete with fluorescent strip lighting. He stopped in front of a door and asked the guard, "Has she been quiet?"

"No, she's been screaming to let her out. But there's not much she can do about it—these cells are warded."

Piers unlocked the door and Tara followed Christian into the room. Piers closed the cell door behind them and leaned against it.

They were in a rectangular room, empty but for a table and two chairs. Ella stood in the corner of the room. She was dressed in tight black leather pants and a black T-shirt and her skin appeared white against the darkness. Her eyes fixed on Christian briefly, then flicked to her, and Tara saw again that same malevolent hatred. But mixed with the hatred was shock. It was obvious Ella was surprised to see her.

Tara knew the witch was guilty—responsible for Chloe's death.

Hatred welled up inside her. Her vision narrowed so all she saw was the other woman. She took a step forward, but

Christian halted her with a warning hand on her arm.

It took a force of will to stop. Blood thundered in her veins and her breath came in quick, sharp pants. She calmed and stepped back to stand beside Piers, who took her hand in his and pulled her against his side. He stroked the skin of her palm with his thumb, which calmed her. Christian sank onto one of the wooden chairs. "Sit," he ordered Ella.

She hesitated for a moment then sat in the second chair.

"So," Christian said, his voice devoid of emotion, "do you have the information I asked for?"

Ella frowned as though it wasn't the question she had been expecting. "The information?"

"The name of the warlock who made Tara's talisman."

Her face cleared, and she nodded. "I think so."

"Think so?" Now his voice sounded deadly.

"I have it. I just can't think straight in here." Her eyes darted back to Piers. "Why am I in here? I've done nothing wrong."

"Don't worry," Christian said and now his voice was soothing. "I'm sure it's a misunderstanding. You didn't know about the lockdown. You won't be here for long."

Ella relaxed and it occurred to Tara that Christian was using his vampire powers on the other woman. It obviously occurred to Ella as well because she jerked herself upright and panic entered her eyes.

"The warlock, Ella, give me a name."

She fought the compulsion hard. Closing her eyes, she shook her head. When she opened them, except for the nervous twisting of her hands on the tabletop, she appeared back in control. "You'll let me go if I tell you?"

"You know that's not up to me, but if you've done nothing wrong there's no reason for Piers to keep you here."

She seemed to come to a decision. "Jonas Callaghan," she said. "The warlock who made the talisman was Jonas

Callaghan."

"You're sure?"

She nodded, the movement jerky. "We have a file on him. He lives in London. There, I've told you. Now can I go back to work?"

Christian sat back in his chair. The mask dropped from his face, taking with it all signs of civilization.

"Hey," Piers muttered, and Tara realized she'd gripped his hand tight, her nails digging into his flesh. She dropped his hand, and he shook it. "You know you have quite a grip for a human."

"Now," Christian said, "perhaps we can get to the other matter."

"What other matter?" Ella sounded shaken.

"The matter of betrayal."

She looked around wildly. "I haven't betrayed anyone."

"I don't believe you. Why were you running?"

"I wasn't running. I just had something I needed to do. I forgot about the lockdown."

Christian slammed his fist onto the wooded table. "Tell me," he growled.

Ella licked her lips. "If I tell everything, will you let me go?"

"No. But I will make you an oath. We have just left the body of a young woman. She'd been tortured, raped, and mutilated. That woman's last few days will seem like a party compared to yours if you don't talk."

"And what happens if I do talk?"

He shrugged. "You're not my responsibility. Piers must decide."

Tara frowned. Would they allow the witch to go free after what she had done? She made to step forward, but Piers shook his head. Tara remained where she was but vowed that the witch would die for Chloe if Tara had to do the killing herself.

The thought surprised her. She'd always hated violence. Now the need for this woman's death was like a living thing.

"Talk."

Ella stood up. She wrapped her arms around her middle and paced the room, coming to a halt in front of the table.

"They approached me six months ago. All they wanted was names, names of people close to you. I didn't know what they wanted them for."

"Did you care?"

Hatred flashed across her face. "No, I didn't care. They paid me well."

"So it wasn't only Tara. You're responsible for Gabriel and Stefan's deaths as well. Who else was on your list?"

"Your little red-headed boyfriend."

"Graham?"

Christian pulled out his cell phone; he flicked it open and pressed in a number. "Graham, don't leave the building until I get back." As he closed his phone, Ella watched him through narrowed eyes.

"So at the time they approached you, you knew nothing of Tara?" Christian asked.

Ella shook her head. "I went to them with that one. I saw the way you watched her that night. I told them if they really wanted to hurt you, she was the one."

"Why?" Tara asked.

Ella glanced at her and shrugged. "Why not?"

"Who were they, Ella? Who did you sell this information to?"

"I told you that night at the bar. If you'd been listening."

"Asmodai?"

She nodded. "He hates you. He'll not stop this until everyone you care about is taken from you."

"Why?"

"The demons I spoke to weren't very forthcoming, but

from what they did say, I gather you'd cost him something he wanted very badly. Something he lost when you banished him to the Abyss after the last wars."

"I remember he asked for a meeting. I ignored his request, but what could he have lost?"

"How should I know? That's all I know." She looked warily at Christian. He stared back.

Piers stepped up beside him and put a hand on Christian's shoulder. "I'm sorry. I should have listened to you and gotten rid of her years ago." He stepped back. "Tara?"

"Yes?"

"You're the one most harmed by this. Her life is yours to take."

She didn't see the knife held loosely in his hand until he held it out to her. For a moment, she stared at the gleaming silver, wicked and razor sharp. She imagined running that blade into Ella, thrusting it through flesh and bone, feeling the life leave her. Then she shook her head. "Just do it."

Ella's gaze darted around the room, frantically hunting for a way out. She halted in front of Christian. "Christian, remember what we once had."

He rose to his feet and turned away. Ella stared after him. She didn't seem to notice Piers come up beside her until he put a hand on her shoulder, and she jumped. She tried to turn but he held her effortlessly in place. Tara watched in fascination as his other hand fisted in the long dark hair. He jerked her head to the side, baring the long line of her throat. Ella fought, her hands scrabbling for release, then the fight oozed out of her, her arms fell to her sides and she stood docile. Her eyes caught Tara's. She held her gaze and for a second they flashed the old hatred.

Piers lunged. This was no gentle feeding. His fangs tore open the flesh of her neck, sank deep into the vein until the blood pulsed from the open wound, and he swallowed convulsively. He raised his eyes and there was nothing human in them.

Tara took a step toward Christian. He must have felt her regard because he wrapped an arm around her and pulled her tight against his side.

She saw the instant the life left Ella. A moment later, Piers released her and she crumpled to the floor. He stared at Tara then wiped his hand across his mouth. Licked his lips.

Tara looked from him to the body on the floor. She'd expected to feel some sort of satisfaction, but she felt numb. Nothing would bring Chloe back.

"Can we go home?" she asked.

Chapter Twenty-One

In the car, Tara gave in and released the tight hold on her feelings. A wave of icy cold washed over her, and she shivered. She hugged her arms around her but nothing seemed to warm her—she was cold from the inside. Behind her closed eyes, all she could see was Chloe's tortured body.

It was impossible to believe that she had spent the last four days worried about losing her chance at a stupid normal life, while somewhere Chloe had been through hell. Chloe had been alive and conscious when the Order found her. What had she suffered in those last four days of her life?

She must have made a small sound because Christian rested a hand on her leg, squeezing lightly, and Tara found she was crying. She put her fists to her eyes but she couldn't seem to stop. She choked on tears.

She didn't notice when the car stopped. Only when Christian unfastened her seatbelt and dragged her into his lap did she realize they no longer moved. Tara curled into him, her fingers clinging to his shirt.

After a few minutes, he got out of the car still holding her.

He didn't release her until he lowered her onto the bed in his apartment below CR International.

His image blurred through the tears. He tugged off her boots, kicked off his shoes, and climbed onto the bed, pulling her into his arms and wrapping her in the folds of the bedspread.

She felt frozen to the core. Tremors shivered through her, and she couldn't seem to stop them. Christian stroked her hair, and after a few minutes, he picked up the telephone beside the bed.

She sensed rather than saw Graham enter the room. He came to stand beside the bed.

"Is there anything I can do?" Graham asked.

"Go run a bath, red hot. We need to warm her up. Then make us some coffee."

"No problem."

Christian stroked her again. "Tara, come on sweetheart, sit up. We need to get you warm."

Tara didn't want to move but she finally struggled into a sitting position. She didn't want to think either, and she followed automatically as Christian led her into the bathroom. At any other time, she would have marveled at the place. It was a sybarite's dream in marble and gold, but it barely registered. Steam filled the air, heavy with the scent of herbs and spices.

She allowed Christian to remove her clothes. He swung her into the enormous bath and she sank down until the hot water covered her to her chin.

"Try and relax," he said.

He turned to go but Tara grabbed his hand. "Don't leave me."

He stared down at her for a moment before stripping off his own clothes. He stepped into the bath behind her, and sat so she could lie in the V of his thighs. The water cooled and he added more hot. Tara washed herself as though she could scrub the smell of death from her skin.

When the water cooled again, Christian lifted her from the bath, wrapped her in a huge, soft towel, and carried her back to the bed. After drying them both, he slipped under the covers with her, and held her until her trembling stopped, and she fell into a light sleep of exhaustion.

Tara woke to utter darkness. Christian still held her tightly against him, and she struggled to free herself from his embrace. She flicked on the small lamp beside the bed. It was already midday.

Suddenly she remembered that Jamie was still searching for Chloe. Oh, God, how could she tell him? What did she tell him?

There was a phone on the table by the bed. She picked it up and stared at it. Then punched in the numbers.

She almost hoped he wouldn't pick up, but he did after the first ring as though he was waiting.

"Tara?"

"Jamie." She paused unable to go on.

"Tara? What is it?"

She swallowed, forcing back the tears that threatened to overflow. She was done with crying. "We found Chloe. She's dead, Jamie." Jamie was silent but she could hear his ragged breathing. "Jamie?"

"Are you still with Christian Roth?"

"Yes."

"Stay there." The line went dead.

She put the phone back. Christian's eyes were open. "Are you going to be okay?"

She nodded. "Not quite there yet, but I think you're safe from anymore tears."

"I don't mind. Cry if it helps."

"But it doesn't, does it? Nothing will bring her back or take away her last days. I have to learn to live with that, and I will, but Christian—"

"Yes?"

"Tell me that we will find the people who did this, and we will make them pay."

He took her hand and kissed her palm. "I promise."

...

The day seemed endless. Tara hadn't been able to sleep any more. She'd gotten up, leaving Christian to do whatever it was that vampires did during the day.

She was pretending to read when he finally emerged from the bedroom that evening. He'd pulled on a pair of black pants but was otherwise naked. His chest was pale, like marble, perfectly sculpted.

"I missed you," he said.

She went to him, slid her arms around his waist, and laid her head on his bare chest. He kissed her, a slow, drugging kiss. Then raised his head and stared down into her eyes. "How are you?" he asked.

"I'm going to be fine."

"Good. Are you up to seeing this warlock?"

"Try leaving me here."

He smiled. "I haven't set up a meeting, I wanted to take him by surprise, and I've had men watching his place all day. They just called in. He's there." He kissed her again, nuzzled her throat, his tongue stroking the sensitive spot where her shoulder met the slender column of her neck. "We can get this over with and then I'm going to bring you back here and make slow love to you for the rest of the night."

His voice was low and husky and started a fire burning, low in her belly. For a moment, he held her close, and then released her. "We have to go."

Less than as hour later, they stood outside a rundown pub in the east end of London. A sign above the door said "The Pointed Hat." This was about as far from the bright lights of the west end as it was possible to get, and Tara scrutinized the building dubiously.

"I thought this was a really successful warlock. He can't be that successful if this is where he hangs out."

"Appearances can be deceiving, which is something you need to remember when dealing with warlocks," Christian said. "Most warlocks and witches aren't attracted by money, but by power. Jonas Callaghan has owned this place for years. It's known as a safe house, neutral ground, and it's a well-known hangout for all sorts of things. It can be an interesting place on a Saturday night."

A surge of hatred washed through her. "Demons?"

He nodded. "Sometimes. Though Callaghan won't serve them alcohol. Try and stay close and don't accept any drinks."

She followed him into the bar. The inside didn't look any smarter than the outside. The lighting was dim, the walls dark, and a pall of smoke hung in the air. Silence descended on the room as they entered, and all faces turned to them as they stood just inside the door. After a minute, everyone looked away, and the low hum of conversation filled the room.

Christian led her through the tables, and she heard his name whispered as they passed—Christian Roth. He stopped in front of the wooden bar that ran the length of the room. Tara studied the man behind it, but he appeared quite normal. The other patrons appeared human to her as well, but if they knew Christian, they must have contact with the supernatural world. Were any of them demons?

"We're here to see Jonas," Christian said to the bartender.

"Jonas isn't here. Now, what can I get you to drink?"

"Nothing. Tell him Christian Roth is here."

"I know who you are, and I told you, he's not here."

Christian moved faster than she could see. His hand gripped the man's throat, pulled him halfway across the bar, and the room went quiet behind them. Christian snarled, the tip of one white fang clearly visible. "Tell him I'm here."

"There's no need for that," a voice said behind them. Tara swung round. An old man stood there, slightly stooped, with short gray hair. "Let him go, Christian, he was only trying to protect his old father."

Christian released his hold on the other man. "As if you needed protection."

The old man raised an eyebrow. "If the Order is hunting you then everyone needs protection." He glanced toward the door. "I noticed your men outside."

"I no longer belong to the Order."

"Don't be naïve, Christian, it doesn't suit you. Once in the Order, you can never leave. I take it you're not here to offer me a job then. I hear there's a vacancy for one of my profession."

"News travels fast. You don't sound particularly bothered."

He shrugged. "Ella was an old student of mine. She was always a treacherous bitch. I'm surprised she lasted as long as she did. So if it's not to offer me a job, why are you here?"

"Can we talk in private?"

"We?" The old man glanced from Christian to Tara. "Are you going to introduce me?"

"This is Tara Collins. I believe you knew her mother."

"I did?" He studied Tara closely. After a minute, his eyes widened. "Well," he said, "I believe I did. Would the two of you like to follow me?"

He led them through a door in the back and into a small sitting room. "May I?" he asked, gesturing to the locket Tara wore round her neck.

She nodded. Jonas picked it up and turned it in his gnarled fingers. "You know," he said to Christian, "I don't like to boast, but this is good work. Out there in the bar, I would have sworn your little friend was human."

"Isn't she?"

Jonas raised an eyebrow. "Well I'm guessing not, at least if she was the one intended for the spell." He dropped the locket. "Why don't you sit down and tell me what you want. I presume this isn't a social call."

He crossed the room to a small table, picked up a decanter. "A drink?" He glanced at Tara and smiled. "Not perhaps for you, that wouldn't be a good idea, but Christian?"

Christian nodded. Jonas poured them both a glass and took a seat opposite. Tara was almost bursting with questions, but Christian sent her a warning look, and she held tight.

"So you admit that you made the spell Tara is wearing?" Christian said.

"I take it there's not a lot of point denying it. Did Ella give you my name? As I said, she always was a treacherous bitch."

"Can you tell us who you made the spell for?"

"You know I can't divulge details about my clients. I'd soon get no business at all if it got out I talked to the Order."

Christian took a sip of his drink. "Perhaps I made a mistake in framing it as a question."

They stared at each other for long minutes. In the end, Tara couldn't take it anymore. She jumped to her feet.

"Please Mr. Callaghan. I want to know about my mother."

"Are you sure about that?"

Tara nodded. "I need to know who I am. I need to know why my mother went to so much trouble to hide me, and from what. Because someone is looking for me now, and how can I hide when I don't know who or what is coming after me?" She took a deep breath. "Besides, I don't want to hide anymore.

I'm finished with hiding."

He searched her face, and Tara held her breath while he came to his decision. Christian would use whatever methods he needed to get the information, but she couldn't stand by and watch him torture an old man. She took a step closer and put her hand on his arm. "Please, tell me what I need to know."

"Tara," Christian said warningly. "Don't make the mistake of thinking that you are dealing with a sweet old man. Ella used glamour for her own ends, as does Jonas. It serves his purpose to appear as he is. Ask him how your mother paid for his services."

Jonas flicked him a cold glance. "She paid in fae blood."

"And plenty of it, I would guess."

"You would guess rightly." He shrugged. "I never said I was a charity, and my work does not come cheap."

Tara dropped her hand and stepped back. "Tell me."

"I take it she's dead, so I suppose client confidentiality doesn't apply."

Tara had known her mother was in all likelihood dead, but still a wave of sadness washed over her at his words. "You know she's dead?"

"She was dying when she left here. She had enough strength left to see you into the world, and that was only through grim determination. She had nothing more."

"What did she come to you for?" Christian asked.

"Two things. A ward for a property to hide those inside and a spell that would make her child appear human. The spell cost her dearly. She needed it to last." He studied Tara as if searching for something. "It would have been easier if the baby had some human blood, but you have none."

Shock flashed through her. "None?"

"There's not a single drop of human blood in your body. I thought you knew. Your mother was pureblood fae. Your father, from the nature of the spell, some sort of demon. I presume she was a casualty of the war. Your mother would have been better off to go back to her people, but the fae would have destroyed you. They don't like mixing their blood." He took a sip of his drink. "They would consider you an abomination and hunt you down. Hence the spell. It's ironic that she gave her life saving you from her own people. Demons are much less fussy about these things."

Tara sank back down into the chair behind her. So she wasn't even a little bit human. That fact would have been a bitter blow only days ago, now it didn't seem to matter much after all that had happened.

"Do you know her name?"

Jonas shook his head. "She never told me, and I never asked."

"What about my father, did she tell you anything about him?"

He shook his head. "Apart from the fact that he was a demon, which I needed for the spell, she told me nothing. It's not in the nature of our deals to share unnecessary knowledge."

Tara tried to assimilate the information. Were they any further forward in finding out who she was and whom she was hiding from?

"So you believe she hid me from her own people, the fae."

"I would think so."

Christian had told her the demons were coming after her. That they congregated whenever she went near CR International. But this man said it wasn't demons but the fae she needed to fear. Her head was about to explode and she rubbed at her temples.

Finally, she took a deep breath. "What was she like? My mother I mean?"

Jonas looked surprised at the question. "She was sweet,"

he said. "And very, very sad."

They left the bar not long afterward.

"So, what do we do next?" she asked Christian as they stepped out onto the street.

"I think we need to approach the fae, but I go alone for that one. I'm not letting you anywhere near them."

Tara shivered. "I'd thought of the fae as the good guys and demons as the bad. Now I find it's the good guys who want me dead. Or maybe they both do. Then again, I suppose I am one of the bad guys. At least half." She tried a smile, but it was a pathetic attempt. "Maybe they cancel each other out, and I'm just sort of average."

Christian took hold of her hand. "There is nothing average about you, you're unique, and I've told you, it's not so simple to say the fae are good and demons are bad. Ask Piers—he'd take a demon over a fae any day."

"You're not making me feel any better here."

"We'll sort it all out, I promise. Now, let's go home."

"Can we go to my place first? I'm worried about Smokey. I don't think he'll let your people near him, and I don't want to leave him there on his own."

"Okay, then home."

The apartment was in darkness when they arrived. Which was as expected. Tara let them in and switched on the light. She was about to enter when Christian put a hand on her arm.

"There's someone here," he whispered.

Chapter Twenty-Two

Tara stopped in her tracks. She hated the fear that ripped through her but couldn't deny it. An image of Chloe's abused body flashed across her mind, and she gripped Christian's arm.

"Is it demons?"

He shook his head, but reached inside his coat and drew his pistol. He held it loosely in his hand and pushed Tara behind him.

"Wait here," he said.

"Not likely." She wouldn't stay anywhere alone. She was sticking close by Christian.

"Okay, just don't cling to my gun arm."

She dropped her hand but kept close as he entered the apartment. He pushed open the door to the kitchen but nothing moved. Backing out, he entered the living room, flicked on the light, and Tara gasped.

"Jamie!"

Jamie was on the sofa, unconscious, his left side drenched in crimson. Blood soaked the fabric beneath him, and as

Christian sniffed the air, a strange expression flickered across his face.

"Is that your friend?" he asked.

Tara nodded. Pushing past Christian, she sank to her knees beside Jamie. His eyes were closed, his face pale. She touched his cheek. It felt warm beneath her fingertips, and she released her breath—at least he was alive.

Christian came to stand behind her.

"Is he going to be all right?" she asked.

"I should think so. Why don't you go look for your cat, and let me see to him?"

"Please don't let him die."

Christian picked up one of Jamie's limp hands and ran his thumb over the pulse point.

"He's not dying. He's lost a lot of blood, but that's not why he's unconscious." He lifted the hair back from Jamie's forehead. A large purple bruise marred the skin. "Go on. I'll get him bandaged up, and we'll take him with us. I don't want to stay around here too long."

He ripped Jamie's T-shirt down one side. What appeared to be claw marks ran across his left shoulder and chest. The bleeding had stopped but the wounds still seeped. Tara watched as Christian probed the wounds, then she scrambled to her feet. Her legs trembled, and she closed her eyes for a moment. She couldn't begin to imagine what she would have done if Jamie had been dead.

"You will save him, won't you, Christian?"

"He'll be fine, but you could get me a clean towel or something to use as a bandage."

In the bathroom, she grabbed a couple of towels from the cupboard and hurried back.

"Here, I don't have any antiseptic or anything—I never need it."

Christian took the towels from her. "No problem, but I

want to stop the bleeding before we move him. We can sort it out once we get to CR."

She gave Jamie one last lingering look. "Good. I'll go find Smokey."

At the door, she glanced back in time to see Christian raise his bloody fingers to his mouth and lick them clean. His eyes narrowed on Jamie and a small smile curved his lips. Tara opened her mouth to question him, then clamped it shut and turned away.

She searched the house but she could find no trace of her cat. Maybe he was hiding from Jamie or Christian. Standing at the kitchen window, she peered down onto the heath but it was too dark to see anything. She opened the window and called. Nothing answered, and after a few minutes, she gave up. She got some fresh food from the freezer and set it on a dish to defrost. Christian came in as while she filled the water bowl.

"He's not here," she said.

"Don't worry, we can come back another time. I'm sure he'll be fine. Cats have a way of looking after themselves."

She followed him into the living room. "You go first," he said. "I doubt we'll meet any neighbors at this time, but just in case."

"Do you want something to wrap him in, so you don't get blood all over you?"

His lips twitched. "I'm hardly likely to be bothered by a little blood." He looked at Jamie. "On second thought, it will save the car. Go get a blanket."

Tara got one from the bedroom and watched Christian wrap Jamie carefully. Jamie groaned and a wave of relief washed over her at the sign of life. He wasn't small, but Christian picked him up easily and held him against his chest. "Lead the way."

It was quiet on the way to the car. Tara scrambled into the

back and Christian handed Jamie in after her so he lay across the seat, his head cradled in her lap.

Halfway back to CR, his eyes opened. "Tara?"

She stroked the hair back from his forehead. "Hi," she said softly.

He blinked up at her, his eyes dazed. "Where am I?"

Christian snorted from the front seat. "Very original line."

Jamie tried to sit up, but Tara pushed him back down. "You're in a car. We're taking you to Christian's place. We found you at the apartment, Jamie—what happened?"

"Chloe's dead," he said.

"I know."

"I wanted to…" He trailed off. "I wanted to kill them all, but there were too many and in the end I ran away."

Tara frowned. "Who did you want to kill?"

"Demons."

"You know about demons?"

Jamie buried his head in her stomach, and she could feel him shaking. She ran her hands through his hair, trying to make sense of what he'd told her.

After a few minutes silence, he rolled his head around to face her. "I wanted to warn you, to tell you everything. I went back to your apartment, but I must have blacked out before I could phone."

"We found you there, unconscious."

"Why did they have to take Chloe? She was nothing to do with all this."

"It was a mistake, a horrible mistake. It should have been me. It's my fault, but Jamie, please don't do anything stupid. I couldn't bear it if I lost you as well."

His eyes were haunted. "It's not your fault, it's mine. I should have done something sooner."

"What could you have done?"

"It doesn't matter now, she's dead, and it's too late to make any difference."

He turned his face away, and Tara stared out of the window watching as the streets flashed by.

None of this made any sense. She'd met Jamie on her first day in London when she'd felt lost and alone. Homesick for Yorkshire—something totally unexpected. Jamie had bumped into her outside the apartment building. They'd started talking, and she'd felt an immediate connection. Had it been a set up? But why? Who was he?

The car stopped. They were back in the underground garage at CR International. Christian glanced at her through the mirror, and she tried a weak smile.

He climbed out and opened the back door.

"Jamie." Tara touched him gently on the shoulder then looked up as Christian hovered in the doorway. "I think he's unconscious again."

Christian reached in and picked him up. Jamie groaned but settled back in the other man's arms. His eyes remained closed all the way up to the thirteenth floor.

Christian carried him into the office and lowered him to the back leather sofa. Jamie was still very pale, his eyes closed, his damaged arm held tight against his side.

Tara sat beside him, took his uninjured hand in hers, and squeezed. Jamie opened his eyes; they were filled with pain.

"Can you do anything to help him?" she asked Christian. "Please, he's lost so much blood."

Christian studied the other man, a slight frown on his face. "Oh, I think you'll find he's quite capable of healing himself."

"What do you mean?"

Jamie stared at Christian with something close to horror stamped on his features. "Are you going to tell her?"

"Don't you think it's about time?" Christian said.

Jamie struggled into a sitting position, wincing at the pain. "Look, I didn't want to deceive her, but I didn't have a choice at first. I promised Kathryn. Later, after Kathryn went, we moved here and—" He shrugged. "She wanted a normal life, and for a while I thought maybe it would be okay. How could I tell her and spoil everything?"

Tara heard the words but they didn't make any sense.

"Everything started to go wrong—demons popping up all over the place, and her wanting to break all the rules. I knew I couldn't cope on my own, and I couldn't tell her the truth about what I really was."

"So you sent her to me?"

Jamie nodded. "I recognized your name. I couldn't believe it. Christian Roth, a private investigator, but you had a reputation for being fair, and she was going to need somebody on her side."

"Okay," Tara said. "Is one of you going to tell me what's going on?"

She looked from one man to the other, and Jamie nodded. A moment later, he disappeared, and in his place sat a large gray cat.

Tara blinked. Christian raised an eyebrow but said nothing. She turned back to the cat. "Smokey?"

The cat strolled across the leather toward her. It rubbed its soft head against her hand. Tara reacted instinctively, as she had so many thousands of times before, and scratched behind his ears. He purred loudly then rolled onto his back, paws in the air. She rubbed his silky tummy, an activity that had so often given her comfort. She tried not to think, did her best to keep her mind blank until a slow, trickling growl sounded behind her.

She turned to see Christian standing over them. He was staring at the exact spot where her hand met the gray fur, and he didn't look happy.

"That's enough," he snarled.

It took her a moment to realize that he wasn't talking to her but to the cat. Smokey rolled onto his feet, blinked his yellow eyes, and sauntered to the far end of the sofa. A moment later, Jamie returned.

She stared at him, her eyes moving over his body. Reaching up, he unwrapped the towel from his shoulder. The wound was still visible, but the healing process had started and the bleeding stopped. His expression was apologetic, and he shrugged.

"You're a cat?"

He nodded.

"My cat?"

"I would have told you."

"When?"

"Soon."

She stared at him through narrowed eyes. "You slept next to me. You watched me in the shower."

Christian growled again behind her, and Jamie threw up his hands defensively. "Hey, I was a cat. It did absolutely nothing for me."

Tara stood up, her legs trembling slightly. Her cat was actually a man. Or was it the other way round? Was Jamie actually a cat? All this time, and she'd had absolutely no idea. *Well, you wouldn't, would you?*

Moving away, she stared out the window at the dark city below. Were there no real, honest to goodness human beings in the world? Maybe the whole notion of normality was a complete impossibility. Maybe normality didn't exist.

When she turned back to them, Christian had moved away from the sofa. He was half-sitting, half-leaning against the desk, arms crossed over his chest. Jamie was still seated; he kept casting quick glances at the vampire.

Tara crossed back and stood looking down at him. "So

what are you exactly?"

"I'm a shapeshifter."

"What does that mean? You can shift into anything?"

"No, not anything."

"Have you always been a shapeshifter?"

He nodded.

She remembered the man in the pub telling her that her mother had a cat. A big gray cat. "You knew my mother, didn't you?"

He nodded again. All the time, the answers to all her questions had been there, right at her side. Tara sank down onto the sofa. "Why didn't you tell me?"

"I told you why, at first I promised, and then you wanted so much to be normal."

"You must have known that wasn't going to happen."

"It might have, if you hadn't been so keen on breaking the rules. I did try to stop you." He frowned. "I promised your mother I'd be your friend. She thought you'd be so alone, and she wanted you to have some chance at a normal existence."

"So you've been watching out for me since I got to London?"

He nodded.

"That night you'd been fighting. Was that protecting me?"

"A demon. Luckily only one."

"And later, in the bar—" She looked at him suspiciously. "Did you put something in my drink?"

"I drugged your wine."

Christian chuckled. "You know," he said. "I almost feel sorry for him."

"How can you feel sorry for him? He drugged me."

"'What was I supposed to do?" Jamie asked. "Let you go on a drunken demon rampage through London? Have you ever seen a demon on an alcohol high?"

"Funny enough—no!"

"I have," Christian said. "He did the right thing."

"No he didn't." Tara almost shouted the words. "He should have told me. Explained."

"Perhaps, but it's too late now. Get over it."

Jamie reached out a hand and touched her lightly. "I'm sorry. I did what I thought was best."

"Don't be too hard on him," Christian said. "Shifters don't think too well for themselves, and they don't do conflict."

Jamie shot him a look of dislike. "We're not usually given much of a chance."

"What do you mean?" Tara asked.

"Shifters are usually tied to one of the other supernatural races, demons or fae."

"Or vampires," Jamie said, and Tara could hear a faint thread of bitterness in his voice.

She looked at Christian. "Like when you mark a human, like what you wanted to do to me?"

He nodded. "Something like that. Except it tends to be hereditary with shifters, they belong from birth."

They were silent for a moment. "Can you tell me about my mother?" she asked Jamie.

"Anything."

"What was she like?

"Her name was Lillian. She was a fae princess, but different from most of the fae. She was sweet and good."

"And Aunt Kathy. Do you know how they came to meet? What happened?"

"Your mother met Kathryn not long before you were born. Kathryn took her in when she was alone. They became good friends. When Kathryn was killed in a car accident your mother had her brought back."

"The perfect guardian," Christian said softly. "It might

not have been much of a life, but it was surely better than the alternative. Or at least seemed better at the time. I wonder if she came to regret the decision."

"No, she didn't. She loved Tara."

"I know that," Tara said. "So you were with my mother before. Do you know what happened to her? Who my father was?"

Jamie flicked a glance at Christian then back to her. "No. She never spoke of him. Ever."

Christian came to stand over him. "But you knew he was a demon, right?"

Jamie nodded. "I was there at the birth. It was pretty obvious Tara wasn't human. Then there were the rules—the alcohol one was a dead giveaway."

"What exactly does alcohol do to demons?" Tara asked.

"It lowers their inhibitions," Christian said. "It brings their inner demon to the surface. They're quite good at being…well good if they want to, but give a demon a drink, and you can guarantee pure carnage."

Sometime soon, Tara would sit down and have a long chat with Jamie. But right now, she had other things to consider. She was half-demon and half-fae, but the truth was she had no clue what that meant.

She still felt normal, but maybe she'd never felt normal in the first place. What did it feel like to be a demon? Both men watched her closely. Jamie obviously worried, Christian looked—she searched his face. At first glance, he appeared expressionless, but closer inspection showed his eyes gleamed—he looked hungry. Her heart sped, the blood pumped in her veins until it throbbed just below the surface of her skin. She remembered the feel of him piercing her body and liquid heat pooled between her thighs.

Christian breathed in deeply as though sensing her arousal. His eyes broke contact, dropped to her throat, and she raised her head slightly, tempting him. His gaze fell lower, lingered on the tips of her breasts, hard and tight under her T-shirt, and down to the junction of her thighs. His lips were slightly parted, and he stroked his tongue over the tip of one sharp white fang. She squirmed on the seat.

Jamie cleared his throat and the sound broke the spell.

"I think I need to be somewhere else," Jamie muttered.

Tara felt out of control, as though she had no say in her body's responses. It knew what it wanted and wouldn't be denied.

Jamie edged away.

"No," she said.

"No?" Christian repeated and his voice was low, smoky, seductive. She swayed toward him but pulled herself up short.

"No. Chloe is dead, and I want to find her killers. I want to know what I am. Why everyone wants to kill me. What have I ever done to them?"

She thought he was about to argue, but the tension left his body, and he relaxed. "You've done nothing, but the fae probably want to kill you because you're of mixed blood. They guard their blood jealously, and it gives you the power to enter both their world and the world of the demons."

"Like I'd want to." She considered what he'd said. "So why do the demons want me?"

"Probably for that very reason—you have the power to enter the Faelands." Christian sighed. "It goes back a long time, before the Accords, when both fae and demons moved freely on the earth. They've always been enemies. At that time, there were constant wars and they were in danger of destroying the earth and all mankind, so the Shadow Accords were signed. It allocated lands on either side of the earth to each race and ensured that neither could enter each other's territories. The Order was set up here to ensure that the two races abided by the Accords."

"And do they?"

"On the whole, they stay put. Demons make the occasional foray onto the earth and the fae keep to themselves. As long as they don't cause trouble and are discreet, we do nothing. Every so often things get out of hand and trigger a war. The last was just before you were born. Probably how you were born, as there would have been numbers of demons and fae around. They were all sent back, and the portals closed, but they always find new ways through."

"So are demons bad and fae good?"

"Demons are," Christian thought for a moment, "impulsive, elemental, they act first and think later. They can be very strong, and they love to fight. They also love the fae women and were notorious for taking them before the Accords."

"So one of them took my mother."

He shrugged. "I presume so. The fae would take the women back, but they considered any offspring to be abominations. They were given the right to destroy them as part of the Accords."

"So the Order wants me dead as well."

"I promise you, no one will touch you. You're mine, and I keep mine safe."

"So what about the fae, what are they like?"

"Proud, beautiful and they can do magic."

"What sort of magic?"

"All kinds. It's thought witches and warlocks have fae blood, though the fae would deny it."

"So if the fae have magic, why did my mother need to go to the warlock?"

"She probably didn't have enough strength left. Like any race, some are more powerful than others, and their powers differ. Some can see the future, some the present, and some can keep things hidden. It's a sort of glamour; it hides what a thing truly is and makes it seem to be something else, but to do that for all these years takes a lot of power."

"Your mother was a necromancer," Jamie said. "She could bring life to the dead."

"That explains Aunt Kathy. But I have none of these powers. I'm not super strong, and I can't do magic."

"My guess is the talisman suppressed the qualities it was designed to hide," Christian said. "Given time your true self would emerge."

"Only I'm not going to be given time." Anger and frustration built inside her. Why couldn't they leave her alone to get on with her life? She slammed her fist down on the table beside her. "It's not fair!"

Jamie jumped.

Christian just raised an eyebrow. "Since when has life been fair?"

"My best friend is dead. The things that did it are out there, maybe waiting to get me and do the same as they did to Chloe." Jamie flinched, but she carried on. "What am I supposed to do, sit around twiddling my thumbs, waiting for someone to come along and finish me off? Well I'm fed up with doing nothing."

Now Christian looked amused and that shot her temper ten degrees higher. Jamie inched away and moved around the back of the sofa, putting it between them.

"Did I mention demons have tempers?" Christian said.

Tara got to her feet and crossed the room to stand in front of him. She only came up to his shoulder. Whoever heard of a miniature demon? She poked him in the chest. "I want to do something."

Christian sighed. "We are doing something. I've put out the word for whoever is after me. That will lead us to the people who took your friend. I'll find them, and I'll kill them.

Then I'll sort something out with the fae."

Tara shook her head. "You're not getting it. I don't want *you* to sort everything out. I want to do this myself. Chloe was my friend. I don't want to wait around for you to make everything right. This is my life."

"You're no match for any of the things coming after you. Trust me." He combed his fingers through her hair. A sensation of calmness washed over her, but she didn't want to be calm. What could she do?

Searching the room, her gaze caught on a small table by the window, with a decanter and glasses. Christian's eyes followed her every movement as she marched up to the table, picked up the decanter, and pulled out the stopper. Raising it to her nose, she breathed in deeply, and the sharp tang of alcohol filled her nostrils. She poured an inch of amber liquid into the bottom of one of the glasses.

"Tara?"

"Yes?"

Christian no longer looked amused. Across the room, Jamie gripped the back of the sofa, his knuckles white.

"What are you doing?" Christian asked.

She smiled and raised the glass. "Releasing my inner demon."

Part Three

REDEFINING NORMAL

Chapter Twenty-Three

Tara stared at Christian over the rim of the glass, and something flickered in his eyes.

"I'm not sure that's a good idea," he said.

"No, Tara," Jamie muttered. "It's a very, very bad idea."

Instead of worrying her, the tremor in Jamie's voice filled her with a wild sense of exhilaration.

She was fed up with being safe.

She'd tried her hardest to be normal, but maybe it was time to accept that she wasn't cut out for normality after all.

She put the glass to her lips and swallowed. The liquid burned her throat like fire.

"Jamie," Christian said, "get out of here, and tell Graham to lock down the office."

The words seemed to come from a long way off.

She expected to see horror on Christian's face. Instead, his eyes were hot and hungry and filled with a deep excitement. She took a slow step toward him.

"Now, Jamie!" he snarled, never taking his eyes from her.

She was vaguely aware of Jamie scuttling across the

room, and the door slamming behind him, but took no notice. Her whole consciousness filled with the vampire and with the inferno in her belly. She needed to do something. Anything. She just didn't know what. Rip something up. Rend something into bloody little pieces.

The need spread through her body, setting her on fire, the flames licking at her breasts, between her legs, and she threw back her head and screamed. It released some of the pressure and for a moment, she came back to herself.

There was a noise behind her, and she whirled. Steel shutters slid down over the windows.

"You can't get out," Christian said softly. "Don't bother trying."

She glared at him through narrowed eyes. "Neither can you."

"Ah, but I don't want to. I have everything I want right in here." He sauntered toward her, circling, sniffing the air. Halting less than a foot from where she stood, he started to unbutton his shirt. He gave up halfway down, ripped it open, and dragged it off his shoulders, throwing it to the floor. "Sex and food."

He smiled, baring his teeth. His fangs were fully elongated, and the flames roared back to life. She stared at his naked chest, the skin so pale, almost luminous, pulled tight over all that muscle. Then down to where his pants hung low on his lean hips. She couldn't take her eyes off his flat belly, ridged with muscle, bisected by a line of black silky hair. Something shifted inside her, and she licked her lips. Christian laughed softly, and her eyes darted to his face.

"Come on, Tara, do you think you can take me? Do you want to try?"

He was goading her. He was insane.

"Come on, honey," he murmured. "You don't really want to fight me. You want to fuck me."

As soon as he said the words, she knew it was true. She wanted him, hard and fierce with none of the gentleness he had shown her the last time. She wanted to unleash the monster she knew was somewhere close beneath his surface, just as her own inner monster strained to be free.

She leapt for him. He stood his ground, and she slammed into his body, hard. It should have hurt, some sane part of her mind told her to stop, but she needed this. It seemed like a lifetime of frustration was pent up inside her, and the feel of his naked skin beneath her hands drove her wild. She clung to his shoulders, her nails digging deep into his satin skin, as her legs circled his waist.

They crashed to the floor, rolling as he tore her hands from his shoulders. He turned her with one fluid move so she lay on her belly, her face pressed into the roughness of the carpet, the long, hard length of him pinning her against the floor. She bucked and writhed beneath him, fighting to get free. His breath brushed over the back of her neck, his teeth grazed her skin, settling at the point where her shoulder met the column of her throat. For a minute, he nuzzled her there, then he bit down sharply. His teeth penetrated her skin, and she went still, her breath coming in short sharp pants.

Taking advantage of her momentary stillness, he raised his body, nudged her thighs apart with his hips, and pushed himself against her core. She thrust back against him to get some relief for the fire raging through her. He was fully erect, and she could feel him pressing into her through the layers of clothing that separated them.

"What, you don't want to fight anymore?" He whispered the words against her skin, and the need to move roared through her once again. She flung herself backwards, taking him by surprise. He rolled off her, and she scrambled to her feet. He followed her up, straightening to his full height, towering over her. Real panic penetrated the thick fog of her brain. He took a step toward her. She breathed in the hot musky scent of him, feral and wild, and the panic washed away on a tidal wave of red-hot desire.

He backed her up until the cool concrete of the wall pressed against her. Another step and he pinned her between the wall and the rock hardness of his body. She writhed against him, and he pushed forward with his hips, his erection thrusting against the soft flesh of her belly.

He stared into her eyes. His were glowing, filled with a ravenous hunger. She needed him inside her any way she could get him, and she raised her head to bare her throat.

He chuckled, and her fury roared to life again. Twisting violently against him, she raked her claws down his back and lunged, sinking her teeth into his shoulder. The blood spurted hot into her mouth, and she swallowed. For a moment, he stilled, then his hands were in her hair, his fist tightening, wrenching her head back so she stared up into his face. She licked the blood from her lips as he bent his head and kissed her savagely, forcing her mouth open. His tongue pushed into her, but it wasn't enough and she thrust her own into his and tasted her blood as her tongue raked over the razor sharp fangs. He sucked on it greedily, and a whimper of pain and pleasure trickled from her throat.

He backed away and she slid down the wall. Slipping his hands between them, he gripped the neck of her T-shirt and ripped it down the middle. Then his hands were on her bare breasts, his palms stroking, his fingers tugging at her nipples until she was almost mindless with desire.

Sliding his hands behind her, he cupped her bottom and lifted her against the hard length of him. She wrapped her legs around his waist, rubbing her core against his erection, until the hot, wet heat of her arousal soaked through the constricting layers of clothing between them.

He carried her to the huge desk, placing her down almost

gently. His hands went to her waist, unsnapped her jeans, slid the zipper down. She kicked off her shoes, lifted her hips from the desk, and he tugged her pants down her legs and tossed them on the floor.

He paused, stroking a thumb over her lower lip. "Are you in there?" he asked.

She nodded. The fire of the alcohol burned in her blood but she was back in her head.

"Good."

He stepped back, peeled off his own pants and stood before her naked, his long hard shaft vertical against his belly. He was so beautiful her breath caught in her throat. She reached out and he came to her. Her fingers trailed through the black, silky hair of his belly, then wrapped around the length of him. His skin was soft and smooth over a steel hard core. She squeezed him hard; his head fell back, and he groaned.

"Give me your throat."

Tara tilted her head and closed her eyes as his fangs sank into the vein. The blood pulsated through her body, throbbing between her legs. His hand moved between her thighs and she moaned. He played with her as he fed, slipping long fingers into the swollen wetness at her core, withdrawing and gliding damp fingertips over her sex, rubbing over the tight little bud that threatened to explode with pleasure. She writhed against him, pushing against his hand, but he held her still with ease. Finally, he licked her neck and drew back.

His hand left her sex and he cupped her breasts and pushed her down so her back rested against the smooth, cool steel of the desk. He played with her nipples, which sent sparks shooting through her body. His hands gripped her knees and parted her thighs so she lay open to him. Lowering his head, he swiped his tongue across her sex and she jerked beneath him. He came up over her and filled her with one lunge of his hips.

"Is this what you want, little demon?"

She bucked under him, but he remained still until she thought she would explode with frustration.

Finally, he slowly withdrew then pushed hard into her, grinding his hips, and she threw back her head and screamed as her orgasm ripped through her.

"More?" he murmured in her ear.

Without waiting for an answer, he drove into her, each thrust sending her higher, and all she could do was hold on tight. Wrapping her legs around his waist, her hands gripped tight to his shoulders and she gave herself up to the savagery of his lovemaking. He cupped her bottom and his movements became even wilder until he slammed into her mercilessly.

She balanced at a strange point between pleasure and pain when his movements slowed. He gathered her in his arms, holding her tight and rocking her against his body as his cock slid into her then withdrew, only to return.

He went still and she opened her eyes to find him staring down at her, his expression fierce and gentle.

"Mine," he whispered against her lips. He thrust once more and spilled them both over the edge.

...

For a moment, Christian thought Tara had passed out. Her eyes were closed, her long lashes fluttering against her creamy cheek. Her mouth was slightly parted and he could see her pink tongue and the whiteness of her small teeth. He carried her to the sofa and laid her on the soft leather.

She opened her eyes as he came down beside her. They were filled with wonder.

"I love you," she said.

His mind ceased to function. Her hand came up to stroke

his cheek, her touch so soft. He turned his head and kissed her palm.

"I don't want you to worry that I'll make a nuisance of myself," she said. "I won't, but I wanted you to know. If anything happens to either of us, I'd hate it if I hadn't told you."

"Nothing will happen," he growled. "I won't let anything happen."

"It's strange, but after Aunt Kathy died, I sort of swore I would never love anyone again, but it's not that easy."

She loved him.

He didn't think that anyone in his whole long existence had ever really loved him. He'd been fond of his wife, but the marriage had been arranged, and love hadn't come into it. Since he'd been changed, he'd had brief affairs but he'd never allowed them to be more than that. In the end, the humans he fed from and slept with were left without choice, puppets to his every command. How could love grow there?

Tara loved him. She wasn't human. He couldn't overcome Tara's mind. He could never control her actions. If she came to him, it was of her own free will.

Love came at a price, as Tara already knew. His mind flashed back to her friend, Chloe. Saw again her tortured body and imagined Tara in her place. Pain ripped through him. He must have flinched because her eyes flashed to his face.

"What's wrong?"

He shook his head. "Nothing." He vowed that he would keep her safe, protect her from those that meant her harm, whatever the cost. "Nothing," he said again. He grinned. "You love me?"

She nodded.

He wrapped his arms around her and rolled her so she sprawled across his body. She wriggled and his cock stiffened between them. She rubbed her sweet little hips against him until he was rock hard, his balls aching for release. His hands on her ass, he positioned her until his cock slid inside her hot, slippery opening. He sighed as she settled on him. Accommodating to his size, she started to move, and he gave himself up to the pleasure.

Chapter Twenty-Four

She'd told him she loved him.

It was the first thought that entered Tara's mind as she woke to the bright light of day. She was in a bed but had no memory of how she'd got there. Christian must have brought her after the last time they made love.

He wasn't with her, but how could he be with the sunlight pouring through the open blinds. She was in the penthouse, and far below her Christian would be sleeping away the day. She concentrated and felt the faint hum of his presence in her mind.

She'd told him she loved him.

She couldn't get it out of her head, and while he hadn't said he loved her in return, he had shown it with his every action. He had made love to her so sweetly and with such intensity, it had made her cry.

At the back of her mind welled a deep, residual sorrow for Chloe. It would probably always be with her, but a sense of excitement for the future now overlaid her grief. A future with Christian.

So he was a vampire, but she was half-demon and half-fae. They would never have a normal life, but so what? They would have a life. Christian had promised he would keep her safe, and she trusted him.

Still, she wasn't going to sit back and let him do everything alone. He would keep her safe but she planned to do the same for him.

Rolling over, she encountered something soft and warm. It was Smokey, and Tara pulled his body against her as she had so many mornings of her life. He purred and her fingers smoothed the soft fur of his head.

Beneath the sheet, she was naked, and it flashed through her mind just what Smokey was. Or rather who he was. She shrugged—he'd seen her naked so many times, it hardly mattered. Sitting up, she tugged the sheet over her breasts and pulled Smokey on to her lap. He stared into her face, his eyes unblinking.

"You and I are going to have a chat very soon," she said. "I'll give you some leeway, because I know you're grieving for Chloe, but prepare yourself. You've got a lot of explaining to do."

She hugged him to her until he meowed, and she let him go. He jumped off her lap but settled on the bed and licked his paws.

There was a tap at the door and it opened, revealing Graham standing in the doorway. He was dressed in a pair of black silk pajama bottoms and nothing else. They hung low on his narrow hips. Tara gave him a brief glance then looked away.

"I thought I heard voices," he said.

"I was talking to my cat."

"The elusive Smokey, turned up at last. When did he show?"

"Last night," she said, not wanting to get into a discussion on the subject.

"I'm glad, I know you were worried. Do you want a coffee?"

Tara nodded. She made to get out of bed but remembered her lack of clothing.

"Don't get up," Graham said. "Christian told me to look after you. He said you'd had a rough night. So wait right there." He paused at the door. "I've got to ask, but what was with the whole lock down thing last night?"

She shrugged. "We were practicing safe sex."

"Right, don't tell me then."

Graham returned shortly with two steaming mugs of coffee. Tucked under his arm was the matching top to his pajama bottoms. He put the drinks on the table by the bed and handed Tara the top.

"I sense you'd be happier covered up, though you don't have to worry about me. You're not my type. Now, that nice friend of yours—Jamie wasn't it—he disappeared last night before we had the chance to get to know one another, but if you want to set us up, I wouldn't complain."

"I'll do that." Tara struggled into the top under cover of the sheet while Smokey squinted up at her through narrowed, yellow eyes.

"Anyway," Graham said, "Christian wouldn't let me stay here with you if he thought I'd make you uncomfortable."

"Just what are you doing here? I thought you had your own place."

"I do, but Christian doesn't think it's safe at the moment, so I'll stay here till he gives me the all clear."

He picked up one of the coffees and handed it to Tara, then sat on the bed next to her, long legs stretched out, and picked up his own.

The coffee was still too hot, but Tara breathed in the wonderful, aromatic scent.

"I only saw Christian briefly," Graham said. "It was nearly dawn when he brought you up here. Did you find out anything useful?"

Tara took a sip of her coffee. "I'm not human."

It felt good to say it aloud. To know that there were people in this new world that she could talk to.

Graham put down his drink and studied her. "So what are you?"

"Half-demon."

He didn't seem shocked. "And the other half?"

"Fae."

"Wow, I've never heard of that before. So are you expecting to turn red and grow horns anytime soon?"

"Do demons have horns?"

"Not always, but some of the fae do."

"I think I would have grown them by now, if I was going to." She took another sip of coffee and frowned. "I hope I would have anyway."

"You know, they're not all bad—demons I mean. In case you're worried that you're half-monster or something."

"Actually, I'm worried that I'm all monster, but I'm trying not to think about it too much."

"Christian will look after you."

A flicker of irritation pricked her. "I don't want to be looked after. I want to be able to look after myself. In fact, you can help me with that."

"I can?"

He sounded so worried that Tara had to bite back a smile. "Yes. I want a gun."

"You do?" He raised one eyebrow. "Christian told me to get you anything you wanted, but I'm not sure he had a gun in mind."

"Can you get me one?"

"Probably, there's an arsenal in the basement. Most of

the security guards are armed."

"Good, and I'll need someone to show me how to use it."

"Well, don't look at me, sweetheart. I'm definitely not your man."

"But do you know of someone?"

"Again—probably. I'll have a word with Carl Hanson. He's the head of security here."

"Does he know what Christian is?"

Graham nodded.

"Is that safe?" Tara asked.

"Well, Carl's not exactly" —he paused as if unsure of the right word to use— "normal."

"What is he?"

"He's a werewolf. Most of the security guys here are."

"Right. A werewolf. Great." She glanced at Smokey, still sitting beside her, listening to the conversation. "Are they the same as shifters?"

"No, they're different. Shifters are born that way, or at least I think so. Weres are born human and turned. A bit like vamps, I suppose."

"I should have guessed there'd be werewolves somewhere," she said almost to herself. "You know, I think I might just pull the covers over my head and go back to sleep. Try to pretend all this isn't happening. That I have my nice, normal life, that I'm not in love with a vampire, and I'm not about to have shooting lessons with a werewolf."

Graham grinned. "You can have a normal life—all you have to do is redefine normal." He frowned. "Hey, did you just say you were in love with Christian?"

Heat washed over her, warming her skin. She nodded.

"You're blushing."

"Am not."

"Am!" He laughed and patted her arm. "I'm glad. I know Christian likes you."

"You really think so?"

"Oh yeah, big time." He swung his legs off the bed and took her empty coffee cup. "I'm going to make some breakfast then get you a gun. God help us all."

Tara stood in reception as the people came and went. The place was buzzing, and she stared, trying to work out what they were, wondering were any of them human. In the end, she had to ask.

"Is anybody that works here human?"

Graham looked hurt. "Hey, I'm human."

"Well anybody else then?"

"Actually, nearly everyone is human, and only a few of them know anything about the vampire stuff—just some of the security guards. It's not hard to keep separate." He glanced down at the cat at her feet. "Does he go everywhere with you?"

Tara picked up Smokey. "Not normally, but he's feeling a little insecure right now."

"There's Carl, come on."

Tara studied her first werewolf. Or maybe not her first. She'd seen other security guards, and Graham had said most were wolves. Carl was a stranger though, and she couldn't help but feel self-conscious as she crossed the room toward him.

He was tall, with short dark hair and an upright posture. He wasn't in uniform like most of the guards, but faded jeans and a khaki T-shirt. His wary green eyes met hers, and he held out a hand. Tara put Smokey on the floor and grasped it. As his palm slid against hers, a frisson of sensation ran through her. He felt it as well, and something feral moved behind his eyes.

"Carl, this is Tara." Graham made the introductions.

"Tara," Carl said, nodding. He brought her hand to his face and breathed in deeply. "Hmm, I can see why Christian likes you."

"Well, I hope it's for more than what I smell like," she snapped, tugging her hand away.

He let her go and grinned. "I'm sure it is. Now, I hear you want a gun. What's it for?"

Wasn't that obvious?

"To shoot things with."

"What sort of things—big things, little things?"

"Demons," she said. "I want to shoot demons. And maybe fae." She thought for a moment. "Make that, probably fae. Does it make a difference?"

"Anything else? Vampires? Werewolves?"

"You never know," she said. "Ask me again in half an hour."

He grinned again. "Come on, let's go down and get you kitted out."

Five minutes later, Tara stood in front of the gun racks and stared at all the weapons. "Wow, what a lot of guns."

She ran her fingers over a few and came to a halt at one particular large impressive pistol. "I really like the look of this one."

Carl ignored the comment and moved along the rack, finally selecting a small pistol. He turned it over in his hands before handing it to Tara.

She took it from him and looked at it dubiously. "It's not very big."

"Has no one ever told you that size isn't everything?" Carl said.

Graham snorted behind her, and Tara scowled. "That's great coming from someone who's six-foot-three," she grumbled.

"It's a Sig Pro 9mm," he said. "And I can give you bullets for that thing that will blow a demon into tiny little pieces."

"Really?"

"Of course, you need to be able to hit something first."

She held the gun out as she had seen people do on the TV, holding it at arm's length and sighting down the barrel. "How hard can it be?"

"Let's go see. The shooting range is right next door, unless you want us to go out and find you a demon."

"The range will do for now."

Tara followed him into a long room almost bare of furniture.

Carl took the gun from her. "You need to insert the magazine, like so. Then to load the chamber you pull back the slide, like this" —he demonstrated— "and release it. Easy. Here you go."

He removed the magazine and bullet and handed the gun and ammunition to Tara. She slotted the magazine, chambered the bullet, and grinned. Carl grasped her wrist, and pressed her hand downward so the gun was aimed for the floor. "Which leads us to the most important rule of all. Never aim your gun at anything you aren't willing to kill."

"Oh."

"Take out the bullets. We'll have a go without them first."

He stood right behind her. "Now," he murmured into her ear, "grip your pistol firm in both hands, but keep your finger off the trigger until you're ready to shoot." His hands rested on her shoulders, he was so close she could feel the heat of his body through their clothes, and a prickle of awareness ran through her.

"Your feet should be shoulder width apart," Carl slipped a leg between hers and nudged them apart. "Stretch out your arms, and lean slightly forward, but stay balanced. Now take a deep breath, exhale halfway, hold it, and squeeze the trigger."

She squeezed, the pistol made a slight clicking noise.

"Okay, let's try it with bullets. Load up."

She took the magazine from him and reloaded while he

pressed a button. Halfway down the room, a target swung into position. Carl stepped back from her this time, and she took up the stance he had shown her, arms outstretched, feet apart. She closed one eye, sighted down the line of the pistol, took a deep breath, and squeezed. Her whole body jumped at the explosion of noise, and her finger seemed stuck to the trigger. She kept squeezing but at least she was facing the right way.

After what seemed like an age, she felt hands on her shoulders. "Relax, Tara, let go of the trigger."

Somehow, she managed to relax her finger. Her eyes were screwed tight shut and her arms trembled. She dropped them slowly to her sides, and opened her eyes.

"Did I hit anything?" she asked.

"Probably, but certainly not the target."

"Oh." Perhaps this was harder than she'd anticipated. Graham was standing in the corner, grinning. He held Smokey, the cat's head hidden in the crook of his elbow. She scowled at the pair of them.

"Okay," Carl said. "Let's go again and Tara—"

"Yes?"

"Try not to panic, this time."

The second time wasn't much better, but at least she kept her eyes open through the whole thing and saw the bullets miss the target.

She stared at the pistol in disgust. "I think it might be broken."

Carl took the gun from her hand, spun round, and shot a bullet into the center of the target without even aiming.

"Show-off," she muttered as he handed her the gun back.

After half an hour, Tara hit somewhere on the target every time. She was moderately pleased and didn't feel quite so helpless. Her hand ached, and she handed the gun over with a sigh of relief. Carl emptied the bullets, slotted it into a holster, and gave it back.

He took her hand and massaged the fingers.

"My advice is, lull them into a false sense of security—"

"How?" Tara interrupted.

Carl eyes drifted over her. "I don't think that's going to be the problem. Just let them get right up close, and then blow them to bits."

"Thank you," she said. "You've been kind."

His eyes were half-closed, a small smile playing across his lips. "Honey, I am never kind." He took her hand, brought it to his face as he had earlier and breathed in. "If you need any more lessons, guns, knives, hand to hand" —he stroked his thumb over her palm as he spoke, and Tara shivered as sensation shot through her— "just let me know."

"What was it with you and the werewolf?" Graham said as they got into the elevator. "All that hand holding shit."

Tara rubbed her hand down her thigh; it still tingled where Carl had touched it. "I was just saying thank you."

"Well, don't say thank you where Christian can see." He looked at her for a moment. "Carl probably just wants to wind him up."

"Is that wise?"

"Hey we're talking about a werewolf here. I'm not sure 'wise' comes into their decision-making process. He likes Christian, respects him, otherwise he wouldn't work here, but there's still friction between the two of them."

"Why's that?"

"Well, vamps can control weres, because they start out as human, and I guess the weres don't like that. But Carl's pretty high up in the werewolf hierarchy, and I doubt even Christian could compel him to do something he didn't want to do."

"So why does he work for him?"

"It's a good job, pays well, and he gets to play with guns."

...

Tara felt the moment Christian awoke, like a light flicking on in her brain.

Minutes later, he strode into the penthouse. He hadn't bothered to dress, just pulled on a pair of jeans, and she stared at him, unable to look away. Then she jumped to her feet, her book clattering to the floor, and ran to him.

He didn't speak, just gathered her in his arms and kissed her. She melted against him, her fingers digging into the bare satin skin of his back. After a few minutes, he raised his head.

"You smell of werewolf," he growled.

"I had a shooting lesson with Carl."

His eyes narrowed. "How did it go?"

"I wasn't very good."

"And did he behave himself?"

Heat spread across her cheeks. "Of course."

Christian smiled. "There's no of course about it. Tell him, if he touches you again, I'll rip his throat out."

"I'm not going to tell him that. He was actually very kind."

A look of complete disbelief flashed across his features. "He's a werewolf. They don't do 'kind.' Now come here."

Tara went into his arms and he kissed her again. After long minutes, he put her from him and stepped back.

"I have to go out. Piers arranged another meeting with the Walker. I'm going to find out what I can about your mother."

"I want to come."

He shook his head. "You're not going to go anywhere near the fae, especially not the Walker. He's an assassin and he wants you dead. Look, this is our best bet to find out what happened. I'm also hoping we can come to some sort of arrangement with the fae—get them off your back for good. You'd be free."

"Well, free of the fae, just the demons to cope with." She forced a smile. "What it is to be popular."

She didn't want him to go—it was impossible to shake the worry that nagged her as he got ready to leave. She followed him into the bedroom and perched on the edge of the bed as he pulled clothes from the drawer and finished dressing.

When he was done, he came and sat beside her, picked up her hand, and kissed her fingers. "If you ever need someone and I'm not around, go to Carl. He's a good guy."

"I don't want to go to Carl, and why won't you be around?"

"It's unlikely, but just in case. I shouldn't be too long. Wait for me here."

He kissed her lips then stood and left the room.

Tara stared after him, biting her lip, and fighting the urge to call him back. For some reason, it felt like he was saying goodbye.

Chapter Twenty-Five

A fierce desire to turn around almost stopped Christian in his tracks. His fists clenched at his side as he fought the need to go back to her, make love to her one last time.

All through the long day without her, he'd gone over and over the facts, searching for a way to keep Tara safe. He'd failed his wife and daughters. He could not fail Tara.

Asmodai was after him, and while the demon hid in the Abyss sending a limitless supply of minions to perform his filthy work, there was little Christian could do to stop him. Images of Chloe's mutilated body haunted his mind. He couldn't let that happen to Tara. He had to find a way to stop Asmodai.

Then there were the fae. As things stood, they would hunt down and kill Tara on sight. Christian had come up with a deal to offer the Walker. If the fae agreed, there was a high chance Christian would never see her again. He could find no way around that, but Tara would have a chance at that normal life she craved. A normal life without him.

He went straight to the weapons room and kitted out,

pulled a long, black leather trench coat over it all, and went up to meet Piers, who was already waiting in reception.

"Hmm," Piers said, as Christian approached, "you smell of your little human. Have you marked her yet?"

"No."

Graham sat behind the desk. But Christian didn't speak to him. If things went badly tonight then in all likelihood Graham would die. The mark would ensure that. What was there to say to him?

He led Piers out into the night. Only when they reached the brightly lit street did he turn to the other man.

"So," he asked, "did you organize it?"

Piers nodded. "Are you going to tell me what this is all about?"

"It's about Tara."

"Your human? What's she got to do with the Walker?"

"Well the problem is, she's not actually human."

Piers raised an eyebrow. "She's not?"

"No. That's what the talisman does. It contains a spell which hides her true nature."

"And that is?"

"She's half-fae."

"Are you kidding me?"

Christian shook his head. "Her mother was fae."

"And her father?"

"Demon."

Shock flared in Piers's eyes, quickly replaced by disgust. "Great, just fucking great," he muttered. "You know what this means, don't you? She's the one they're hunting for. She's the abomination."

"Don't call her that," Christian growled.

"Okay, but you admit it—she *is* the one they're looking for?"

"Yes. They must have sensed her months ago when she

took off the talisman the first time. They've been searching for her ever since."

"And couldn't find her because she'd put it back on. Which is why they came to us." Piers ran a hand through his hair. "You swore an oath to destroy her."

"It's not going to happen."

"Look, if you can't do it, I will. I'll make sure it's painless. She won't even know it's going to happen."

Christian stopped, swung round, and placed a fist in the center of Piers's chest. "If you lay one fucking finger on her, I'll rip you apart."

"You could try," he said. "It might even be fun. We've never really known which one of us would come out on top in a fight. You want to go for it?"

They stared at each other for long minutes, unaware of the stream of humanity that parted around them. Finally, Christian dropped his hand. "No."

Piers rubbed at his chest. "I won't touch her."

"Good."

"But you'd better have a bloody good plan or this has all the potential to plunge us back into the dark ages. You remember the dark ages don't you, Christian? Chaos and mayhem."

"I thought you liked chaos."

"That was before I got respectable."

Christian almost smiled at the idea. Almost, but not quite. The problem was, he did remember. He remembered it well, and even for Tara he couldn't justify plunging the world back into that. He had to find a way to neutralize the fae without tipping them over the edge into war. He suddenly became aware that they were on a busy street. People gave them a wide berth, but still they were drawing attention.

"Let's get moving. I'll tell you on the way. Where are we meeting?"

"At a bar, around the corner from here. I thought it might be better to be somewhere public."

"The Walker was okay with that?"

Piers shrugged. "He agreed. So what's this plan of yours?"

Christian spoke as they walked.

"You think she'll agree?" Piers asked when Christian fell silent.

"It's what she's always wanted, and I can give it to her."

"You won't be able to see her again. You'll have to cut yourself off completely."

"I don't know how else to convince the fae. Do you?"

"I'm not even convinced this will convince the fae, but it's worth a try. And if that doesn't work I vote for killing him."

"The Walker?"

Piers nodded. "At least it will give you more time with her and me a great deal of pleasure."

"And bring the whole fae nation down on us."

"Might be worth it. I've always hated that guy." He grinned. "I know. I'm a man with responsibilities now. I can't go around killing people just because I don't like them, but maybe we could make the odd exception." He came to a halt. "Right, we're here. Last chance to back out."

Christian shook his head and followed Piers into the bar. The room was almost empty and a heavy silence hung in the air.

"He's over there," Piers said, nodding in the direction of the back of the room.

The Walker sat in the shadows, facing the door, and his eyes glowed in the dim light.

"I need a drink," Piers said. "Christian?"

Christian shook his head and waited, impatient, while Piers ordered a beer. The Walker rose to his feet as they approached. Christian studied him, searching for similarities, and once you knew to look, they were there to see. The Walker had Tara's green eyes, her fine bones, even the blond hair was the exact color and texture. How could he have missed that Tara was fae?

"I hope this meeting is to tell me you have solved my problem and the abomination is dead."

Piers took a sip of his beer. "Not quite."

The Walker's eyes narrowed, and his mouth formed into a thin line. "Then why am I here?"

"Sit down," Christian said. "Both of you."

Kicking a chair out from the table, Christian sat and looked pointedly at Piers. After a few seconds of uncomfortable silence, Piers sank into the chair next to him. Finally, the Walker took his seat. "I sense you want something from me?"

Christian nodded. "I want you to release me from the vow I made."

"I can't do that."

"Of course you can," Piers said.

The Walker cast him a look of intense dislike. "Okay, I *won't* do that."

"I think you will," Christian said.

"I expect such treachery from this one." The Walker nodded at Piers, who grinned and flashed his fangs. "But you are held to be a man of honor, a man who carries out his oaths."

"There are some things that even I would consider more important that my honor."

"And those things are?"

Christian remained silent.

"Love," Piers said.

"Love?"

Piers shrugged. "He's in love with your abomination."

Christian stared at him, a growl trickling from his throat.

"Hey," Piers said. "I'm trying to appeal to his better nature."

The Walker watched them, a frown on his face as though he didn't quite know what to make of the whole thing. "My better nature?" he mused. "Do I have one?"

Piers shrugged. "Well, I have to admit it was a long shot, but—"

"Shut up, Piers," Christian snarled. He turned to the Walker. "I wasn't aware of the facts back then."

The Walker raised one arched eyebrow. "And you are now?"

"Most of them. I'm hoping you can clear up the last few things."

"I'm interested in this love thing." He studied Christian. "I wasn't aware that vampires were capable of love."

"It's irrelevant."

"I don't think so. Tell me about her. I presume it is a 'her.'"

Christian searched the fae's face. This was not a direction he would have chosen to go without Piers's intervention, but perhaps it would help. Or hinder. It was too late to stop now.

"We were told she looks like her mother," he said. "And she has your eyes."

"What?"

"Her eyes, they're green like yours, and her hair is blond, almost silver."

"And she looks like her mother?"

Christian nodded.

The Walker rose to his feet, his body rigid, his fists clenched at his side. Piers glanced at Christian in query, and Christian shrugged. The Walker turned back to them. His eyes filled with a deep sorrow. "Her mother was my brother's child."

It was Christian's turn to be stunned. "What?"

"My people do not produce many children, and Lillian was the last."

"What happened to her?"

"The demons took her. She was much loved by our people. She was a beautiful child and grew into a beautiful young woman. All who saw her wanted her."

"How?" Piers asked. "She should have been safe in the Faelands."

"Lillian was fascinated by earth and humans. She was always crossing over. The last war was on, my brother tried to keep her at home, but she slipped away and must have been seen by demons. They love to take beautiful things and destroy them."

"That's when you came to us?"

He nodded. "My brother was frantic, but it was too late. When the war was over and the demons banished, we thought we might find her. We hoped she would return home to us, but she'd disappeared, and we believed her already dead."

"Instead, she was pregnant and running from you because she knew you would kill her unborn child. Would you really have killed an innocent baby?"

The Walker didn't hesitate. "Yes."

"And people believe demons to be evil." Piers shook his head.

"We cannot allow demons access to the Faelands. It is why the child had to be killed, why she must die now."

"That's not going to happen."

"She's part demon and can enter the Faelands. They will use her against us."

"She's also part fae, doesn't that matter?"

"It can't matter. We have to protect ourselves."

"They can't use her if they don't have her," Christian said. "If I can guarantee they will never know of her existence will you back off? Let her live."

The Walker appeared thoughtful. "How could you do this?"

"Have you been able to find her?"

"No. We felt the presence once, months ago, and again ten days past. We sensed its dual nature and we've been hunting since, but found nothing."

"She's not an 'it.'" Christian growled.

The Walker shrugged. "It never occurred to me that this could be a child of Lillian's. We thought it a human with traces of fae and demon blood. But a half-demon, half-fae, she could go anywhere—enter the Abyss, the Faelands. The Accords would not hold her."

"She has no wish to enter the Faelands or the Abyss. She's grown up believing she's human, and all she wants is a normal life."

"Are the demons aware of her existence?"

"Only to the extent you are. They sensed her, but she's hidden to them now."

"How is she hidden?"

"She wears a talisman. It hides her true nature." He paused. "Her mother had it made. She paid for it with her blood and her life. Would you have that sacrifice made for nothing?"

The Walker pursed his lips. "She's part demon, there will come a time when she will cause trouble."

"Not if she never knows what she is, who she is. What if we arrange it so she truly believes she's human? If she remembers nothing of the worlds of fae and demons?"

"You mean more magic?"

Christian nodded.

"Would she agree to this?"

"It doesn't matter. It would be done."

"The demons could still find her, use her."

"Not if she continues to wear the talisman. We can increase the compulsion in the spell. She won't ever take it off."

"Let me think this through."

He walked away from them, and Christian watched him go.

"Do you realize Tara is his niece?" Piers asked, and Christian nodded. "If he says no, what are we going to do?"

"Kill him."

Piers laughed softly. "Let's hope then."

The Walker came back. He sat down "You do this," he said to Christian, "and you lose her forever. She must forget you along with all the rest."

"I know."

He frowned. "Is this real love? The willingness to let something go."

"I'm giving her what she wants."

"Does she love you, this daughter of Lillian?"

Christian thought back to Tara lying beneath him, giving herself so freely, her soft words of love echoing in his ears. He forced them from his mind. "It doesn't matter."

"If she's a true child of Lillian's, she won't thank you for this."

"She won't know. I'm giving her the chance of a normal life."

"You have your deal, Christian Roth. The child of Lillian will not die at the hands of the fae, but she will forget all. But if she ever removes the talisman, the deal is off, and I will kill her myself."

A rush of mingled emotions ran through Christian. Relief that Tara would be safe, but also a deep, dark vein of regret that she would be lost to him forever. "I'll see that it's done."

The Walker rose, nodded at Christian, ignored Piers, and left.

"Damn," Piers said, staring at the door as it closed behind the Walker. "He agreed. I can't believe it. My chance to kill the bastard gone."

"I'm sure there'll be another." Christian ran a hand through his hair, the energy leaking out of him. He was halfway there. The fae had been the tricky part. It was always uncertain which way they would go.

"So what now?" Piers asked.

Now was the easy part. Like Piers said, there was nothing tricky about a demon. He was going to face Asmodai. He was going to fight, and in all likelihood, he was going to die.

Because they would meet in the Abyss.

While on Earth, they could meet on equal terms, and there was a chance he could beat the demon, in the Abyss, the demon's power would be almost limitless. But if Asmodai agreed to his deal, at least Tara would be safe.

The thought of his probable death drove his desperation to see her one last time, to hold her again.

"I need to see Tara, tell her the fae are off her back."

"Can't you phone?"

"No." He rose to his feet. "Afterward, we need to see Jonas Callaghan, make sure he's okay with doing the spell."

"He'll want something in return."

"Then we'll just have to give it to him."

...

A deep sense of foreboding nagged Tara. She wanted Christian here, where she could see him, touch him. There was a connection between them, growing stronger, which translated into anxiety when he wasn't with her.

She tried reading a book, switched on the TV, switched it off again.

Finally, she fastened the holster to her belt, pulled a jacket on to hide the gun, and took the elevator down to the shooting range. She practiced until the bullets hit the target each time, sometimes even close to the center. Then she tried a couple of rapid draws, like she'd seen in the movies, and missed totally.

Glancing at her watch, she realized an hour had passed. He should be back soon. She pulled her jacket on and headed back up to reception. As the elevator opened, Christian walked through the sliding glass doors with Piers. He came straight over to her before she could step out of the elevator.

"Come on," he said, stepping in beside her. "We need to talk."

As he pressed the down button, Tara slipped her hand into his and peered up at his face. His expression was closed.

"Did it go okay?" she asked.

He didn't answer, but at that moment, the elevator stopped, and he pulled her into his apartment, slamming the door behind them. She could sense his urgency and frowned.

"What is it, Christian. Did it go wrong? Are the fae coming after me?"

"The fae have agreed to leave you alone. I'll tell you the details later. I have to go back out with Piers because we've one more thing to do so you'll be safe. But before I go I need to—"

He picked her up and carried her through to the bedroom, laid her on the bed and stripped off his clothes before coming down beside her.

He undressed her slowly, kissing her skin as it was bared to him. He made love to her. Slow, intense, erotic love, as though he wanted to imprint himself on her body for always. As she drew close to her orgasm, he burrowed his face in her throat, sinking his fangs deep into her. He drank as his hips thrust leisurely into her, grinding relentlessly against her, until she came in a flood of pleasure so powerful that for a moment she blacked out.

As she came to, Christian's arms were wrapped around her, and he was kissing her neck, licking the wound, healing her. When he realized her eyes were open, he gathered her tighter and kissed her lips. "That was sublime," he said.

She snuggled closer, but after a few minutes, he sat up and pulled her with him.

He removed her arms from around him and stood. She watched as he pulled on his clothes. A part of her wanted to call him back, but another part needed him to go, to get her situation settled so they could be together without the constant worry that someone or something was coming after her.

He dressed in silence, then crossed the room, pausing for a moment in the doorway. As he looked back at her, foreboding swept through her once more, settling low in her belly. She swung her legs onto the floor to go after him.

"I love you," he said, and she went still at his words. "I might not have mentioned it yesterday, but I wanted you to know. I've never loved before. I'm new to this. I just hope I get it right."

Then he was gone.

...

Christian kept his mind blank as he rode the elevator up to reception.

Piers leaned against the wall, looking pissed. Graham was behind the desk studiously ignoring him.

"Are we ready to go?" Christian asked.

Piers raised an eyebrow. "I've been ready for the last half hour. Just hanging round here, while you shag your girlfriend."

"Leave it, Piers."

"I'll get the car." He pulled out his cell phone.

As they left the building, a black SUV pulled up beside them. They got in the back and the car merged into the traffic. It stopped ten minutes later outside The Pointed Hat. Christian climbed out, followed by Piers. All around, the street was quiet, nothing moved.

The bar was empty of customers. The barman glanced up as they entered, a scowl forming on his face. Christian ignored him and took a seat at one of the tables.

"I could do with that drink now—Scotch."

Piers brought back a bottle and two glasses. He sat and poured them both a drink. "So, what now?"

The door to the back room opened and Jonas Callaghan entered. He crossed to them and sat in the chair opposite. "Did the fae agree?" he asked Christian.

"He did."

"I'm impressed."

Christian smiled. "Piers appealed to his better nature."

"He has one?" Jonas sounded impressed.

"Perhaps," Christian said. "So are you ready?"

"I'm ready. All I need is for your friend here to agree my terms."

"I haven't mentioned them yet."

Jonas raised an eyebrow. "Well, perhaps now would be a good time."

Christian turned to Piers. "Jonas has agreed to do the spell on Tara, but he requires something in return."

"I'm guessing that something affects me. As long as he's not after my blood, I'll consider it."

"No, your friend here has agreed to contribute that part of the bargain. What I require from you is a job with the Order. I believe you have a vacancy."

"A job doing what?"

Jonas shrugged. "Whatever the Order requires."

"I don't want to appear suspicious here, but why would you want a job with us?"

"You have access to resources I could never get alone.

There are certain things I am working on that could benefit us both."

Piers turned to Christian. "Can you vouch for him?"

"I wouldn't have considered the deal otherwise. You need a witch or warlock on the staff to replace Ella. It's unrealistic to think you'd get one without their own agenda, but I don't believe any agenda of Jonas' will harm the Order."

"Unlike Ella," Piers added caustically. "Okay, I have no objections. How do we do this?"

"You do it tonight," Christian said.

"Are you going to tell her?"

"I won't be there, but I have a letter for her. She won't be a problem. She'll do what she has to."

"And where will you be while all this is going on?" Piers asked.

"I'm going to meet with Asmodai."

"Why?"

"Tara's friend was killed on his orders because of me. They were trying to get to me like they did with Gabe and Stefan. Tara won't be safe until whatever is between us is resolved."

"He won't meet with you."

"He'll have no choice. I'm going after him. I'm going to the Abyss."

Piers stared at him. "You're out of your mind."

"Perhaps." Christian swallowed the rest of his drink and poured another. "But it finishes tonight. I'm going to offer him combat. I defeat him, or I die. Either way Tara will be safe."

"You really are in love, aren't you?" Piers shook his head in disgust. "You'll die for this. You can't fight a demon in the Abyss. Certainly not one of the seven."

"I can try."

"You know I can't come with you," Piers said. "It would

be a declaration of war."

"I don't want you to come with me." Christian finished the drink and put down the glass. "I want you to wait until you hear from me, but if I don't get back by an hour before dawn, take Jonas and go to my place. Do the spell." He took an envelope from his pocket. "Give this to Tara. It explains everything."

Piers nodded.

Christian rose to his feet. He clasped hands with Piers briefly, then vanished.

Chapter Twenty-Six

Christian loved her.

She should be radiantly happy. Instead, Tara couldn't rid her mind of the fear that something was terribly wrong.

Finally, she got up, pulled on her clothes, clipped the gun holster onto her belt, and went up to reception.

It was quiet, just Graham sitting behind the counter, and next to him, Smokey. They both watched her as she crossed the floor.

"I'm going crazy," she said.

"He'll be back soon," Graham replied.

"Don't try and sooth me. I don't want to be soothed, and I have a gun."

"Yeah, but you can't hit anything, so I think we're safe."

"Ha, ha."

She looked at her watch again. Another ten minutes had passed.

"Why don't you go through the back and make us all a coffee?" Graham said.

"You're trying to sooth me again."

"Yes, but I would like a coffee."

Tara shrugged. "Okay." She turned to Smokey. "Do you want one?"

"Your cat drinks coffee?"

Tara glanced between the two of them. "I thought you two were getting pretty matey." She came round the back of the counter and stroked her hand along Smokey's back. "Why don't you think about telling him your secret, while I'm making the coffee?"

Smokey jumped off the counter and followed her through into the small kitchen behind the reception area, weaving between her legs. Tara put the coffee on and leaned down to stroke him. "You can tell him, you know. He likes you."

"Meow."

"Yes, well. I suppose that's up to you, but I want to talk to you anyway, so you can't stay like that forever."

She puttered around putting milk in the cups. She was pouring the coffee when something snapped in her head and she cried out. The coffee jug fell to the floor and smashed, hot liquid splashing up over her legs. Tara collapsed to her knees as Graham burst in through the door.

"Tara!" He came down beside her. "What is it?"

"He's gone."

"What do you mean, he's gone?"

"I can't feel him. He was there in my head, and now he's gone."

Graham reached out to help her up, but stopped abruptly as Jamie appeared out of nowhere.

"What the fuck!"

"Shapeshifter," Jamie said and went down on his knees beside Tara.

"You're the cat?"

Jamie nodded. He pulled Tara against him. "Come on, Tara. It's probably nothing."

"No." Panic clawed at her insides. "Christian's not there, it's like he's vanished. He's dead, I know he is."

"Tara, he can't be dead," Graham said.

"How can you be sure?"

"Because I'm still alive. I know Christian's explained about the vampire marks. Christian dies and I die. And do I look dead?"

She shook her head, trying to drag herself back from the edge of despair. Glancing around her, she realized she was sitting in a puddle of cooling coffee and broken glass.

Graham reached out a hand to her. She took it, and he pulled her to her feet. "Come on, sit down. I'll make more coffee, and we'll try and work out what's happened."

Tara didn't argue as he pushed her down into the chair. She remembered what Christian had told her about the marks. She bit her lip to stop the trembling. "Okay."

Jamie cleaned up the floor while Graham made the coffee.

"We can try his cell phone," Graham said, handing her a mug.

Tara watched as he phoned. Jamie stood behind her his hands on her shoulders. She knew there would be no answer.

"I'll try Piers. Christian left with him. Maybe they're still together." Graham punched another number. "Piers? It's Graham. Is Christian still with you?"

Tara strained to hear the reply, but couldn't.

"Okay, well thanks."

As Graham started to put the phone down, Tara ran forward and snatched the receiver from him. "Piers, it's Tara."

"Tara, how lovely to hear from you, but I don't know where Christian is."

"When did you last see him?"

"Tara, I'm not his keeper. I'm sure he'll be back to see you when he's ready." He hung up on her.

She stared at the receiver for a moment then threw it down and glared at it through narrowed eyes. "He knows where Christian is."

"He says he doesn't."

"He's lying."

Graham raised an eyebrow but didn't say anything further.

"I'm going over there," she said.

"Over where?"

"To the Order."

"You can't. Christian said not to leave the building without him."

"Christian's not here, is he?"

"There might be demons out there."

"Well we'll just have to stay away from them. We can drive over there, and it should be safe enough. It will have to be, because I'm not waiting here, doing nothing when Christian might be in trouble."

Graham sighed, but nodded. "I'll see if Carl's still around. He can drive us over, but they might not let us in."

"I'm going as well," Jamie said from behind her.

Graham frowned. "You're a cat?"

"Get over it."

Carl was leaning against the side of a big black SUV when she came out of the elevator. "I hear we're going visiting."

"Do you know where the Order is?"

He seemed surprised at the question. "I worked there when Christian was in charge."

"Good."

"Got your gun?"

She pulled her jacket aside to show the holstered pistol, and he smiled. "Let's go."

Jamie and Graham were already sitting in the back when Tara climbed into the front seat next to Carl.

"I phoned Piers," Graham said. "I told him we were on our way. He didn't sound too pleased."

"Is that supposed to bother me?" she asked.

Carl laughed softly from beside her, and she glanced at him. "What's funny?"

"Well, most people I know would be a bothered if Piers Lamont wasn't too pleased with them."

"People with any sense, that is," Jamie muttered from the back.

"Well, he should have told me what I wanted to know on the phone then."

"Oh, this is going to be fun," Carl murmured and started the car.

Tara tried to decide how to get Piers to talk to her. There was still the blank space in her mind where Christian should be. What did it mean? Was he unconscious somewhere? She held onto the thought that he couldn't be dead, which made her peek behind her at Graham.

"Still alive," he said, and waggled his fingers as if he knew what she was thinking.

The entrance into the Order's underground garage opened as Carl drove up. They were expected and at least allowed into the building. Carl parked the car.

"Looks like we have a welcoming committee," he said.

Two men walked toward them across the concrete floor. Both dressed in the uniform of security guards. Both big and dangerous. "Are they vampires?" she asked.

Carl nodded. "Come on, let's go."

They all got out and stood as the two guards approached.

Carl shook hands with the two men and held a quiet conversation. "Piers will see you," he said to Tara.

A wave of relief washed over her. She'd overcome the first obstacle. She followed Carl and the two vampires to the elevator, Jamie and Graham at her back. Tara's nerves tightened as they sank lower and lower beneath the building. When the doors slid open, Piers was waiting for them.

He did not look happy. But when did he?

In fact, he radiated menace, his arms crossed over his broad, black-clad chest, his mouth a thin, tight line, his eyes narrowed. He must have just returned to the building because he still wore the long, black leather coat.

Tara refused to be intimidated and lifted her chin.

Piers's gaze shifted from one member of their group to the next, settling on Carl. "Carl." He nodded at the werewolf. "You shouldn't have brought them here."

Carl shrugged. "They would have come without me anyway."

"That might have been better for you." Piers turned to glare at Tara. "Well, if it isn't the little abomination." His eyes ran over her small figure. "All the way back here, I've wondered how something so small could cause so much trouble."

Tara ignored the comment. "Where's Christian?"

"Not here." He sighed. "I planned on paying you a visit later. You could have waited."

"How was I to know that? Besides, I need to know now."

"No, you don't *need* to know. You *want* to know. I told Christian I would take care of you, which is the only reason you're here."

Why should Christian have asked Piers to take care of her?

"I do not need anyone to take care of me," she ground out. She didn't want to be taken care of, but if anyone was going to do it, she wanted it to be Christian.

Piers raised an eyebrow. "Baby, you're right at the number one spot on the fae's most wanted dead list. On top of that, there's a whole shitload of demons ready to make your life a living hell just to get at Christian. Personally, I'd let them have you." He paused, his eyes wandering over her, lingering on her throat. "Or maybe I'd just finish you off myself—because I've got a feeling you're a whole load of trouble."

Tara shivered, recalling the moment Piers had killed Ella. Saw again that sensual mouth ripping out her throat. That same mouth smiling at her now as if he noted her reaction and it pleased him. It wasn't a nice smile.

"But as I said, I promised Christian I would look after you, otherwise you wouldn't have gotten through the doors. So come with me, keep your mouth shut, and I might tell you what's going to happen." His eyes took in the rest of the group. "But you can leave your bodyguards here." He headed off down the corridor.

"No." Carl spoke from behind her. Tara glanced at him thankfully; she didn't want to go anywhere alone with the vampire.

"No?" Piers asked softly.

"We stay together," Jamie said.

Piers whirled to face him. "Ah, the shifter. I've never met a shifter yet who would stand his ground when the going got tough." He took a step toward Jamie. "Can you?"

Jamie looked a little green, but he stood his ground and nodded. Tara slipped her hand into his and squeezed gently.

Piers regarded them for long minutes. Finally, he lifted one shoulder in a careless shrug. "Whatever. Let's get this over with."

They followed him down the corridor. He stopped at a door, opened it, and beckoned for them to enter. He was still watching her as she stepped past, his eyes puzzled as though she hadn't acted as he expected.

They were in some sort of unused office. Blank white walls, a bare desk, and a few chairs. Tara's legs trembled, and she sank into one of the chairs.

Piers took off his coat and dropped it onto the desk.

Underneath, he wore black leather pants and a black shirt, over which was strapped a double shoulder holster with a pistol at each side.

"So," he said, "what do you want to know?"

Tara thought for a moment. "I've been able to feel Christian in my head since we—"

"Fucked?" Piers supplied. "Shared bodily fluids?"

Tara scowled at him. "Anyway, I can feel him, and then all of a sudden he was gone." She waved a hand at Graham. "We know he can't be dead, but I need to know where he's gone. Is he hurt? Unconscious."

"No, to all those things. Well at least he wasn't when I last saw him. Of course, that could have changed by now. He's in the Abyss."

"The what?"

"The Abyss. Realm of darkness, home of the demons and all that sort of thing. It's also another dimension. You can't feel Christian because he's not in this world anymore."

"Why's he gone to the Abyss?"

"You."

"What have I got to do with it?"

"Christian's got this idea that as long as there is someone targeting him, you're not safe. He saw what they did to your little friend, and he can't face the thought of the same thing happening to you. So much so, that he's willing to die for it. He's on a suicide mission." His eyes were bitter. "And it's all for you. Does that make you feel good?"

"I don't believe you."

"Oh, believe me."

"Why did you let him go?"

"Because it was what he wanted. A fool in love."

"Couldn't you have gone with him? Can't you go after him now?"

"Well you see, there's a little problem with that. The

demons have made this thing with Christian personal. He's within his rights to face them. I'm not. The Order goes to the Abyss, and they'll take it as a declaration of war."

"Then we have to get him out of there."

"No we don't. Christian was very clear on what he wanted, and I'm afraid that you mounting some pointless rescue mission was not on the list."

"So what is it that Christian wants?" she asked.

"He wants you to be happy. He's gone to a lot of bother, probably sacrificed his life, to give you the one thing he knows you want."

"And that is?"

"A normal life."

She stared at Piers in amazement.

"I'm half-demon, half-fae. I was brought up by a dead woman. Just how's that going to translate into normal?"

"It's been arranged."

"Well unarrange it. I don't want normal. I want Christian."

"Unfortunately, sweetheart, we can't always have what we want."

Panic rose up from some place deep inside Tara. She remembered the way Christian had made love to her earlier, so sweetly, as though it could be the last time. The look he'd given her as he walked out the door. "What has he done?"

"He's made a deal with the fae that will keep you alive."

"What sort of deal?"

"You're to forget everything. Cut off all ties with our world."

"I don't want to forget."

"You won't have any choice, and it won't be so bad. After all, you won't even know what you're missing."

"I won't let you do it. Christian will be back, I know he will."

"He doesn't expect to come back." Piers's voice was harsh

and Tara realized he was more upset by this whole thing than she had thought. After all, Christian was his friend.

"And think," Piers said. "What sort of life could you ever have if the fae are always after you?"

Tara opened her mouth to say she didn't care when there was a tap on the door. It swung open. Jonas Callaghan stood there, and Tara realized what they meant to do. They were going to cast some sort of spell on her to make her forget Christian. She jumped to her feet, putting the chair between her and the warlock. She glanced around the room. Graham looked sick, Jamie alarmed, only Carl seemed unaffected. She sidled to stand beside him.

"If he comes anywhere near me, shoot him," Tara said. "In fact, if he does anything at all, shoot him."

Jonas smiled at her. "Don't be so melodramatic, my dear. I only have your best interests at heart."

"Jonas is our newest employee," Piers said. "I see you've already met."

"Keep him away from me."

Piers sighed. "I knew you were going to be trouble. Here read this. Perhaps Christian will be able to persuade you."

He pulled an envelope out of his pocket and handed it to her. Tara stared at it, could hardly make her fingers work enough to open it. She tried to focus on the handwriting.

Tara,

Do what Piers says. It's for the best. We will not meet again.

Christian.

As love letters went, it was sorely lacking. She crumpled it up and threw it on the floor. How dare he make decisions about her life? How dare he presume that he knew what was best for her?

"So," Piers said. "Are we on?" He glanced round the room, his eyes settling on Jamie, then back to Tara. "You're going to have to say goodbye to your shifter friend."

Jamie moved a step closer to her.

"What?" Tara asked blankly.

"No ties with our world, remember."

Tara shook her head; Piers actually believed she'd let them go through with this.

"Perhaps I'll keep him myself," Piers continued. "Shifter blood is always a pleasant change. And you might as well say goodbye to your red-haired friend. If Christian doesn't come back, he's finished as well." Graham looked even sicker.

"At least," Piers said, "we'll have proof that Christian is well and truly dead."

"I thought he was your friend," Tara said.

"He is my friend, and I'll abide by his wishes."

"Well, I won't just sit here and wait for proof that he's dead."

Jonas moved into the room and the door swung shut behind him. Tara watched him warily.

"It doesn't matter, Tara," Jonas said. "Even if Christian defeats Asmodai, he has agreed that he will no longer be a part of your life. Let us do the spell as he wanted."

No way.

She wouldn't let it happen, would fight against it with everything she had. But glancing from the Warlock to the vampire, she knew her wishes wouldn't be enough. They were going to steal her very memories from her. She would rather die than let them take her time with Christian away from her.

"Tara." She turned at the sound of Jamie's voice. His eyes were wide and panic flashed across his face.

"What is it, Jamie?"

"Asmodai?"

"That's the demon who's been going after Christian. His

people took Chloe."

Jamie looked sick, and a wave of alarm washed over her. She didn't want to hear what he was going to say. She wasn't capable of any more shocks tonight, and she had a feeling, from the look on Jamie's face, that this was going to be a whopper.

"Asmodai is your father."

She swayed. Carl's arms came around her, holding her steady, and she leaned against him as shock thundered through her.

"What?"

The question came from Piers. He stared at her, but she couldn't define the expression on his face.

"Oh, this is so good," Jonas murmured.

Tara pushed at Carl until he released her. She licked her lips.

"Say that again," she ordered Jamie.

"Asmodai is your father."

"You're sure?"

He nodded.

"You said you didn't know who my father was."

"I lied. I promised your mother I wouldn't tell, and besides, I didn't know Asmodai had a vendetta against Christian. I would never have sent you to Christian if I'd known that. Oh God." He put his head in his hands. "It all makes sense. That's why he hates Christian."

"Well, I'm glad it all makes sense to you," Piers drawled. "But it makes absolutely none at all to me. Why does he hate Christian?"

"Christian was head of the Order. He defeated Asmodai, banished him back to the Abyss. Lillian was fae—she couldn't follow him. She was left stranded on earth, pregnant and alone. He would never forgive Christian for that and would blame him for Lillian's death."

"I thought he kidnapped my mother. I thought she hated him."

"The fae would like everyone to believe that, but they loved each other. Why else would she have gone to such trouble to keep you?"

Tara tried to get her head around the idea that her mother and father had been in love and not bitter enemies. That her own father had been responsible for Chloe's death and even at this very moment, he might be killing Christian. And Christian hated Asmodai. What could he ever feel for the daughter of the monster who had killed his family?

"Where do you come into this?" Piers asked Jamie.

"I belonged to Asmodai. He gave me to Lillian as a gift."

"So, just what sort of shifter are you?"

"I'm a cat and..." Jamie paused.

"And..." Piers prompted.

Jamie shifted uncomfortably. "A hellhound."

Piers hooted. "Half-demon, half-fae, brought up by a dead woman and now you have a pet hellhound. No, I wouldn't describe you as normal."

"What's a hellhound?" she asked.

Piers grinned. "Do you want to show her?"

Jamie disappeared. In his place was a huge dog-like creature. Graham choked behind her, but she ignored him and examined the creature. His head was level with Tara's as she gazed at him in awe. His fur was reddish brown, with a black ridge along his back, his body lean, with powerful forelegs ending in vicious inch-long claws. He had pointed ears, yellow eyes, and the longest, sharpest teeth she had ever seen. He stared back at her and something shifted in his eyes. Tara reminded herself that this was Jamie. Her friend. She stroked the fur on his head. It was soft, and he pressed against her hand.

A moment later, Jamie was back.

"Well, that was fun," Piers said. "But it doesn't change anything."

"It changes everything," Tara said.

Piers frowned. "How do you see that?"

Tara tried to get her thoughts straight. "We were thinking the demons wanted me to get back at Christian. But what if Asmodai wants to find me because I'm his daughter, and he loved my mother?"

"So what?"

"Maybe he would listen to me. Maybe he would agree to leave Christian alone if I asked him to."

"How do you expect to ask him? You'll never find Christian without me, and I can't enter the Abyss. And I sure as hell can't see Asmodai coming here."

"I can."

Piers ran a hand through his hair. "Why do I have a feeling I'm not going to like this?"

"I'm going to take off the talisman. The demons will sense me the way they did when I took it off before."

"Great idea!" Piers said, and Tara could hear the sarcasm in his voice. "Do you know who else will sense you?"

"The fae?" she asked.

"Right first time, and this would make them very unhappy. One of their conditions for not killing you was that the talisman never comes off. That way the demons never know of your existence."

"We'll just have to deal with the fae."

"How do you suggest we do that?"

Tara stood and confronted Piers. "This is a chance to save Christian, and I'm doing it. So get used to the idea."

Piers curled his lip. "You do realize I could just kill you all and go home to bed."

"You could, but you're not going to."

He was quiet for an age. Tara waited for him to speak.

"Shit," Piers said. "What the hell? I always wanted a go at the Walker anyway."

Tara didn't dare hope this would work, but it was a chance.

"We can't do this in here," Piers said. "There's so much magic built into the place that I'm not sure they'd read you."

"Where then?"

"The roof."

At the last minute, Tara reached down, picked up Christian's note, and smoothed the paper. She was about to prove Christian wrong—they would meet again.

Even if it killed her.

Chapter Twenty-Seven

This meeting had been a long time coming. Too long, perhaps.

It was dark in the Abyss. Christian breathed in the cool crisp air, sharp in his lungs but clean and fresh. He liked it here. He always had. Overhead, the sky was full of stars and a half moon hung low against the horizon, casting its dim light over a landscape of mountains and deep rugged gorges.

He knew where to find Asmodai, but he'd manifested a good way from the fortress. He needed to acclimatize to the thinner air. It was slightly warmer than London, and he shrugged out of his coat and left it crumpled on the ground. He had no need to hide his weapons and the coat would slow him down, hamper him in a fight. He thought about leaving the guns as well; bullets would be no use. In the end, he decided to keep them on the slim chance he made it out alive. He also kept the sword down his back and the knife at his thigh.

He saw no one, but was aware he was being watched, and when he reached the fortress, the gate was already raised.

He was expected.

He'd tried not to think of Tara. Now he allowed himself one last image of her. Sprawled on the black silk sheets, her eyes smiling as she told him she loved him. He could imagine how furious she'd be, but he trusted Piers to handle it. She would be safe, and eventually she would be happy. He pushed her from his mind and stepped into his enemy's stronghold.

The entrance to the fortress was a narrow tunnel, utter darkness that gave way into a courtyard. It was light here; flaming torches formed flickering shadows that danced across the stone walls.

A figure stepped out of a doorway. It approached, bowed low.

"Christian Roth," it said. "My Lord Asmodai awaits you."

He followed the hooded figure into the building, along a stone corridor and into a great hall. A huge fire burned at one end, and seated on a wooden chair was the demon prince. Two hellhounds flanked his seat. They raised their heads and growled, their hackles rising as Christian approached.

Asmodai stroked the hounds until they quieted, then rose to his feet. Standing almost seven feet tall, with black, feathered wings furled at his back, he bore little resemblance to the minor demons who served him, those inhuman creatures who filled the nightmares of man. He was lean and handsome with pale skin and dark impassive eyes.

Christian came to a standstill a few feet away. For long minutes, the two men stared at each other. Christian had hated this being for so long, but now, standing before him, he was unsure of what he felt.

There was no fear, but rather a feeling of inevitability, as though his life or rather his death had been leading up to this. He couldn't destroy Asmodai, but he could weaken him so he'd be stuck in the Abyss for a long time to come.

On the other hand, Asmodai *could* destroy him and

probably would, but if he agreed to Christian's terms then Tara would be safe.

"So," Asmodai said, "what do you want here, Christian Roth?"

"I want you to finish this."

"This?"

"You've been killing innocents when it's me you want dead. It's a coward's way."

Asmodai shrugged. "I didn't ask for details, just that they go after the ones you love." His dark gaze ran over Christian, and the first signs of emotion showed in his eyes. Black hatred, deeper than the Abyss itself. The wings at his back unfurled, framing him in darkness. "Oh, yes, I want you dead, but first, I want you to understand what it feels like to have those you love ripped from you."

"You showed me that many years ago."

A frown flickered across the demon's face. "I did?"

Disbelief swept over Christian. He'd always held Asmodai accountable for the death of his wife and children, and now it appeared the demon wasn't even aware of it. "You probably don't recall all the humans you slaughter."

"Actually, I very rarely slaughter humans, myself. I have no taste for the sport. At least the fae or even vampires show a little spirit." He studied Christian carefully. "I killed someone close to you?"

"You killed my wife and daughters."

"Humans?"

Christian nodded.

Asmodai paced the room, deep in thought. When he returned, he was frowning. "When you insisted on my banishment after the last wars, was that in revenge for what I did to your family?"

"No, you were banished because you broke the Accords. You started a war."

"I asked for time."

"I chose not to give it."

"Because I murdered your wife?"

Christian forced himself to acknowledge the truth. "Perhaps."

"I understand revenge," Asmodai murmured. He sank back onto his chair, rested his chin on his fingers, regarding Christian through heavy-lidded eyes. "Are you aware why I have ordered the death of those close to you?"

"No."

"Do you wish to know before you die?"

"All I require is that it ends here. That you won't pursue those close to me after this night. Fight me now, and whatever the outcome you leave my people alone."

"Fight you?" Asmodai seemed amused at the notion. "You know there's no way you can defeat me here."

"I can try," Christian snarled.

Asmodai smiled. "Are you aware of the closeness of bravery and stupidity?" He studied Christian, and his eyes narrowed. "I see it. There is one you love. One you seek to protect. You have no choice in this."

Asmodai stood again and paced the room, then came to a halt in front of Christian. "Very well. I take into account the ones I have already taken from you and will consider the books balanced with your death."

Christian released his breath. Tara was safe. He'd never thought much about dying, or whatever it was vampires did when their time was over. Would he be reunited with his soul, or was this end of everything? For a long time now, he'd thought he could go out with no regrets. Now, he realized that he wanted to live. He wanted to spend an eternity with Tara, but that would never happen.

A rush of hatred almost swamped him, followed by a wave of unexpected excitement. He was going to go out fighting. The bastard would pay for Gabe and Stefan. For Tara's friend.

He drew the long sword from his back. The blade glittered in the flickering light from the fire.

Asmodai smiled. He strolled to the wall where a huge sword hung. He pulled it down and dragged the blade from the scabbard. It glowed crimson as he held it up two handed in front of his face.

Something moved in the corner of the room as demons slipped into the hall. They hung close to the walls, their eyes gleaming in the dim light. He turned back to concentrate on Asmodai, saw the moment he made his move and swung the huge sword around to bear on Christian.

Christian raised his blade to counter. As the swords clashed, he staggered under the force of the blow. Pain ripped down his arm. He ignored it, gritted his teeth, and attacked.

. . .

Nobody appeared willing to make the first move. Tara caught Piers's eye, he grinned and raised an eyebrow. It was obviously up to her.

She realized the warlock was still with them. "You don't need to be part of this, Jonas."

"I wouldn't miss it for the world," he replied. "Don't worry, I'll keep out of the way."

"And don't you dare do that spell while I'm not looking."

"I wouldn't dream of it."

Graham was still green, as though he was about to throw up at any moment, and Jamie didn't look much better. She crossed over to them. "You two, stay down here." She wanted them safe.

"No way," Jamie said. "I'm coming with you. I can shift and fight if I need to."

"I don't want you dying because of me."

"Do you know how many demons I've fought since you moved us to London? You don't want to know. I'm not giving up now and letting the fae have you."

"And I'm not sitting around waiting to spontaneously combust or whatever it is happens to me if Christian dies. I can't shift into anything, but I can shoot a gun," Graham said.

"Okay." She gave Jamie a hug. Then turned and embraced Graham.

"I'm coming as well," Carl said. "Do I get a hug?"

"When we get back," she said.

"Let's go get more guns," Piers said.

They followed him down the corridor and into the gun armory.

"I've got one," she said as Piers gave her what looked like a sub machine gun. She passed it on to Graham who peered at it dubiously, but slung it over his shoulder. Jamie shook his head. "I'm going to shift remember? Paws don't work too well with triggers."

Piers handed her a jacket. "It's Kevlar. Bullet proof." He handed one to Graham as well.

Tara looked at it doubtfully. "Are they going to shoot us?"

"Who knows, but Graham has a gun, and he doesn't know how to use it, so it's probably best to be prepared. Put it on." He turned to the werewolf. "Carl, you want one?"

"Nah, unless they've got silver, which is unlikely, I'm okay. A jacket will slow me down too much, and I might want to shift."

"Okay, that's it." Piers came over to Tara as she struggled with the jacket. He brushed her hands away and tightened the buckles. She shrugged her shoulders to get comfortable, but it was heavy, constricting.

"I can't move," she said.

"Of course you can move." He yanked the last buckle even tighter. "But you don't need to move. You need to stay out of the way when the fae come."

"Do you think they will come?"

"No doubt about it and I promised Christian I would keep you safe. So no stupid heroics." He leaned down and kissed her on the mouth. He took her by surprise, his tongue gliding between her lips to taste her, drawing back before she had a chance to object.

"Mmm, delicious," he said, against her mouth. "I've wanted to do that since the first moment I saw you. Thought I'd better do it now, just in case."

Presumably, just in case, everything went wrong, and they all died up there.

Piers slung a sub-machine gun over each shoulder and headed out of the door. Tara took a deep breath and followed.

They rode the elevator to the roof. Tara stood between Carl and Piers, the top of her head somewhere close to their shoulders. The air between them thrummed with excitement. Like they were going to some sort of party. A small smile played around Piers's lips—he was looking forward to this.

Suddenly she was overwhelmed. Standing between the werewolf and the vampire, she felt small, insignificant, and immensely vulnerable. She was supposed to be half-demon and at that moment, would have given anything to feel a little more demon-like.

"I want a drink," she murmured to herself.

She fiddled with the necklace at her throat. It had always been part of her. Now she planned to take it off, and this time it wasn't going back on.

The time to hide what she was had passed.

From now on, people could take her as she was and if they didn't like it they could—her thoughts ground to a halt. The fact was, not many people did seem to like her, except

Christian, and he might very well be gone forever. She forced herself to finish the thought—they could kill her.

"So, who is this guy who wants to kill me? This Walker?"

Piers glanced down at her in surprise. "He's your uncle. Well great-uncle I suppose. His brother is your grandfather."

"And he wants to kill me?"

"He will do as soon as you take that talisman off, but don't take it personally. He wants to kill a lot of people. Me for one."

Tara glanced at him, and he grinned.

"Why does he want to kill you?" she asked.

"Oh, I'm just popular, I guess. Here we are."

The elevator door opened and Tara stared out into the dark night. The sky was clear, the air cold. She stepped out after Piers. They stood on top of the tallest building in the area. All around them lay the sprawl of London, the Thames winding its way through the heart of the city, the London Eye glowing red across the water, but up here, it was as if they were alone, cut off from the rest of the world.

Everyone watched her. It was time. She remembered removing the talisman with Christian, how he had distracted her with his kisses. Tears stung her eyes, but thoughts of Christian also filled her with urgency. Even now, he could be fighting with Asmodai. Fighting with her father. Would her father sense her, and would it be enough to stop him, or maybe at least divert him? Would he come for her? According to Jamie, he had loved her mother. Would he feel something for her because of that?

Enough to give her back Christian, the man *she* loved.

She put her hand to her throat, lifted the necklace, and slipped it over her head. She opened up the locket and took the strand of hair from under the clip. It was the only part of her mother that remained, and she didn't want it destroyed. Then she dropped the locket to the ground at Piers's feet.

"Finish it," she said.

He glanced at her in surprise. "I can see it now. How amazing—you're a demon and the fae is there as well." He looked from her to the talisman at his feet. "Are you sure you want to do this? Once you do, there's no going back. What you are will be out in the open."

She nodded. "I'm sure. Destroy it."

Piers raised his foot and ground his heel on the crystal. She heard the crunch as the thing disintegrated. "Is that enough?" she asked Jonas. "Is the spell broken?"

"It's more than enough."

"So what happens now?"

"Now we wait and see who finds you first."

...

Falling back under the storm of savage blows, Christian accepted it was only a matter of time. Blood trickled from a cut on his forehead, blinding him, and he wiped it clear with the back of his hand. The attack was relentless now, soon it would be over, but something inside him refused to give in. He rallied, cursing and slashing with his blade, standing his ground.

Asmodai threw back his head and laughed.

"You've been a good opponent, but you can't beat me."

"Fuck off," Christian snarled and raised his blade.

Asmodai came for him. The crimson sword beat him down until he stood exhausted, breathing hard. Asmodai raised his sword for what Christian knew would be the final blow. He held it high above his head but at the last moment, he stumbled and fell to his knees in front of Christian.

Christian stepped back. He raised his own sword and was about to bring it slamming down when something stopped him.

Triumph gleamed in the demon's eyes.

"My daughter is alive," he said, and his voice rang with wonder. "She has destroyed the spell. She is no longer hidden from me."

Christian frowned. He was getting a bad feeling about this. He watched warily as Asmodai rose to his feet.

"Put down your sword, Christian Roth. I have no time to kill you now. My daughter might need me."

"Your daughter?"

"Yes. Mine and Lillian's."

Christian's sword clattered to the floor. He stared at Asmodai, rank horror churning in his belly. Shock washed over him, threatening to drown him in a tidal wave of disbelief. He searched Asmodai's face, hunting for any small hint of similarity, but there was nothing of Tara in him. "It's not possible."

Regarding him curiously, Asmodai put down his sword. "What, exactly, do you find impossible?"

Christian laughed, but the sound was void of humor, harsh in his ears. Why had it never occurred to him? Then again, why should it? He was in love with the daughter of his worst enemy. The daughter of the demon who was about to finish him off.

"Shit," he said. How would Tara feel? Her own father had, if not murdered her best friend, at least arranged and condoned that murder. And now her father would be responsible for killing the man she loved. He laughed again and Asmodai's eyes narrowed.

"Speak," he growled. "Or I will kill you."

"And will you tell your daughter that you killed me? At the same time you tell her you ordered the death of her best friend? It would have been her, you know. It was only by error that she wasn't taken. Your own daughter raped, mutilated, and killed at your command."

"What do you know of my daughter?"

Christian smiled. "She looks like her mother."

"What?"

"She's beautiful, and she has nothing of you in her."

Asmodai's dark eyes glittered. "Tell me what you know of her."

"I love her. I came here tonight to save her life."

"What is her name?"

"Tara," Christian said and grabbed his blade. Asmodai tensed, but made no move when Christian sheathed the sword. "Kill me if you like. If not, I'm going to see if I can get to your daughter before the fae kill her."

"The fae know of her?"

"The Walker is already close by. He'll have sensed her at the same time you did and he will kill her."

"You know this for sure? She is his niece."

"I spoke with him tonight. We made a deal. Part of that deal is that Tara never takes off the talisman, never reveals what she is."

"So why has she removed the spell?"

"My guess is she's found out what I'm doing and this is her way of calling me back." Christian's frown deepened as something occurred to him. "Or maybe, she's found out about you, that you're her father, and she's calling out to you. Maybe she thinks she can appeal to your better nature."

"Why would she wish to do that?" He searched Christian's face. "Let me ask you one question, Christian Roth. You claim to love my daughter. Does she love you?"

"Oh, yes." Christian smiled. "She's going to be really pissed that you killed me."

Asmodai pursed his lips. "Well, perhaps I should wait until I know her a little better, and perhaps, until she knows you a little better, by then I'm sure my killing you will be far more understandable."

"No doubt. So what now?"

"I'm coming with you. I need your help to exit the Abyss."

"One of the reasons I came here tonight is to prevent a full-scale war breaking out."

"There will be no war. I will find my daughter, prevent her death, and bring her back where she will be safe from the fae."

"You plan to bring her back here?"

"Of course. She's my daughter."

"She was brought up believing herself to be human."

"Thanks to you, I know nothing of her." He sounded bitter. For the first time Christian saw things from the demon's point of view. To be dragged from the woman you love and to be able to do nothing to save her.

"Did you know Lillian was carrying a child?"

Asmodai nodded. "She was excited. When I knew we would be separated, I wanted her to return to her people, but she refused. She said they would take her back but only at the price of our child. It was a price she was unwilling to pay. I thought they had both perished. Once the portals opened again, I sent whoever could go to search for them, but I found no trace. Until a few months ago when I sensed her."

"She took off the talisman, a spell her mother had made for her, that hid her true nature."

"Lillian is dead?"

Christian nodded. "She died giving birth, all her strength was gone."

"I felt it. I knew she was dead. So will you assist me, open the portal so I may enter your world?"

Christian nodded. "If you swear to return here afterward."

"I swear." Asmodai picked up his sword. "Now, let's go."

. . .

Tara kicked the shards of broken crystal littering the ground at her feet then glanced back up at the faces surrounding her. They were all examining her as though she were some sort of peculiar laboratory specimen. She scowled.

"It's quite amazing. So obvious really, it seems like we should have been able to see it all along." Carl studied her face closely. "You don't look any different, but you are different."

"What?" she snapped. "Never seen a half-demon, half-fae before?"

"Demon-fae, they used to call them," Piers spoke softly.

Tara's eyes widened. There was actually a name for what she was. Perhaps she wasn't such a freak after all. "There are others like me?"

"There were, long ago. It was inevitable—demons have always had a hankering for fae women." His eyes drifted down over her body. "Not that I blame them." He licked his lips and leered.

"If they're immortal, are they still around?" She could hear the eagerness in her own voice.

Piers shook his head. "Not anymore. The fae hunted them down and slaughtered them as part of the Accords. They claimed that as long as the demon-fae existed, the Faelands would never be safe from attack. The fae have always hated to mix their blood."

A shiver ran down her spine. "I'm beginning to dislike the fae."

"Join the club."

They fell silent. Up here, high above the streets, all was quiet. Far below, she could hear the faint hum of traffic. She rubbed her hands up her arms. Her body was rigid with tension and a tight knot of nausea burned in her belly. She wanted something to happen. Anything was better than this waiting. Though most of all, she wanted Christian to magically appear, and everything to be all right.

She raised her head. There was a change in the air.

Piers stepped closer. "Do you feel it?"

She nodded. "What is it?"

"Our first visitors, and I'm guessing it's not your dad."

"Don't call him that. He'll never be anything to me."

Piers pointed. "Over there."

At first, Tara saw nothing different. Then the air thickened until it was a tangible thing, like smoke and mist. She stared as the figures formed within the mist.

Tara's hand dropped to the gun at her waist, she fingered the grip. "Can't we just shoot them now?"

Carl laughed softly behind her. "I think I might have mentioned it before, but you're a bloodthirsty little thing, aren't you?"

Tara glowered at the "little." "You're not the one they're here to kill. I don't see anyone referring to you as an abomination."

"Not and living. And no, unfortunately, we can't shoot them yet. Bullets would go right through."

The figures solidified.

"Now, we can shoot them," Piers said. "Though it's hardly a permanent solution—kill them here and they just remanifest in the Faelands. I think we'll see what they have to say first."

"Is one of them the Walker?" Tara asked.

"The tall one in the middle. He has a bit of the look of you, don't you think?"

Tara studied the man. This was her uncle, and he was one of the most beautiful beings she had ever seen. Tall and willowy, pale blond hair pulled back from his face to show high cheekbones and slanted grass green eyes. Her eyes.

He was dressed in tight black pants, long leather boots, and a loose white shirt. A long sword hung buckled from his waist. At each side stood another armed man.

All three were expressionless.

"Stay here," Piers said and stepped forward. "Walker."

The Walker's eyes locked with Tara's. They widened as he took in her appearance, and she saw recognition flare in his face. She resisted the urge to stick her tongue out, or draw her gun and shoot him, but she let the hatred show clear in her eyes. She wasn't going to cower, or beg for her life. This was the man ultimately responsible for her mother's death. If it hadn't been for him, and beings like him, her mother would have gone home and been safe and cared for. How different would Tara's life have been?

"If looks could kill," Carl whispered in her ear.

Tara forced her gaze away. "I don't like him," she said.

"I think the feeling is mutual."

"Yes but the difference is I've got a good reason to hate him, whereas he's just a narrow-minded, bigoted bastard."

He laughed softly. "Shh," he said. "Let's hear what they have to say."

"Where is Christian Roth?" The Walker asked.

Piers looked around the rooftop with exaggerated care. "Not here."

"It's only hours since he gave his oath and it is already broken."

"He had a little demon problem to sort out, and your niece refused to cooperate with the plan. I guess being a pain in the ass must run in the family."

"My niece?" His gaze ran over Tara, coming to rest on her face. "It's curious, but obviously fae blood is stronger than that of demons. She could pass as fae."

"No, thanks," Tara muttered.

His brows drew together in a frown, and his eyes narrowed. The Walker turned back to Piers. "Hand the abomination over to us and we will forget this. You and your people can go."

"Thanks," Piers said dryly. "But they're not 'my people,' and I'm curious. What do you plan to do with 'the abomination'?" He glanced at Tara as he spoke and winked.

"Destroy her, of course." He gave Piers a considering look. "Unless you prefer to kill her yourself. Her blood should be..." He studied Tara for a moment. "Interesting. I remember you had a fondness for the demon-fae."

"You're a piece of shit, Walker, you know that?"

His eyes cold, the Walker stared back. "So you refuse to give her to us?"

"Yup."

"You have a duty as head of the Order, to follow the Accords."

Piers shrugged. "I was bored with the job anyway."

"Is she worth risking another war for?"

"Probably not, but I promised Christian I would keep her safe and I'm going to do that. If it means killing you three and hiding the bodies, well..." He shrugged. "I can live with that."

The Walker smiled. "You really don't think it will be that easy, do you?"

The air thickened behind them, white haze forming. Dense patches of mist formed all around them, and groups of fae materialized from the mist. Hundreds of them drew their swords in unison.

"Oh, shit," Carl said. He raised the gun onto his hip. "Better hope your dad comes soon."

"Don't call him that," Tara snarled, but her heart pounded as her gaze darted around her small group. Her hand slipped to the pistol at her waist, her fingers tightening on the grip to stop their trembling.

Panic clawed at her—she had led them into this. They were all likely to die, and it was her fault. A hand clasped hers. It was Jamie, her friend all her life, and she might just as well be murdering him. She squeezed his fingers. He pulled away. A moment later, he vanished, and the hellhound stood in his place.

She wished she could tell him to run, save himself, but knew he wouldn't go.

"Looks like we're on," Piers muttered, stepping back and pushing her behind him. "Stay there, don't—" He broke off as one of the fae leapt toward them. The roar of gunfire filled the night, and the fae collapsed to the ground. Tara stared in horror, but the body faded into mist and was gone.

The whole seething mass of bodies shifted toward them as one. The fae moved faster than she could follow, their blades gleaming in the dim light, only to be mown down by gunfire. But, however many crashed to the ground, more replaced the ones who vanished into the fog.

Everything slowed, until Tara could see the fierce expressions on their hauntingly beautiful faces as they lunged, the bullets as they cut through the bodies. The noise faded until she was cocooned at the center of a world gone to chaos. Legs braced, Piers and Carl stood in front of her, their guns spraying a continuous burst.

Tara crouched behind them, her pistol out, but couldn't find a target. To her right, Jamie leapt for an incoming fae, knocking the sword from his hand and sending them both sprawling to the ground. He clamped the fae's throat between his wicked jaws and shook his head, so the blood sprayed, hitting her in the face, warm and wet. On her other side, Graham stood with his eyes closed, gun held in his outstretched hand. One of the fae leapt toward him. Tara squeezed her trigger, and he went down.

Still more came.

They couldn't win, and despair threatened to swamp her.

Christian wasn't going to make it, and if he did, it would be too late. The fae kept coming, their swords drawn. She searched the sea of faces and found the Walker standing off to the side, watching through narrowed eyes.

And she knew what she had to do.

She straightened and took a step forward.

"Stop." She spoke quietly, but Piers swung in her direction, his lips curled back, his expression savage.

The Walker's gaze locked with hers and some unspoken agreement passed between them. He raised his hand...and everything stopped.

Piers swung to face her, his eyes accusing.

She swallowed. "I'm sorry. But I have to stop this. I never expected you all to die for me. I thought—"

What had she thought? That Christian would come along and save her? That her uncle would realize he didn't want to murder her after all? That her father—well, what could she hope for from her father? Absolutely nothing.

She looked around at her friends. Carl bled from a wound in his arm; Jamie stood, head hanging down, his muzzle smeared with crimson. The others were untouched, but that wouldn't last. She'd already lost Christian. She couldn't lose more.

"It doesn't matter what I thought, but it's over." She put a hand on Piers's arm. "Stop this. I'll go with him." She heard a low growl from the hellhound. "Jamie, I can't die knowing that I've caused your deaths as well."

He whimpered, and Carl put a hand on the huge head. "I'll look after him."

"He'll kill you," Piers said.

Tara's gaze took in the fae surrounding their small group. "Can you honestly say there's any chance that I'll live, anyway?"

Piers followed her gaze. "Maybe not, but it's better to go down fighting."

"Keep your fighting for when it can do some good.

Tonight, save my friends instead."

Fury raged across his face. For a moment, she thought he wouldn't agree, but then he nodded, once. "We'll stay with you. Don't worry, they'll let us go once—"

"Once I'm dead," she finished for him. "If Christian comes back, tell him... It doesn't matter, he knows."

She stepped past Piers and stood in front of the Walker. "So Uncle, how do we do this?"

He held out a long, slender hand. Tara took it and he drew her close, turning her so she faced her friends once more. She closed her eyes, as she couldn't bear to see the pain in their faces. A fist grasped her hair and dragged her head back. She tried to think of Christian, tried to be brave, but she didn't want to die and the tears spilled down her cheeks. She heard the rasp of a blade as it was drawn from its scabbard.

Chapter Twenty-Eight

"You can find her?" Christian stood in the courtyard of the fortress, Asmodai beside him, and all around them milled a hoard of lesser demons.

Asmodai nodded. "She has my blood."

Christian drew his gun and gripped it in his right hand as he held his left out to Asmodai. "Hold on to my arm. I'm going to open the portal. Concentrate on where we need to be, and get us as close as you can."

The Abyss faded as the portal opened. The temperature dropped as they left the Abyss behind and rematerialized in London. He recognized where they were–the rooftop of the Order's building. His heart stopped once he made sense of the scene in front of him. Asmodai had indeed brought them close to Tara.

He swung up his gun and placed the barrel at the base of the Walker's skull.

"That knife moves and I blow your head off," Christian growled.

The Walker tensed, but his arm remained motionless and

the knife in his hand rested against Tara's throat. The Walker held her immobile, one hand clamped in her hair. Her head was pulled back, baring the long line of her throat, and her blood pulsed in the veins beneath the blade. Her eyes were closed, but her lids fluttered open as he spoke. She tried to turn to him but the knife cut into the tender flesh of her neck, leaving a crimson line. She gave a slight intake of breath then stilled.

Christian inhaled the scent of her blood, and his hand tightened on the trigger. He'd never wanted anything in his entire life more that he wanted to blow the Walker away, but Tara stood too close and might be hurt.

"Lower the knife," he snarled.

"Christian Roth, oath breaker," The Walker said. "I see you have returned from Hell and brought a new friend with you."

"Lower the knife." When the Walker didn't move, he pressed the gun harder against him. "If you kill her now, Walker, I will shoot you down, then I will search the Faelands and kill everyone who has ever meant anything to you."

"They will not allow you to do this."

"You think I need their permission?" Christian held his breath. For a moment it seemed like the Walker would not comply, then he lowered the knife. "Let her go."

The hand holding Tara fell away, and she turned to him. He saw the tracks of tears on her pale cheeks. Her enormous eyes locked on him as though she couldn't believe what she saw.

Asmodai stood at his side, his gaze fixed on his daughter. Christian handed him the gun. "Keep the Walker covered."

Christian ran his finger over the small cut at her throat. He opened his arms, and she fell into them, trembling as he held her tight. He trembled too; he couldn't believe how close he had come to losing her. A minute later and he would have arrived to find her butchered. His grip on her tightened.

Christian's eyes narrowed on Piers. "What part of the plan didn't you understand?"

Piers grinned. "If you shack up with a demon, don't expect her to toe the line. She didn't like your plan."

His eyes searched out the others, Graham, looking pale, and Carl standing with his hand on the head of a huge hellhound he guessed to be Jamie. His eyes widened when he saw Jonas Callaghan behind the small group.

The fae, their swords drawn, surrounded them. Piers nodded his readiness to fight; they had guns, but the fae outnumbered them.

The air shimmered and a stream of lesser demons swarmed through the open portal, taking up positions around them.

The Walker remained impassive as he returned Christian's stare. "We will have a reckoning for this, you and I."

"Perhaps, but not tonight."

"According to the Accords, she is ours."

Christian sighed, every bone ached, and exhaustion threatened to overwhelm him, but they were still alive, and Asmodai was off his back. The demon continued to stare hungrily at the girl in his arms, but he wasn't getting her. She was Christian's now. Only the small problem of the fae remained.

Tara couldn't spend her life looking over her shoulder, expecting attack. He looked the Walker in the eyes, eyes so similar to Tara's.

"You can't have her," he said softly, "She's mine. We reach an agreement or we fight now."

Piers strode over to stand next to him. "I vote we fight now. Let's just kill them."

Christian raised an eyebrow. "Well?"

"What sort of agreement could we reach with a man who broke his oath only hours after making it?" The Walker asked.

"What sort of agreement would you want?"

"We need assurances that she will never enter Faelands."

"That's not a problem."

Piers snorted. "I doubt she's going to want to visit with her Uncle Walker anytime soon."

The Walker ignored him. "I cannot take your word for this."

"So what do you want?" Christian asked.

"You have proved untrustworthy, but the girl has honor. She offered herself tonight so her friends might live. We need a hostage to her good behavior. If she provides that and gives us a blood oath, we will consider it binding."

• • •

Tara clung to Christian's solid body. She burrowed her head against his hard chest and breathed in the scent of him. Warm, musky, he smelt of sweat, blood, and his own wild, masculine flavor.

She had been so sure she was about to die. She could still feel the hand gripping her hair, the icy coldness of the blade at her throat, and tremors ran through her body.

As though from a distance, she heard her name. She looked around, her eyes widening. All about them stood not only the fae, but figures from her nightmares. Some appeared human, others bore little resemblance to anything she had ever before seen, including creatures like Jamie—hellhounds. Their eyes glowed with hunger as they paced among the throng.

Her gaze was drawn to the tall figure standing next to Christian. Knowing who he must be, she looked away. She couldn't cope right now.

"Are we going to fight?" she asked Christian, pleased that her voice sounded firm. She loosened her grip on him and tested her legs. They'd stopped trembling and she thought they would hold her up. Probably.

"Maybe, maybe not. It depends on you."

She wasn't up to making any more decisions tonight. Fighting would be easier than thinking, but who were they going to fight?

The fae? The demons? Everyone? Perhaps the fae and the demons would fight each other and their little group could slip away in the ensuing chaos.

"What does he want?" Her eyes skittered over the tall fae, the Walker and the knife he still clutched in his hand.

"If you give them a blood oath and swear you will never enter the Faelands, they'll leave."

She frowned. "It seems a little too easy."

"Apparently you've impressed him."

"He didn't act like he was impressed. He acted like he wanted to kill me." She thought for a minute. "What does a blood oath involve?"

"Blood, obviously," Piers said.

"How much blood?"

"You'll live."

"Well that's a novel idea, but what exactly do I have to do?"

"You swear on your blood, but they also want a hostage."

How could she give them a hostage?

The Walker eyed up their small group. His eyes settled on the hellhound who growled softly. The Walker smiled.

"The shifter will come with us. She cares for him. He'll stand for her good behavior."

A flare of anger shot through her. "You're not taking Jamie."

The Walker shrugged. "Then the deal is off."

"I guess we're going to fight, after all." Piers sounded positively cheerful. Tara cast him a dark look. She slipped her hand into Christian's and held on. A hollow pit nestled where her stomach should be. If they fought, some of them would die, but she wouldn't hand over Jamie.

She took a deep breath. "Yes, we fight."

The night charged with tension. Demons shifted restlessly, eager to begin, and the fae raised their swords. Christian's hand tightened in hers and he drew her closer into the protection of his body.

The hellhound vanished, and Jamie stood in its place. He blinked, shook off Carl's restraining hand, and stepped toward her.

"I'll go with the fae," he said.

Tara frowned. "You can't."

"Why not? It's not as though they're planning on doing anything unpleasant to me. At least, I presume they're not."

"He'll be well treated," The Walker said.

"You don't need me anymore," Jamie said. "And Chloe's gone. It will be good to get away, see something new. I've heard the Faelands are very beautiful."

Tara bit back her tears, but she couldn't argue with him. She stalked toward her uncle and pushed her finger into his chest.

"Swear to me that you'll be good to him?"

A flicker of amusement crossed across his features. "It will be part of the oath. As long as you do not enter the Faelands, he will be safe and unharmed."

"You won't keep him locked up or anything?"

"No, he'll be free."

She returned to Jamie and hugged him. "You're sure?"

He nodded.

"I'll never see you again," she said.

"Never is a long time. Who knows what will happen in the future?"

She tried to hold on to that thought. "Can I see Smokey one last time?"

He smiled and vanished. She scooped up the huge gray cat, burrowing her nose in his soft fur, and listening to the deep, rumbling purr. She squeezed him hard to her, then let him go. He leapt to the ground and padded over to stand beside the Walker.

Tara bit her lip. "Let's get this over with."

"Come here."

She eyed her uncle warily but took a step closer. He raised the knife. "Hold out your hand."

Christian came to stand behind her and his warmth and strength flowed into her. She raised her hand and held it palm up, managing not to flinch as the razor-sharp blade sliced through her tender skin. Blood welled from the wound. The Walker raised his own hand and cut his palm. He held it out to Tara, and she took it so their blood mingled. A weird sensation ran through her from the point of contact. Her eyes rose to his face. A strange expression crossed his face.

"Promise, on your blood and the blood of your friend that you will never attempt to enter the Faelands."

"I promise," Tara said. The fae made to pull away but she held on. A flash of surprise crossed his features. "Now, you promise that you'll keep Jamie safe. Keep him happy."

The Walker glanced down at the cat at his feet. "I promise to try."

Tara nodded and released his hand.

Christian took Tara's hand in his, raised it to his lips, and ran his tongue along the cut. Immediately, the sharp pain subsided and she felt the healing begin. He kissed her palm and kept hold of her hand. "Go," he said to the Walker. "If you ever try and touch her again, I'll kill you."

The Walker shrugged. "No hard feelings."

"Piss off."

The fog gathered around the fae, swirling swathes of white. They merged with the mist, their edges blurring. Smokey blinked at her one last time and vanished.

"He was my friend for so long, now he's gone."

"Despite what you've seen of them, the fae aren't complete monsters, and the Faelands are beautiful."

"Are there any mice? Smokey likes to hunt mice."

"I'm sure they can magic him some."

Piers snorted behind them. "Yeah, of course they can, and I'm sure they will. Because underneath it all, admittedly a long way underneath, the Walker's a really great guy."

"Shut up, Piers."

Piers raised his hands. "Okay, maybe they will make him something to chase. Who knows?" He gestured around the rooftop. "Now, how are we going to persuade the rest of these guys to head home?"

The roof swarmed with demons. They kept their distance but circled like hungry sharks, their eyes gleaming in the darkness. Christian turned to the tall figure at his side. "Get rid of them."

Asmodai flicked his hand and the demons vanished. Only he remained.

Tara studied him. This was her father. He could pass for human except for his height and the wings. His body was long and lean, his face held a harsh masculine beauty, hawk-like with sharp cheekbones and a large nose. His mouth was full and sensual, his dark hair glinted with hints of ruby, and his eyes gleamed golden. Tara could see nothing of herself in him, and she was glad. He was responsible for Chloe's death; she would never forgive him for that.

He stood impassive under her regard. When she didn't speak, he took a step toward her. She made to move back, but

Christian blocked her retreat.

"You look like your mother," Asmodai said.

"So I've been told."

He reached out and cupped her cheek. She flinched, and then froze.

"Do not fear me," he said. "I wouldn't harm you. You are my blood."

"I don't fear you," Tara said. "I hate you."

He studied her as she had studied him, head tilted on one side as though considering the best way to approach her. "You hold me responsible for the death of your friend."

"Yes."

"I didn't know her, and I didn't know she was your friend."

A wave of fury washed over her. "You think that makes it okay? Why was she killed?"

He shrugged. "She was a means to an end. I wanted to hurt Christian Roth the way he hurt me. We believe in an eye for an eye, and he took your mother from me. I wanted him to know how that felt before I killed him."

"It doesn't justify murder."

A frown creased his face. "You behave like a human."

She glared at him. "I thought I was a human."

A look of distaste crossed his face. "Hopefully that abnormality will pass, but then what will you be, I wonder. The demon-fae were always unpredictable."

She wasn't sure she liked the sound of that. She might have accepted she wasn't human, but unpredictable sounded like it could throw up some nasty surprises. She glanced at Christian.

"Don't ask me," he said, "I've never met one. They were all killed before I was born."

"I've met them," Piers said. "And yeah, unpredictable just about covers it." He grinned. "I liked them."

"Well, that makes me feel all warm and fuzzy." She turned back to Asmodai. "Why are you still here?"

"I came here to offer you a home with me. A place at my side."

She stared at him in disbelief. "I want only one thing from you."

"And that is?"

"Leave Christian alone."

His glance flashed from her to Christian. "Don't worry about your vampire lover. We've already reached an understanding. He's safe from me." He looked back to her. "Do you know where the vampires came from?" She shook her head. "Well perhaps one day I will tell you, but I think a vampire is a fitting mate for one such as you. Now, I'll go."

"Wait," Tara said. "Did you love my mother?"

For a brief moment, his face softened. "Oh, yes."

"Did she love you?"

"She gave up her people to be with me. She gave up everything and she would have followed me to the Abyss had she been able. She gave up her life for my child. Yes, she loved me." He reached around his neck and pulled out a ring on a chain. "This was hers. She would have wanted you to have it."

Tara took the chain. The ring was a simple white-gold band, studded with glittering stones. She draped it over her neck so it rested where the talisman had lain for so many years.

"One day," Asmodai said, "you might want to know more about her. When that time comes, you are welcome in my home. Your vampire knows the way. No doubt, he will escort you and make sure you get safely back."

He leaned across, kissed her briefly on the forehead, and was gone.

Her Father. Chloe's killer. Christian's worse enemy.

All that remained of the demons was the faint tang of

sulfur hanging in the air. A breeze blew across the rooftop and even that scent disappeared. Rain started to fall and she shivered.

"Do you hate me?" she asked Christian softly.

Surprise flashed across his face. "Why should I hate you?"

"Because of who I am. What I am."

He pulled her to him, wrapping his strong arms around her, warming her. "No, I don't hate you."

Graham walked across the rooftop. "Thank you," he said to Tara.

"For what?"

"For saving my life. If Christian had died tonight, so would I."

"Christian wasn't going to die."

"Asmodai would have beaten me." Christian said. "If you hadn't destroyed the talisman, he would have killed me."

Tara trembled. Christian must have felt it because he lifted her in his arms and cradled her to his chest. She nestled against him. "Don't ever, ever, do anything like this again," she whispered.

He bent his head and kissed her. His lips were cool against hers, but his tongue was scalding hot as it slipped into her mouth and feasted on her. It was long minutes before he raised his head. "You asked me if I hated you."

She stilled.

"I've lived for over five hundred years. In that time I've often questioned what I am, wondered whether I was evil. I am a vampire. I have no soul. I should have died many, many years ago, but tonight, for the first time I accepted what I was. For the first time, I have no regrets about the decision I made so long ago. I also had no regrets about giving up my life if it meant that you could have yours." He raised her hand to his lips and kissed her palm, his tongue flicking against the sensitive skin. "All I'm trying to say is I could never hate you, whatever you are. I love you."

Tears pricked her eyes as he spoke the words.

"I love you, too," she said.

He smiled and kissed the tears from her cheeks. "I accept what I am now, and I want you to do the same. Don't hate yourself for what you are. I suspect you're going to change—the talisman suppressed what you are and that's gone now."

"Do you think I might sprout wings or grow a little taller?"

"I don't know, but don't be afraid to look inside yourself. I've come to believe there is no such thing as pure evil or pure good, and maybe no such thing as a normal life."

Tara forced a smile. "Don't worry. I'd already decided—I'm going to be a normal demon-fae."

"Good. Now I think we should go home and celebrate." She flashed a quick glance at his face. His eyes were hot and hungry. "There's a bottle of champagne in the fridge at my place."

"Champagne? Is that wise?" But fire sizzled through her veins as she remembered the last time she had drunk alcohol with Christian.

"Probably not. But who cares?" He dropped a kiss on her lips. "I reckon it's an important part of accepting your inner demon. Anyway, Graham can lock us in—let us out in a year or so."

"I'm not sure a year will be long enough."

"Ten then, or a hundred…we have forever."

He was right. No doubt, there would be repercussions for tonight but for now, she could relax, spend some time discovering who and what she was. Suddenly she was impatient to start. She looked around her; they were alone. It was raining harder now and everyone else had disappeared.

"Come on," she said. "Take me home."

Acknowledgments

To Liz Pelletier at Entangled publishing for her fabulous covers, her wonderful editing, and her limitless enthusiasm. And to the ladies at Passionate Critters for reading my stories and letting me know what they really think. And finally to my gorgeous husband, Rob, for not getting too fed up when I spend most of my life playing in made up worlds.

About the Author

Nina Croft grew up in the north of England. After training as an accountant, she spent four years working as a volunteer in Zambia, which left her with a love of the sun and a dislike of nine-to-five work. She then spent a number of years mixing travel (whenever possible) with work (whenever necessary) but has now settled down to a life of writing and picking almonds on a remote farm in the mountains of southern Spain.

Nina writes all types of romance, often mixed with elements of the paranormal and science fiction. If you'd like to learn about new releases, sign up for Nina's newsletter here.

www.ninacroft.com

Don't miss the rest of the **Order** *series*

BITTERSWEET MAGIC

BITTERSWEET DARKNESS

BITTERSWEET CHRISTMAS

Also by Nina Croft

THE DARK DESIRES SERIES

BREAK OUT

DEADLY PURSUIT

DEATH DEFYING

TEMPORAL SHIFT

BLOOD AND METAL

FLYING THROUGH FIRE

THE BEYOND HUMAN SERIES

UNTHINKABLE

UNSPEAKABLE

CUTTING LOOSE SERIES

FALLING FOR THE BAD GIRL

BLACKMAILING THE BAD GIRL

THE THINGS TO DO BEFORE YOU DIE SERIES

HIS FANTASY GIRL

HER FANTASY HUSBAND

HIS FANTASY BRIDE

THE BABYSITTING A BILLIONAIRE SERIES

LOSING CONTROL

OUT OF CONTROL

TAKING CONTROL

THE MELVILLE SISTERS SERIES

OPERATION SAVING DANIEL

BETTING ON JULIA

BLACKMAILED BY THE ITALIAN BILLIONAIRE

THE DESCARTES LEGACY

THE SPANIARD'S KISS

Discover more Entangled Select Otherworld titles...

NIGHT'S CARESS
a The Ancients novel by Mary Hughes

When artist Brie Lark left her vampire ex and hometown for New York City, she promised herself two things: she'd never go back, and no more vampires. But her FBI boss needs her undercover back home—with a vampire. FBI Special Agent Seb Rikare has cut all emotions to protect himself and leads a deliberately steady, almost sterile life. But as much as Brie irritates him, he finds himself drawn to her.

DRAKON'S PLUNDER
a *Blood of the Drakon* novel by N.J. Walters

Archeologist Sam Bellamy doesn't believe in dragons, but the secret society called the Knights of the Dragon do, and if she can get one of the artifacts they're searching for away from them, she'll consider it payback for killing her mentor. Four-thousand-year-old water drakon Ezra Easton knows just because he pulled an injured woman from the ocean, doesn't mean he gets to keep her... When she wakes up, she has a tall tale to share, and it seems the Knights are after her. But this drakon won't give up his treasure.

Printed in Great Britain
by Amazon